RENEGADE MAGIC

(LEGACY SERIES BOOK 3)

MCKENZIE HUNTER

McKenzie Hunter

Renegade Magic

© 2017, McKenzie Hunter

mckenziehunter.author@gmail.com

ISBN: 978-0-9903441-9-3

ACKNOWLEDGMENTS

I feel like I'm starting to sound redundant but I can't help but thank Stacy McCright for all her support, encouragement, and help throughout the years. Many thanks to my awesome beta readers who continue to offer constructive and useful feedback to help improve my stories. Thank you so much: Angie "Nana" Hatcher, Kylie Kniese, Kathryn Beard and Vanessa Jorgensen. I want to offer my appreciation to my family for being there for me through this journey.

I want to express my gratitude to Luann Reed, my editor, and Orina Kafe, for my beautiful cover art.

To my readers, I appreciate and thank you for giving my books a chance and choosing the Legacy series.

CHAPTER 1

*A*very glanced up at me several times, the last for a few seconds longer and with a flick of irritation that I would dare to ask him to work at a job he believed was a punishment and his uncle considered repayment for damaging his car. Although there was just a vague physical family resemblance between nephew and uncle, they were practically twins in their characteristic obstinacy. Uncle Gareth had perfected his over decades, and his position as head of the Supernatural Guild only reinforced it. Avery had spent only eighteen years on his.

"Is your uncle in his office?" I blew out a sigh of exasperation as he returned to his phone, sending a text.

"I don't know."

I looked for Beth, who usually worked the reception desk of the SG. The kind fae knew her job and did it well.

"Isn't it your job to know where he is?" I asked, frowning.

He placed his phone on the desk, leaned forward, and gave me the sad puppy-dog eyes that Gareth accused him of using on his mother to get away with virtually everything. While they were widened into his impression of a male

Blythe doll, I momentarily found myself looking past his mussed man bun and his overly casual dress of t-shirt, jeans, and flip-flops that I became aware of when he propped them on the desk.

"I'm indentured. I can't do anything, and I go to school in a couple of weeks."

"Aw. I would feel really sorry for you if you were actually doing your job and the big, mean lion was being unreasonable. Have you ever thought about actually doing the job really well and seeing if he'd let you off easy for good behavior?"

He made a face as he considered my suggestion but gave it just a few seconds of his time. "Doesn't seem to have worked for you." Then he gave me another sly smile. Even if it *had* worked for me, I suspected he would have ignored my suggestion. Avery and Gareth seemed to be embroiled in a subtle battle of dominance and stubbornness. Based on what I'd seen of Gareth, I was going to put my money on him. Avery wasn't his uncle's equal, and with all his years of dealing with him, he should have figured that out. He picked up the desk phone, dialed a number, and listened for a while. "He's not in his office. He was in one of his moods this morning. When he's like that, he's usually trotting about the city in his animal form or taking it out on anyone stupid enough to spar with him. People around here are pretty smart now." He shrugged. "I'd check the gym." He reached into a drawer, pulled out a visitor's badge, scanned it, and then handed it to me. He wasn't incompetent, he just wanted everyone to think he was.

"Where's the gym?"

"The bottom floor."

Avery was right: I heard the aggressive grunts and followed the sounds and ended in a large gym. Gareth, shirtless with a pair of sweats, laid into the heavy bag. With each movement, his muscles contracted and sweat ran down the peaks and valleys of his back, chest, and abdominal muscles. I averted my eyes. We'd had several moments that hadn't gone very far. Once, I'd stopped it and had lived to regret it. The last time, we'd been interrupted with news that Trackers had taken the Legacy that the SG had captured with my help. Now I couldn't get in touch with Gareth. Two days calling and texting had gone unanswered. I'm not sure why it bothered me, as it was his MO. I took a step closer to the massive gym, which didn't look any different than the typical gym except for the thicker, more solid equipment. Probably necessary when dealing with shapeshifters, who were stronger and faster than most.

"Hello Levy," he said, his back still to me, before he hit the bag again. Then he turned.

Oh yes, the infamous enhanced sense of smell.

I kept my eyes fixed on his as he advanced toward me. His smooth, graceful movements were constant reminders that I was dealing with an apex predator. The shifter ring that pulsed around his eyes was several shades darker than their crystalline blue. The ever-present smirk on his lips indicated he could tell the effort I was putting into looking at his eyes and there only. This was a business meeting.

He beckoned me to follow him. He led me past the locker rooms to another elevator, different than the one I'd used earlier. He swiped a keycard, and the elevator opened.

"You have your own elevator?" I asked derisively. Had they met this guy? He didn't need an ego boost, and giving someone their own private elevator was definitely a way to inflate one.

"You're Batman," I teased as the door closed and we started to ascend. Towel in hand, he wiped his chest and arms and then ran it over his head. Once again, I directed my eyes to anything other than the half-naked man in front of me.

He made a face. It was obvious he wasn't a comic book fan: each time I'd made a reference I'd gotten the same tilt of his head and a quizzical look.

The elevator opened to a small room behind his desk. Each time I visited his office I was surprised by its massive size and the floor to ceiling windows that gave a beautiful view outside. There was a small kitchenette in the corner, and he had a shower. His office was basically a small apartment.

"This is a business visit. I'm not going to take a shower with you!"

He stopped midstep and turned to face me. Looking faintly amused, he regarded me for several moments. "We can *talk* while I'm in the shower. The shower and dressing area are separated. I didn't invite you to take a shower with me, but it seems like you would like me to." He strode toward the shower, the haughty little kink in his lip that I'd become far too familiar with firmly in place. I cursed the warmth that inched up my face.

Do I follow him in? There were so many inappropriate things about this situation, I had no idea where to start with the list.

After a few minutes of hesitation, I followed him. As soon as we were over the threshold of the bathroom, he slipped off his sweatpants. I turned my head.

"Surely you've seen a naked man before?"

"Of course, and it's because of shapeshifters—driving past Forest Park, I've seen enough naked man and woman parts to last a lifetime. I understand nudity doesn't really bother you all, but there is a social contract. A person should at least get a name before they start showing their goods or at least charge people for the look-see."

"Who made that rule?" he asked, stepping through the door that separated the shower area from the dressing room. The wide-open door didn't offer a lot of privacy so I kept my eyes averted to the khaki-colored walls of the dressing area.

I turned when I heard the water running and shower door closing.

"Society," I offered, rolling my eyes.

"Well, if it's any consolation to you, if I hadn't received that call the other day, I had planned on seeing you naked. Every inch of you," he pointed out in a low purr.

He wasn't wrong; I had every intention of that as well, but I didn't want to think about our lascivious intentions. There were more important issues we needed to discuss. "What are you going to do about the Trackers and the Legacy?"

For a long moment, all I heard was the sound of water splashing. I waited longer. Even over the water, his enhanced hearing would have allowed him to hear me.

After several long beats of silence, he finally said, "Nothing."

"What?" I nearly opened the glass shower door. I needed to see his face as he told me that the Supernatural Guild was going to allow seven Legacy and Conner to die at the hands of Trackers. Anger simmered inside of me and I was unable to tamp it down. The steamy fog filling the room didn't help and only made things seem claustrophobic and stifled. I didn't have any sympathy for Conner—there wasn't any redemption for him, certainly not from me. Nor for Evelyn, who had become his most devoted acolyte. They were a threat and I could see how the others were as well. Perhaps I was being naïve, but they'd been persuaded by the promise of something other than a life of hiding in the shadows waiting for Trackers to pick them off the moment their existence became known. I didn't agree with their alliance with Conner or how easily they'd been seduced by his idea, but I understood how it had happened. I felt sure they could be dissuaded; maybe not as easily as they'd been convinced, but at least it was possible that they could switch sides. For a brief moment I considered how I would have responded if Conner had approached me after my parents were killed. Blocking out the image of their lifeless bodies lying on the floor when I'd returned from school one day was hard. I blinked back the tears that were threatening to stream down my face.

I averted my eyes when Gareth stepped out, otherwise I would have gotten a full frontal view. He made an annoyed sound and said, "I'm covered now; you maintain your virtue," with a huff of sarcasm.

He was standing just a few inches from me, and it was becoming increasingly difficult to keep my eyes from drifting down to look at the towel. Knowing he was probably going to drop it, I brought my eyes to his face. Although I was done pretending I wasn't attracted to him—I was—now wasn't the time to make that stand. Whether or not he was deliberately trying to distract me with his appealing body, I didn't want to be distracted. This was important, and I wasn't going to let my libido get in the way.

"You're going to let the Trackers murder them and do nothing about it?" Ire hardened my words and intensified the glare that I'd fixed on him.

He remained silent, the only sound the gentle ruffling and movements of him getting dressed. However, he held my gaze as he slid on dark blue slacks and a light blue button-down shirt. It wasn't until he started to button his shirt that he spoke. "It wasn't a decision I came by lightly—but it's a good one," he finally said in a flat tone, which just fueled my irritation.

"And you are okay with their murders?" I managed to keep my voice down but the words were hissed out through gritted teeth. Clothed, he looked so official, and the look of quiet resolve that he gave me made this seem more like a professional meeting in which he was giving me intel. It didn't matter if I liked it, that was his decision, and he was just informing me of it.

"This isn't right."

"What's not right is for us to use resources for a massive hunt to get back people no one believes exist. This is a good decision—my final decision."

The rage was more than a little flicker of discomfort; it was a fiery uncontrolled blaze and I was having a difficult time trying to contain it.

"Is that your decision or Harrah's? Protecting the humans and controlling the narrative at all costs seems like a play out of her handbook."

As the head of the Magic Council, Harrah was instrumental in maintaining the alliance between the humans and the supernaturals. Fully trusting her was difficult because she'd do anything to keep up the appearance that supernaturals were harmless. Anyone who was capable of the sleight of hand that she'd used to maintain that illusion, all while keeping a plaintive genteel smile, couldn't be trusted. I suspected behind her seraphic appearance was someone whose personality and agenda were anything but. She'd ordered the Supernatural Guild to murder someone so the world wouldn't find out about his betrayal in assisting Conner to perform another Cleanse after acquiring a Necrospear.

"It was her suggestion, but I made the decision to do it."

At least he was being honest with me about who'd come up with such a cruel idea. My eyes narrowed on him. I was a cynic by nature—my past had made me that way— and I wondered how close he still was to the Trackers. He'd *been* one once, but he'd said that their "kill on sight no matter what" policy wasn't something he could abide by. Was that same dislike of my kind so deeply instilled in him that agreeing to such a callous and cold decision had been easy?

"How did they find out?" I asked.

The same incensed look of betrayal that had been mine claimed his appearance as my question lingered in the air.

"I'm still looking into that and when I find out—" He bit down on his lips, and the shifter ring that flashed in his eyes was a less than subtle reminder that behind the nice, professional clothing a predator still lurked in him.

"The idea of you having a leak in the SG is a problem but—"

"Levy, I urge you not to make this personal. This isn't an affront against you. I will keep you safe—"

"I've managed to stay safe this long without you, I'm sure I'll be fine. For all I know you might have a bad day and lead them to my door."

I turned and headed out of the dressing room. My frustration over the situation was making me unnecessarily volatile. I tried hard to master it, but I couldn't get over how cavalier they were about the murders of Legacy and Vertu, our stronger counterparts. Everyone was just so flippant over the loss of our lives and it was hard to ignore the feeling of betrayal because of it. I'd come out to the world as a Legacy myself and hoped that the Supernatural Guild would work on the redemption of the others who were in SG custody. I'd envisioned a mutual display of goodwill that would lead to us being part of the fabric of society instead of being forever feared and hunted as the people who'd done the Cleanse. The stories of it would be just part of our history and regarded as such. Never to be repeated, but to remain a mutual cautionary tale for humans, supernaturals, and Legacy.

Ignoring Gareth calling my name, I headed for the elevator, and by the time it opened to the main floor I'd devised a plan. It wasn't much of one. I was going to go find the Trackers who'd taken the Legacy. I didn't have the element of surprise because they knew who I was. That left me at a disadvantage, but I didn't care. As I moved down the hallway, my thoughts were consumed by violent retaliation and the many ways I planned to exact it. I had no intention of implanting false memories in their heads when I was finished. I wanted them to remember and possibly have nightmares for days to come after my visit.

As I made my way to the door, I was met by four people who blocked my exit. Two very powerful mages—I could feel the waves of magic that wafted off of them—and two shapeshifters. One of the latter definitely had to be a bear. Arms the size of tree trunks rested at his side, and his broad body was going to be hell to get past. Even if I managed to duck around him, I wouldn't stand a real chance against the other shifter, who was lean, sinewy, and undoubtedly fast.

"Ms. Michaels." The mage spoke, approaching me slowly, sparks of gold and turquoise twining around his fingers. A congenial smile rested on his face, but his eyes were hard, deadly—dangerous. Out of habit my hands slipped to my back where I usually kept the twins, my sai, but I'd left them in the car.

He said my name again, lower—a warning as magic twirled around my fingers, accumulating and forming a small ball in my hands. He watched me carefully and so did the other three. *Do I want to do this?* I did, even if it was a show of force, a demonstration that they didn't want to screw with me—a Legacy. But that was the problem. No one wanted to deal with us, which was why it was okay for some rogue group to take incarcerated Legacy and kill them.

"Mr. Reynolds has instructed us not to let you leave the building."

"Really? I had no idea! That's what the fanfare was all about," I said sarcastically.

"Come with us," requested the bear-shifter as he positioned himself in front of me. The other shifter flanked me on one side and one of the mages on the other. The first mage moved to secure me from behind.

They took me to an interrogation room, which didn't help with subduing my irritation with the whole situation. I sat for a few minutes and then paced the length of the room feeling like a caged animal, taking long strides, looking at the double-sided mirror wondering if anyone was on the other side.

The room was better than the ones I'd seen on TV, but this was the only one I'd actually ever been in. A long table had six sturdy-looking wooden chairs placed around it. But unlike those in the TV shows, which usually had plain white or some muted-color walls, this room was covered with sigils. You'd have to be pretty strong to get past them to perform any magic. There was a fire extinguisher behind a windowed steel door that seemed too big for containing just that. I assumed there were other things that they housed there "in case of emergency," like dealing with a misbehaving supernatural malcontent. Or someone who dared not to respond to the arrogant Supernatural Guild's head when he called her name.

I can't believe I almost slept with this jackass!

I stopped pacing and stood in front of the two-way mirror. Glaring at it, I said, "This is a flagrant abuse of power."

Yep, he'd been on the other side, because the moment the words came out of my mouth, he stepped in. Haughty amusement skated over the defined planes of his face as his lips curled into a grin.

"Would you like to file a report, Ms. Michaels, detailing

my gross abuse of power?" He rested against the wall, one leg crossed over the other and his arms folded in front of him. He waited patiently for me to answer. He was obviously finding a peculiar pleasure in this moment, as the indigo shifter ring brightened around his light blue eyes.

"Will you put in the report that I had the audacity to try to protect you from yourself and keep you from getting yourself and others killed?" He pushed up from the wall and stood just inches from me. "Perhaps you will document your obstinacy and how you refused to let me explain things but instead left in a little huff. Will you add that you rolled your eyes and stomped out of my office? Well, that can't possibly make me look bad, now can it, Ms. Michaels?" I hated when our conversations were reduced to him calling me by my last name. We'd passed professional courtesy weeks ago.

He'd inched so close that I could feel the warmth of his body as he brushed against mine. His breath wisped against my cheek as he spoke. "Would you like me to get someone to take your statement, Ms. Michaels?"

I took several steps back. "Levy," I offered.

He studied me for a few minutes before he spoke. "It's not you," he said softly. "No one wants you dead, but are you willing to risk the safety of the people in this city on a wish that the other Legacy are better than what they've presented? I understand your desire to make things better and to be able to live openly without the threat of someone trying to hurt you. I want that for you, too. For all of them, but not the ones we had in custody."

"You think it will stay in the dark? That there won't be speculation or whispers of it among other Legacy? If it becomes one of those things that Harrah so handily spins the optics about and reduces to nothing more than just an 'incident,' what are you telling others? What they will see is that the SG supports our assassination—legally sanctioned murder. And those who never would have considered joining a person like Conner might see him as the type of savior they need. When another Conner pops up with even more followers, I guess you can unleash the Trackers and hope they get to them before they actually do a Cleanse for no other reason than to retaliate."

"You think I didn't consider all that? We will be monitoring Trackers—all of them. Hopefully, you will work with us to find the Legacy and form an alliance before someone like Conner does appear. It will be a preemptive operation. You're out, and they will see that there isn't an issue."

"It's a limited 'out.' You all know, and the Magic Council knows." Then I considered the situation and shrugged. "Perhaps you're right. Since you have a leak, there's no telling who else knows about me." I gave him a hard look. I really didn't want to take my frustrations out on him, but his casual attitude toward the situation bothered me. I wasn't sure whether the professionally stoic face was a mask that he presented for my benefit and that of his staff, but it made him seem indifferent and cold. I'd rather have seen him riddled with apprehension and uncertainty. Now I just saw him as a killer of my kind, no different than when he was a Tracker.

"Do I have your word you aren't going to pursue this?" he asked.

"Of course. After all, I wouldn't want you to threaten to arrest me for the umpteenth time." I made an attempt at a smile but failed. I wasn't sure why controlling my emotions was such a challenge. Perhaps I expected and needed things to end differently. This incident wasn't neat and tidy as I'd expected it to be. My gut was telling me to be afraid, and I hated feeling afraid. Cautious, yes. I lived that way, but I hated fear. Fear made people behave irrationally, and no matter how much they understood that, they were unable to react otherwise.

He smiled. "Okay, Levy."

"Oh, we're back to friendly repartee, are we?"

"I was always there. You were the one who was in a mood. I just let it play out."

"No, you didn't. You put me in an interrogation room!"

He made a face. "There's that mood again." Laughing at my scowl, he said, "I'd like to see you tonight."

"I can't tonight." I held his gaze. It wasn't officially a lie and I wondered if he could tell or not.

"Do you have plans?"

If sitting in my room sulking was a plan, then yes, I had plans.

I nodded.

He gave me a simple, plaintive smile. "Have fun." He walked over to the door and unlocked it, opened it, and extended his hand, inviting me to leave.

CHAPTER 2

I looked at my phone as I opened the door. My boss, Kalen, knew I was going to be late, but he probably didn't expect me to be *this* late.

"Sorry, I was locked in an interrogation room," I blurted as I walked into the office. I halted when I saw Blu sitting on the desk leaning into the screen that he'd turned in her direction. His coffee cup was on the table; hers was in her hand. Smiling, Midwest Barbie and Ken were both dressed like they were ready for a photo shoot. As usual, he was in a suit. Midnight blue slim fit, white shirt with the first button undone. She had on silver heels, a long, pink hooded cardigan paired with a little white shirt, and slinky black pants that hugged her curves. Pink gloss accented her supple lips and complemented her walnut-colored skin. Thick liner rimmed her eyes, and mascara created a lush veil of lashes. Corkscrew ringlets of dark brown hair tipped with blue blended well with her ensemble.

Kalen shifted his gaze from the screen to me, and his silver eyes narrowed to slits. "She's what I'm talking about," he mumbled to Blu, the witch who had not used a spell to enchant him, but her smart fashion sense, which was the surest way to his heart.

She flashed a genial smile as they both gave me the same assessing look, starting with my green Converse sneakers, moving to my jeans, and going on to the light green tee I had under my multicolored plaid shirt.

Oh, look, now there's two of them.

Blu kept smiling as she hopped off the table. I liked her, mostly because since she'd come into our lives Kalen hadn't bothered asking me to go to whatever designer was having a show that I didn't give a damn about. Blu loved them. When we found antiquities that she could use, she was given a discount—but it came out of Kalen's half because I hadn't agreed to give her the pretty-fashionista price. She always bartered something for them. Usually she'd make *herba terrae*, the witches' version of pot, and pseudo-magic protection amulets that did a fireworks presentation for show when the right magical word was said. Humans really loved both, and they were easy sells in the shop.

"So what weird game were you and your boyfriend playing, and why did it involve an interrogation room?" Kalen asked, taking his focus off Blu, who was now leaving. He waved at her as she ducked out the door. Again giving me a derisive once-over, he lifted his finger, and I glared at him.

"If you change anything I'm wearing, the pigtails come back to stay."

He shuddered, affronted at the very thought of the hairstyle. That was probably why I used it as a threat so often.

"You and Gareth were playing your little games, and then he did . . ."

I took up roughly the same position Blu had held just moments before, but instead I crossed my legs as I explained everything that had happened over the past three days.

Although I left out the intimate details about Gareth and me, I was sure Kalen had already inserted his version.

Although he feigned a lighthearted interest in my love life, Kalen couldn't conceal the obvious concern he had for me. He was still dealing with the new knowledge that I was a Legacy and I could see the effort he was putting into fully comprehending it. This was one of those moments because he was reminded of what we could do and what Conner and his newly formed crew *wanted* to do. They were not only planning another Cleanse but recruiting others who were Legacy and the stronger version of them, Vertu, to help. And they weren't above enlisting the help of other supernaturals who were willing to betray their own in an effort to gain favor with them and live in a world where few rivaled their power. I found it just as disturbing as Kalen did. High-level mages could do a small Cleanse if they used one of the magical objects Legacy had made along with pulling magic from another mage, witch, shapeshifter, and a fae—which they did by killing them.

The more I thought about it, the more it didn't seem like such a bad idea to have the Trackers handle this situation. However, I still lived with the apprehension that they would be emboldened by the Supernatural Guild's complicity and it would have devastating results.

"I agree with Gareth's decision," Kalen said softly after several minutes of contemplation of everything I'd told him. A reluctant resolve shrouded his features after the struggle for acceptance of such cruelty played across them. But at least there had been a struggle, moments of indecisiveness, consideration. It bothered me that Gareth hadn't displayed any of that.

"I'm sure Conner was very persuasive, but the fact that those following him could be swayed into doing it says a great deal about where their loyalties lie," Kalen continued,

"They are dangerous and can't be trusted." I started to speak, but he raised his hand to stop me. "Levy, I wish there was a perfect answer that didn't end with violence, but Gareth's job is to protect the majority. The Legacy are a threat."

"I'm not a threat."

"You're not. And there are others that aren't and I'm sure he will stop the Trackers if they go after those. The ones that were captured weren't innocent, Levy. You said some of the SG died trying to capture them—trying to stop them from doing something heinous. Conner and the others need to be held accountable for those deaths and their crimes."

Kalen was echoing much of what Gareth had said and I was just as reluctant to hear it from him, but somehow it didn't seem so bad now. At the end of the day, the SG, Gareth, the Magic Council, and Harrah had an agenda— Kalen didn't. His only goal was to keep himself and his friends safe.

"If by chance he did stop the Trackers from executing the Legacy they currently hold captive, are you sure you'd be safe from them? Are you sure they don't consider you an enemy, one who betrayed her own kind and the cause? Have you considered that he's doing it to keep you safe as well?"

His words were a reminder of how fear made people illogical—this time, I was the one suffering from it. Conner had dropped me in the middle of no-man's-land and left me to fend off a supernatural freak animal. He hadn't expected me to survive, and when I did, he'd been willing to take my life himself. His devotees followed him blindly; one command from him and they would have done the same.

Kalen was right. Gareth was right. Humility was too bitter for my palate.

Instead of going home after work, I ended up in the pit cave I'd found years ago, where I'd performed magic, hidden from everyone. Well, I should have been, but both Lucas, the vampire Master of the city, and Gareth had found it. Before I did anything, I waited. I was out of the closet, exposed to the Supernatural Guild, but I still didn't feel comfortable performing magic in the open. I'd retreated to the cave when my curiosity had gotten the best of me. Were Conner's followers dead? It had been several days now. They probably were, but I needed confirmation.

Taking a knife out of the bag I kept it in, I sliced the blade over my hand. Wincing at the pain as blood welled and dripped on the dirt, I recite the locating spell. I watched as my blood curdled around the rocks, brightened, and spread over the area. Magic blanketed the dirt, forming a small map that represented almost one hundred miles and would reveal the location of any magic similar to mine. I used to employ this spell to make sure I wasn't near another Legacy, which would have made it easier for us to be detected. I tamped down the raw, cold feeling of being a coward for having done so. I looked at the map: clear, empty of any small dots except a few on the far edges, away from me, that couldn't be Conner and his sympathizers. I stared at the blank empty spaces where there should have been clustered dots representing them and then averted my attention to the pale lines that divided up the city. Despite the thrum of magic that came off the map, there was a cold emptiness of nothing being present. The heaviness of what that meant was hard to shrug off no matter how I tried. There weren't any Legacy near me. I didn't think about Conner and his acolytes' agenda. That should have been at the forefront of my mind. It should have consumed my thoughts and drowned out everything—but it didn't. I thought about the fact that the very people who'd killed my parents had been allowed to kill others. That's what the empty map meant to me.

It took an hour-long drive for me to find some acceptance of the situation. Conner was dead, and so were the others. It was the consequence of the choices they'd made. Period. It was over, and I decided I wasn't going to fixate on it anymore.

I drove up to my building and saw the Tesla, now scratch free, parked behind Savannah's car. I debated whether to keep driving. Tenacity and pure stubbornness wouldn't allow me to do that, so I parked my own car and went to my apartment. Casually strolling in, I found Gareth in the kitchen with Savannah. He was cutting up tomatoes, and she was checking on the food in the oven.

"I wasn't expecting a guest tonight," I said, my tone cool and even. Gareth turned around, a smile slowly spreading over his lips, defiant and amused. "You don't have company, Savannah does. I thought you were busy?"

"I am."

The grin broadened. Smug. A subtle challenge. "Well, then pretend I'm not here."

As if I could. His all-consuming and overpowering presence was hard to ignore, and I didn't doubt for one minute that he knew it.

"Gareth called to see how things were going with the Shapeshifter Council since I am now allied with them." She gave me a congenial smile. She was always kind and welcoming, but she'd been firmly on Team Gareth from the very beginning. Her adoration had earned her a position as president of his fanclub.

"And he brought this." She picked up a bottle of wine from the table, turned the label to me, and flashed another smile. I returned it, widening my eyes in pseudo excitement, mirroring her enthusiasm, wishing I knew what I was faking excitement about. Savannah was the wine connoisseur, one of the few indulgences she considered worth the empty calories. That was her vice, wine and hot zombies, or rather vampires.

Gareth kept drawing my attention. The smirk wavered a little before he spoke. "How was your day?"

I shrugged. "Another day, another threat from a conceited tyrant threatening to arrest me when I dared to not do what he wanted."

"Did he ask nicely?" Once again I was treated to the little kink in his lips. The blue eyes sparkled. When I glared at him, his smile widened.

Savannah's narrowed gaze bounced between the two of us, but she remained silent. From her knowing look, I thought she had figured out that Gareth had done something more than be bossy and domineering. But I wasn't sure if she regretted inviting him over. I doubted she would have been able to extend her trademark kindness if she'd known before the invitation. Who was I kidding—this was Savannah. She probably would have still extended it, but it would have been accompanied by a thorough haranguing. When I excused myself to go to my room they both looked concerned.

Reading while lying on my bed was enough of a distraction. Once I'd decided that Saturday I'd look for the other Legacy who'd shown up on the outskirts of the map, my mind cleared and escape into my book's world of espionage was easy.

Staying in that world wasn't quite so effortless. Every once in a while, my thoughts slipped to trying to figure out what I'd do once I found the mapped Legacy. I needed to talk with the Magic Council, and it would benefit me if I learned to play nice with Gareth. His position as head of the Supernatural Guild and a member of the Magic Council made him an asset. A complicated, arrogant, sexy asset, but an asset nonetheless.

I returned to my book, ready to be immersed in a life that made mine pale in comparison when there weren't many things that could do that. I considered ignoring the light knock on the door, but after the second one I invited the person in.

"Peace offering," Gareth said, bringing in a plate and a glass of wine.

Sitting up, I looked at the plate. Only Savannah would think it was okay to serve a shapeshifter—a lion—eggplant parmesan and a salad. I grinned. He had the very look I'd expect to see on his face.

"Are you sacrificing your meal for me?" I teased.

"No, we finished eating earlier. This is yours." After I took the plate from him and started eating, he took a seat on the chair in the corner.

"How did you like your vegetarian entree?"

He shrugged. "I guess I'll go take down a buck on the way home and get myself a proper meal."

His voice was even, without a hint of humor, and I wasn't sure whether or not he was joking. An easy smile settled on his lips, which didn't help me determine if he was being facetious or not.

I took a sip of the wine and immediately figured out why Savannah was so excited. It was good—very good—and I was sure it had to be way out of our budget.

"Do you like it?" he asked.

I shrugged. "It's okay."

"Hmm. You should tell your face that. You seemed to have enjoyed it."

"I like it. It's a wonderful choice." It was time to play nice with Gareth, who just made it more difficult than it had to be.

"See, you can be amicable when you really set your mind to it."

The glare I shot in his direction just pleased him even more.

"What happens next?" I asked after moments of silence. "With the Council," I specified when his brow rose.

"We wait for things to settle with Conner and then—" He stopped for a moment as if he was choosing his words carefully. "Harrah thinks it's a good idea for you to come out, publicly. You've been out front and center handling some of the most chaotic occurrences recently. The agents at the SG hold you in high esteem and so does the Council. It would be a good choice for you to be the Legacy who comes forward."

"I'm also riddled with scandal." I pointed out that I'd been charged with murder at one time. "I think most people will only remember that about me."

"It never made the news, Harrah made sure of that."

I knew that; Savannah had told me that before. I was looking for an excuse. I didn't want to be the Legacy poster girl and be paraded in front of the cameras as the innocuous version of my predecessors. A neutered version of what we were. And with the Trackers out there emboldened to murder us with the support of the SG, I didn't want to be a walking target.

"I don't want to do that."

"I didn't say I agreed with her. I told you what she wanted, and she will press the issue because it's what she wants."

"What do you want?"

Again, the devious smile emerged, and he gave me a once-over. His tongue ran lightly over his lips before he bit into them. I doubted it was to bite back any more innuendos.

"What do you want me to do *regarding coming out*?"

I appreciated that he considered the question for an

extended period of time. "I don't agree with Harrah that it's the right time to do this. I think you should locate the others and talk to them, get an idea of what they want. You can't speak for all Legacy. The people that know about you—or *think* they know about you—will be ridiculed because the story won't be corroborated by anyone else."

"There are people who will believe it."

"The ridicule is going to happen no matter what we do. There were always people who suspected there were still Legacy, and they weren't all part of Humans First or Trackers. They're the people who still claim to have seen Nessie and Bigfoot. To the general population, they are conspiracy theorists and nutjobs and won't be taken seriously. The Magic Council is now tasked with mounting a believable case that Legacy exist and managing the death of the head of the HF and several of their members"—he paused for a while —"among other things."

I assumed under the umbrella "among other things" were concerns that they had a leak and someone who was colluding with Trackers in the SG. I was absolutely sure that "among other things" were cleaning up the situation with HF: the dead members, the arrests associated with members having kidnapped me, and the disbanding of any remnants of the organization. There wasn't any doubt that magic, strong and illegal, would probably be involved. Magic was banned among the general population, but used by the SG and the Magic Council.

Gareth's lips were pulled into a thin, taut line and I didn't expect to get any more information from him, but I still tried. "Have you spoken with your cousin about how the Trackers found out you apprehended Conner and the others?" I squeezed out the question through clenched teeth as I broached the subject that was the point of contention between us. A crisis of conscience had caused him to leave the Guardians of the Order, known to me as Trackers, but he'd remained linked to them through his cousin who was an active member.

"Yes, we are discussing the matter," he confirmed coolly. The baleful glint in his eyes and the dark shadow that was cast over his face were reminders that beneath all that Gareth presented to the world, he was a predator. A dangerous one.

"Where is he?"

"I have him in custody." His tone had become dark and ominous. A subtle hint for me to drop it. If only I could quiet my curiosity. "In custody" was a vague answer. I felt the poorly controlled anger that emanated off him. He'd been betrayed by his cousin, that I was sure of, and I didn't think he was handling it well—or legally.

"Your cousin, is he in custody at the Haven?"

"I didn't say he was in SG custody. I said he was in custody." He stretched out on the chair, linking his fingers together behind his head.

"What? Is he locked in your basement being waterboarded?" I asked, half-jokingly. The stern look that overtook his features didn't make me feel confident that he wasn't.

"When do you want to start looking for the other Legacy?"

I see what you are doing. He'd not only changed the subject but invited himself on my excursion.

"Let's start next week." I had every intention of starting before that week, without him. It was an unknown situation, and I wasn't ready to do it with a partner. It was bad enough that I was probably going to have to sneak out so that Savannah didn't volunteer to go, weighted down again with her "quest" bag.

He nodded. "When you start looking for them this weekend, should I just tail you or are you going to 'fess up now and invite me along?"

I inhaled a sharp breath.

"I can hear the changes in your breathing and the increase in your heart rate. But we can continue pretending that I can't." In a graceful wave of preternatural movement he came to his feet and closed the distance between us. He leaned down until he was at my eye level. "I personally enjoy the game of cat and mouse," he said before he walked out of my room. I took another drink from my glass, hoping that Savannah had left more wine in the bottle.

CHAPTER 3

ocused on getting to work on time, I simply looked down at my phone when it rang. It was an unknown number, not Gareth's as I'd been expecting. It had been two days since he'd shown up at my apartment for dinner. Since I had no intention of him accompanying me to find the other Legacy, I hadn't seen the point of taking his many calls. I figured it was only a matter of time before the threat of arrest was sent or maybe another cadre of badass SG officers teeming with magic and frustration ready to make me comply with Gareth's demands and try to convince me to stop being a pain in his butt. Just before I could retrieve the message left by the unknown caller, a sedan darted out from a side street, blocking me. An SUV pinned me in from the rear. Craning my neck, I looked for other cars. I always took back roads to work to avoid traffic, and the very reason I loved them was the very reason I might be in trouble: no one was around. I could maybe count on a car or two to pass but I wasn't sure how long that would be.

When a woman jumped out of the SUV behind me, I grabbed my sai. A rust-colored shifter ring danced around her eyes, but I focused on the scowl etched on her face. I did a quick assessment. She had me by at least three inches, and being a shifter she had extraordinary strength and agility that gave her an advantage. But hubris caused her to approach me without a weapon, which wouldn't be beneficial for her.

For a split second, I wondered if she was SG, but I didn't see a badge. The two men that hopped out of the car that had blocked me from the front wore the same scowl as the shifter, along with similar looks of contempt and disgust. Trackers for sure. I remembered that look, it never changed. Abhorrence was woven so deeply in their thoughts and emotions that the very sight of us evoked their hate. I considered maneuvering to drive off, when another car crept along, coming from the other direction. I was completely blocked in. There wasn't enough space to navigate between them, and my car wasn't powerful enough to push the SUV behind me out of the way.

The men approached me with caution. The moment the woman was close, I opened my car door and sprang out. I jammed the left sai into her thigh. She howled in pain and dropped to her knees, grappling to pull it out. Four against one didn't afford them restraint. They'd planned to kill me, and I planned to send a message to the Trackers to leave me the hell alone. I punched the right sai into the neck of the shifter Tracker before she could remove the first one. After that I withdrew the sai from both her neck and thigh. She choked a breath. Her eyes widened as she reached for her neck. Her hand came away crimson and wet with blood.

I didn't turn fast enough to get to the other two. I was hit hard with a blast of magic. It smashed into me, heat spread over my body, and sharp aches of pain shot through me as I moved. *Mage.* I turned to move away from the other one, who lobbed another ball of magic in my direction. *Damn.* I didn't want to deal with two magic wielders. I pushed out a wave of magic, the powerful kind I usually reserved for Conner, but I didn't care. The stronger and deadlier the better. They both went back, hitting their car with a thud, their heads rebounding against it. I went to the car that was blocking me on the side; when I was just inches away, the female driver sped off. I looked at the license plate, trying to commit it to memory.

I spun around. The mages were trying to come to their feet, and I kept them pressed against the car with another wave of magic. Sunlight gleamed off the blood-soaked blades as I approached them with the twins in hand.

They struggled against my magic, trying to pull themselves from the car.

"Now you're the ones captured," I said in a low drawl. Feeling the surge of magic as it wrapped around my hand, I contemplated what I would do to them. I took in the rage; how confident they must have been knowing they had caught me and were just going to kill me, four against one. They wouldn't have given me mercy, and I wasn't prepared to offer them any.

Flashes of the blank map overtook my thoughts and I couldn't shrug them off.

"I don't mind dying for our cause. You will prove what we've all thought of you. You all are murderers, unable of being anything else," one of the mages spat.

The hypocrisy enraged me. I'd killed one Tracker, the one who had killed my parents. I'd only erased the minds of the others I'd encountered, making them think they'd killed me. I had shown mercy to no avail. Now that the shoe was on the other foot, they had none to give me. They had orchestrated an assassination. I got a glimpse into the window of the mages' car. A small arsenal of weapons was in the back: blades, firearms, magical objects, vials, large manacles. If they hadn't killed me here in the middle of the street, there was no telling what they would have done to me.

"Do your worst," he challenged.

I smiled; dark, cold, ruthless. "Thanks for your permission. I plan to."

I studied them as the many ways to die from stab injuries ran through my mind. I glanced at the other fallen Tracker lying faceup, eyes still widened in shock, lips parted slightly in death's awe. I drew back. Stabbing someone when the adrenaline was high was admittedly easier. It made things a blur, the act nothing more than reflexive, the body's need to survive at all costs. This was intentional, and there was a part of me that was a little concerned that my conscience was silent, on a hiatus, prepared to give me a pass on this behavior. Perhaps the voices of anger and umbrage were too loud, drowning out my conscience. I drew back, prepared to deliver the killing strike into a neck. Mages could heal themselves so I'd need to inflict enough serious wounds that they wouldn't have enough magic to counter them all. The first mage had depleted some with his initial assault on me.

"Levy, stop," I heard Gareth command from the distant left. He was too far away; his voice carried in the wind. Even with his preternatural speed, he wouldn't reach me in time to stop me. When he called my name again, he sounded closer. I shot a look over my shoulder before releasing the mages from their pinned position against the car. They dropped forward onto their knees. I relaxed the sai down at my sides.

As I knew they would, instead of surrendering, they attacked. The one closest to me drew his hand back first: magic twirled around it but stopped and quickly withered away when the blade of my sai sank into his stomach. I jammed the other one into his partner's neck and he met the same fate as the shifter. My hands and shirt were covered in blood. When I turned, it took me a moment to meet Gareth's intense gaze. The blue of his eyes was barely visible as they narrowed and homed in on me like a scope. For a few minutes he stared at me in weighted silence. Eventually he allowed his gaze to rove over the three bodies lying in the middle of the street in broad daylight. I glanced up at the sound of an approaching car from the side street. Moving at snail speed, the occupants looked at the bodies in the street and my blood-covered weapons.

"You could have moved away from them," Gareth offered.

"That wouldn't have stopped them." For a moment I felt indignant. They had come after me. I'd protected myself.

Before I could inquire why he'd tracked me, he said, "I wasn't looking for you, but we received a call about this. A. Call. You were seen by a human."

"I used magic, nothing different from the mages'." I didn't mean to sound so indifferent, but that's the way it came out. Callous and cold.

"To observers, a supernatural just killed someone in the street. That's what you did to the 'woman.' That's what they reported. The shifter ring can't be seen from a distance by most humans. But throwing spheres of magic and pinning someone to a car without touching them is a dead giveaway." His tone became rougher with each word, blistering and stern, and his eyes remained on me.

"They blocked me in, I had no choice." Once again, my words sounded flat and apathetic.

His lips disappeared into a line as he assessed me. "Of course," he delivered with the same disbelief evident on his face. He pulled out his phone and made a call. Minutes later SUVs and official cars had surrounded me and the bodies. Some of the agents were in uniform, some in protective equipment as they took pictures of the scene and assessed the situation. I couldn't ignore the glances in my direction. They knew what I was, and I wondered if some of them held the Trackers' view that I deserved to be hunted and killed. One look around the immediate area and I saw how they could think that. How they could see me as the very monster that the history books had depicted us as.

Gareth's arms remained crossed over his chest, and a pondering look shrouded his features. A man with gloves and shoe covers approached me with a large red bag. "I need your weapons."

I looked in Gareth's direction. His expression hadn't changed, and I knew I wasn't going to get any assistance from him. Slowly he started to pace the small area, answering calls as they came in. *Surely this can't be that big of a deal.* That initial thought quickly vanished: there were three dead bodies. A human had seen me use magic and then murder at least one person they thought was human. This was a crapstorm and I couldn't imagine how it was going to play out. I watched as people moved around me, clearing away the bodies, cleaning the area. It became such a disturbing distraction that I didn't see the two agents approaching me with cuffs.

Again, I looked in Gareth's direction. "She'll go on her own, no need for those."

Their brows rose, and they both had the same look of anger and dissension. I had already caused enough problems. I extended my arms out and let them put the cuffs around me. They weren't the typical iron cuffs. These were the ones used on the Legacy a few days ago, large iridium manacles. In silence, they escorted me to their car. When we drove away, I looked back at Gareth, who was still on the phone.

I paced the small room that I'd been escorted to. Each time I moved, I was aware of the blood that encrusted my shirt making it stiff. The metallic smell of it wafted in the air, and I could still feel dried blood on my face. They'd given me a damp towel to wipe it off my face and hands, but it required more than that. I needed a shower.

Magic strummed through me and was worsened by my increasing anxiety. I felt caged as I replayed everything over and over in my head. I wanted to feel remorse, to have just a hint of regret that I could display when I was questioned. I delved deep into all the emotions I had and kept coming up empty on the ones that I needed to show if I was going to get them to show the slightest amount of leniency in this situation.

Standing in front of the two-way mirror, I was aware that someone was probably watching me. I probably looked horrid, covered in blood, unable to control the magic that curled around my fingers, and pacing the floor while occasionally taking a moment to look at the mirror. I was happy for the bright colors that spiraled around my finger and hands. It was the only life in the drab room. White walls, long white desk, and small wooden chairs that looked more uncomfortable than they actually were.

When the door opened I expected Gareth; instead Harrah walked in with an SG agent. His cropped hair was just a few shades darker than his eyes, which watched me carefully. He had a short-sleeved button-down, his slacks crisp and his demeanor distant, professional. A kind look was something he wouldn't give freely.

"Hello, Levy." Harrah greeted me with the smile and gentleness that the agent couldn't manage.

Harrah was camera ready, as she always appeared to be. Her eyes were lightly lined, making them look wider, entreating, and kind. Bowed lips had just a hint of peach and complemented the gentleness of her smile that welcomed people into the supernatural world and suggested it was a lot less scary than they'd imagined. Her voice had an ever-present delicate timbre that lured people into trusting whatever came out of her mouth. I'd learned not to believe most of anything that she said. Because of her, I didn't believe what was reported in the news about incidents that involved supernaturals. I knew that she'd bleached and sanitized the situations until they were unrecognizable. As a fae, she had the gift of cognitive manipulation. Just as I could wipe and implant new thoughts and memories, so could she. But fae could manipulate them as well, and compel actions. Did someone really commit a crime or suicide, or was there a fae nearby urging them into that behavior? It was illegal to do, and punishment for it was severe. When it came to handling the optics of a situation and changing the narrative so that it was palatable for humans, the SG and Harrah seemed to skate over those little restrictions that were in place to protect those same humans. Harrah's unyielding desire to maintain the illusion that supernaturals were all innocuous peddlers of magic and the extent to which she would go to maintain that impression made her untrustworthy.

Harrah remained in the corner, watching me as I took a seat in front of the agent. Shifters could determine if someone was telling the truth, but it wasn't necessary when a fae was in the room working her magic to make it happen. I didn't fight it. I erected no shields to protect myself. I welcomed the magic as it laced around me, overtaking my mind. The soothing touch of it relaxed me to the point that I knew nothing of doing anything other than providing the truth.

The agent shuffled his papers and looked down at one in particular. "State your name."

Fuck. This again. "Anya Kismet." His eyes lifted and he studied me for a long time but didn't seem surprised.

He continued, "Are you a Legacy?"

Being forced into telling the truth didn't make the questions any less annoying. My mind felt open, and I knew Harrah kept her magic flowing over me. Savannah once expressed concern about Harrah and her strength and abilities because she could manipulate the memories of everyone in a club just by walking past them. There always seemed to be a slight indicator when magic was being performed, even if it was just a slight strain on the wielder's face, a tick of their lips, a raising of fingers to direct it, or something. With Harrah, there was nothing. She performed magic as if it was as natural and automatic as breathing.

"Tell me what happened today when you were attacked," he commanded in an even voice.

I told him every detail, even the parts that I should have been remorseful about. My tone matched his—I didn't bother to show emotions that weren't there.

"When Mr. Reynolds told you to stop, did you?"

"Yes, but I knew they would attack the moment I released them."

"And you knew you would have to kill them?"

"I wanted to. I've lived my life in fear because of them. They killed my parents. Why do you think they were there, to invite me to brunch? They were there to kill me."

"So, you thought you'd seek your own justice," he asserted coolly.

I scoffed. "Should I have waited for you all to do something?" Then I looked at the two-way mirror, certain that Gareth was behind it watching. "I'm sure I could have counted on you to do nothing, since that seems to be what you all do when it comes to them and us."

Harrah spoke. "Do you know that Conner and four others escaped and none of the Trackers responsible for taking them survived the incident? Would you like to see pictures of the scene? It's nothing compared to the mess you left in our streets today." For a brief moment, her gentle intonation had hardened. I assumed not because of the deaths but over the mess she was going to have to clean up because of that and Conner's escape. He was supposed to be dead, they'd wanted that. Now he and his followers were on the loose, and they had to be pissed and ready to make people pay—including me.

I could tell the wheels were turning as she figured out what to do. Did she still think it was a good idea for me to come out? It didn't matter, because I was sure Conner and his gang of magical elite crazies were about to make it difficult for anyone to admit any connection with Legacy, much less come out as one.

"I searched for them a couple of days ago and couldn't find anything."

"They didn't want to be found, Levy. I don't think you want them to find you either." She warned in a soft voice.

I remembered the flashes of Conner's angry glare as I'd subdued him. He'd considered me his future consort, a worthy companion. When he'd realized I wasn't going to give in and concede to his romantic ideas and his Captain Crazy Pants plan of doing the Cleanse again, he'd become disenchanted with me.

For a fleeting moment I hoped his agenda had changed. If he had to be a sociopath with a cause, I hoped he'd started an anti-Tracker movement. Had everything that had transpired over the past few days changed him? He might not be as dangerous. He had fewer allies than he'd had before. Although I could see how he'd charmed the others, I wasn't sure he had the time to do it to another group of people to increase his followers.

"Levy, I may need your assistance in fixing this," Harrah admitted.

My head barely moved into the nod and I controlled the

frown that was threatening to form and the wary glare that I wanted to direct in her direction. I didn't want to assist Harrah. I didn't even want to be around her. I'd seen her direct Gareth and an SG agent to make sure someone didn't survive to be questioned or contradict the web of deceit that she would construct. She'd told outright lies and woven in lies of omission, all while she smiled for the cameras, docile and sweet. I really didn't want to have anything to do with her.

She nodded at me and then to the agent. She left first; the agent remained behind.

"Don't leave town in case we need you for more questioning." He looked down again.

"If a person were trying to evade the SG, what would be the best way to do it? I'm asking for a friend." I grinned, an attempt to coax a smile or even a smirk from him. His eyes were harsh as they looked back at me. The lines of his brow pulled even tighter together.

"I'm glad you find killing three people a joking matter. Do you think the human that witnessed it found it as funny, Ms. Michaels?"

His scathing look of contempt lay heavily on me.

"They were going to kill me. You do realize that's why they were there? Would you have preferred it to be me lying in the street?" I countered. The guilt wasn't there, and I was doubtful it would ever be no matter how he attempted to shame me for it.

"Do you have any family or friends that we can contact if we aren't able to reach you at home or work?" he asked, ignoring my question.

I shook my head.

"These are the potential contacts we have." He went on to name Kalen and Savannah and rattle off the addresses of their siblings and parents. I gaped at him as I realized how much they had delved into my life and what they knew about me. Was that typical, or was it a subtle threat to encourage compliance? I nodded.

"Good." He nodded his head and left, leaving the door open behind him. I didn't move initially, but when no one came in to release me, I slowly stood up. When I walked out of the room and passed the one adjacent to it, I saw Gareth standing still peering into the two-way mirror, listening intently to what the agent who had just left me was saying to him. They both glanced at me, and the agent said something else. Gareth responded, in a lowered voice; I wasn't able to make out the words.

"Your car is at your home. Would you like me to take you there or do you want to call Savannah?" Gareth asked. Just like Harrah and the agent earlier, his tone was professionally cool.

I accepted his offer.

Once in the car, time ticked by as we drove in silence. The silence made the thirty-minute drive seem longer. Much longer.

"You're *asking for a friend*—Levy, what's wrong with you?" he demanded. At least it managed to coax a smile, albeit a small one, out of him. He kept his eyes on me, although I wished he dedicated more time to looking at the road.

"I was attempting to make him laugh hard enough to dislodge the stick that was firmly wedged up his ass."

Gareth chuckled and shook his head. When he stopped, he hadn't settled into his typical relaxed demeanor: something was bothering him. I supposed coming upon someone with three bodies lying at their feet might be a little alarming. But he'd seen worse. Maybe not from me, but I was sure he had.

"I want you to put a ward up in your apartment."

"Why?"

"You're probably going to be attacked today," he admitted.

That is not something that should be said casually.

"Seems to be happening a lot lately," I responded briskly, not caring to hide the irritation. It had taken up residence in me several days earlier. There wasn't any need to pretend it wasn't there.

"There will definitely be Trackers. I think I've found the leak." He failed at his attempt to keep the frustration out of his voice as he pushed the words through clenched teeth. "I've narrowed it down to two people. One of them thinks you will be staying at one of the SG safe houses, and the other knows you will be going home."

"Is the latter the stick-up-the-butt agent from earlier?"

He nodded and frowned, his anger showing as he accelerated, passing the cars that had the audacity to go the speed limit. "It's harder to discern when another shifter isn't being truthful, and I'm always cautious around those who can lie without any noticeable differences in their vitals. It serves them well when working on behalf of the SG, but I have always been leery. One mage and the shifter have been particularly concerned that you all still exist and have made comments about the numbers they expect there are. It seems that they are privy to information that only"—his eyes slipped in my direction—"you and Trackers would have."

The muscles of his neck bulged as he clenched his jaw. I wasn't sure if he was silent out of embarrassment that he had a leak or because he thought his agents would be more open-minded about Legacy.

I didn't hurry taking a shower, despite the fact that Gareth was waiting for me in the living room. The warmth of the water was relaxing enough, but it didn't help the way I'd expected it would. Of all the times for them to rear their unwarranted heads, guilt and remorse crept into the many emotions I was feeling. It was getting harder for me to force them out. I had been conditioned to be better. My parents had taught me to fight, but instilled the mandate to preserve life when possible. Years of being hunted and seeing the lifeless bodies of my parents and their friend made me advocate for preserving life even when people didn't deserve it. I based this stance on how others felt about us—we didn't deserve it. "You're not a murderer," I'd heard my mother tell me over and over. I now realized she'd done it because I would constantly be told tales of how my kind were nothing but ruthless, callous murderers. I'd internalized a "do no harm" philosophy to my detriment. I should have killed the Trackers who'd come after me earlier instead of wiping their memories.

I didn't own the guilt and remorse for killing the most recent Trackers, and by the end of the shower, I had a better perspective of what I planned to do. It included finding Conner, ending his plans, and finding the other Legacy before Conner or Trackers did.

I opened the door of the bathroom to find Gareth in the chair on the opposite side of my room, his legs stretched out in front of him as he thumbed through the pages of one of my graphic novels.

"Please, make yourself at home," I said sarcastically.

He looked up, baring his teeth in a roguish grin. "I did. Thank you." He returned to the novel and flipped through several more pages as I cinched the towel tighter around me and gathered some clothing out of the dresser. When I turned around, he was scrutinizing me.

"Are you okay?" he asked.

I nodded. He rose from the chair, his eyes remaining on me. His head angled and he continued to study me as he cleared the few feet between us. "What's wrong?" he asked, his tone softer and concerned.

It felt ridiculous that I had a problem telling him that I wasn't going to feel sorry for what I'd done to the Trackers. I inhaled deeply, but instead of it being cleansing I became aware of Gareth. Our proximity, the masculine musk that was uniquely his, the primal nature of his existence. When he placed his hand on my waist, the touch was soothing. I was almost positive I could feel the heat of his caress through the fabric. The pads of fingers hugged my stomach and I leaned into his touch needing to feel more of him.

His mesmeric blue eyes stayed fastened to mine.

"I guess it won't do any good for me to just make something up?" I said.

He shrugged. "Hasn't really stopped you before. I find your stories entertaining. What do you have for me?" he teased. With each word he'd inched closer, taking up any space that had managed to remain between us. His lips brushed against mine as he spoke the last ones. I leaned in, pressing my lips against his. Seconds before, I'd stopped lying to myself that the chemistry between us was a distraction. I wanted Gareth. He responded fervently, kissing me hard, the weight of his body urging me back against the wall. His fingers grasped the towel on each side, pulling me closer to him. I ran my fingers through his hair, kissing him harder, exploring his mouth and tasting him.

One tug and the towel dropped to the floor. Pulling back for a second, he gave me a long, lingering once-over, slowly roving over me inch by inch. His eyes blazed with raw sensuality as they raked over me. He leaned in closer, kissing me fervently as his fingers stroked lazily over the bare skin of my shoulders and arms and then lightly stroking over my breasts. He sucked in a ragged breath and I could feel the rapaciousness of his need in his touch as his hands roved over me, exploring further. His tongue flicked out to taste me, gliding over jaw, neck, shoulder, and breast. Panting, I tried to catch my breath as he eased over my stomach, my thighs, and between them. He pulled away and yanked off his clothes in one sweeping move.

He pulled me to him, and I wrapped my legs around him as he carried me to the bed and lowered me onto it. He resumed his fervent exploration of my body, and when he moved up to my face, I kissed him again. He pushed away for a moment, his gaze slowly roving over my body as he moistened his lips. Again, he kissed me- harder, hungrier and more commanding. He slipped between my legs, sheathing himself in me. He rocked against me, languid and easy at first. He writhed inside of me, bringing me to new heights of pleasure as my body willingly succumbed to the animalistic nature of his movements and raw sensuality. His touch was still gentle as his breath breezed against my lips, but his thrusts became more vigorous as we found our sensual rhythm. Gareth shuddered as my fingers grazed over his skin. His body was a blanket of warmth as he relaxed more of his weight into me. His movements were frenetic, filled with a need to find our pleasure. I couldn't stop running my hands over his body, craving even more of him. A feeling that was definitely mutual as his kisses became hungrier, more voracious before trailing over the rest of my body: my neck, my shoulder, my breast. My fingers curled into his back as we reached our pleasure together, and then he relaxed on top of me. He whispered my name into my ear.

I recalled him teasing me about my desire to hear him purr—the lazy way he said my name wasn't far off. I liked it.

He continued to languorously run his fingers over the curves of my body. After a few moments of silence, he asked, "Are you able to put up the ward, or do you need a nap?"

This guy. "I think I can gather the energy to walk down the hall and put up a ward to stop a mage."

"Now who's the arrogant one," he teased, rolling to his side and taking me with him so that we faced each other. His hands never left my body, keeping contact with me. I looked into his eyes and the carnal sensuality I saw there evoked an urge to repeat what had just happened.

He kissed me long and hard as if he was thinking the same thing. He kissed me again and then flicked his tongue against my lips and pulled back. "Ward," he reminded me. "You put up the ward, and I'll fix us something to eat." He rolled out of bed and headed for the door.

I cleared my throat before he could exit, and he raised an eyebrow in inquiry. I stared at him, allowing my eyes to travel the length of his body and come to rest on an area I was sure Savannah wouldn't want to see when she entered the apartment.

"What?" he asked.

"Do you think you might want to put on your clothes?"

"Not really"—he flashed me a crooked smile—"and based on what I'm picking up from you, I don't think you want me to, either."

"Your humility is inspiring," I responded, rolling my eyes. His movements were graceful and fluid as he grabbed up his pants and slipped into them. I watched him the whole time.

CHAPTER 4

Three hours after the ward was erected we sat in my living room as Savannah's attention bounced between Gareth and me as we explained everything that had happened and she peppered us with questions we couldn't answer. When I explained why I was warding the apartment, she looked more concerned.

"Who are we really warding the house against?" She cast a dark look in Gareth's direction.

"It could be someone at the SG or even Trackers. I'm not sure they haven't been given your information," Gareth said.

"Unless Conner gets here first," Savannah said with an edge to her voice that I hadn't ever heard before. Our eyes widened at her rigid snarl. She was worried and rightfully so. The risk of being attacked by Conner was just as great as being captured by a Tracker.

"Most of his people didn't make it out," Gareth said.

This information didn't change Savannah's mood or the intensity of her rictus. Her stormy gray eyes kept moving from us to the door, expectant and frustrated. Gareth directed the same watchful concern he'd had for me at her now. I hated that she felt anything other than ease in her home, but she seemed to have a heightened awareness and if something was going to happen it would serve her well.

"We're both here, nothing is going to happen."

She nodded, stood and left out the room, and returned with the blade I'd given her weeks before the first time we took her to track Conner. She held it like someone with experience; unfortunately, I'd seen her use it when we'd practiced. At least she looked formidable, and that might be enough. At first sight, anyone who came through the door would have taken her for a knife-wielding slayer who was going to dice them up into bite-sized pieces. They wouldn't suspect that she would probably lose it the moment they started to fight.

Once the first four uneventful hours had passed, I expected Gareth to leave, but he didn't. By ten o'clock that night nothing had happened and we all went to bed. Sleep came easier than I'd expected with Gareth next to me. When his arms wrapped around me, I wished we were skin to skin, but remaining clothed probably was more practical in the event someone did try to break in. It wasn't until magic—strong magic—struck against my ward that I woke with a startle. I grabbed the twins and ran to the front of the house. The ward was stronger than I would have typically used, but if they were coming to kill me, they weren't going to send just one weak mage. They would send their best, and they did. Each time magic battered against the ward, I could feel it as though it was physically pounding into me. Our running to the front door had woken Savannah up and she was now standing next to me, holding the blade.

"Savannah, please go back in your room," I urged.

She glared at me. "I will do no such thing. We are in this

together," she barked, baring her teeth. *Damn, she looks menacing.*

"Fine, play lookout from your room. Make sure no one is coming through the back," I suggested.

Cutting her eyes at me, she gave me an "are you kidding me" look.

The intruders kept working on the lock, pushing more magic into it, and I was afraid to look out of the window to see how many there were.

"Let the ward down," Gareth instructed me. He changed his stance, moving into a defensive position.

"Ready?"

He nodded. I dropped the ward, the door blasted open, and Gareth lunged forward. He shed his human form like it was a coat, and tawny fur covered his body in place of his tanned skin. Massive claws stretched from his flexed fingers, and the cocky smile that he usually wore was replaced by a powerful jaw and sharp canines. The assailant closest to the door didn't stand a chance as the massive cave lion careened into him, knocking him to the ground. One strike against the neck, and blood spurted as the man slumped to the ground. I could hear sirens, and I hoped it was the SG and not the human police. I didn't remember seeing any SG cars having sirens, which made sense as they tended to prefer discretion when apprehending people. Their cars usually only had a small unobtrusive emblem on them.

Magic hit me, sending me stumbling back. Another blast struck Savannah, and she flew back into the wall, hard. I heard the sound of crumbling plaster but I couldn't give them the advantage of being distracted by looking. Her pained sounds served as an indicator she was alive, but I wasn't sure how badly she was injured. A wave of magic came off me, an aggregate of it, sending three men back onto the lawn. I ran out of the house, sai gripped firmly in hand, ready to inflict pain and damage. The battering I'd given myself from not feeling guilty about killing the other Trackers was long gone. I had every intention of killing these as well. The fewer of them left trying to kill my kind, the better things were going to be. I hit them with another jolt of magic. One gritted his teeth, but refused to scream out in pain. The others wailed loudly. The police would soon arrive, and the neighbors were out on their lawns watching the magical show and the savage monster lion mowing down and mauling a supernatural. They were gawking at me as I hurled magic at another magic wielder. Concentrating on the mage in front of me whose fingers were encircled by vibrant colors, I waited, preparing to put up a shield to protect myself from whatever he was about to do. Then I felt the magic of someone in my head, crowding my thoughts, making an attempt to manipulate my mind, something that I'd done to other Trackers who had come for me. They pushed, I blocked. They pushed even harder, and I looked around for the fae who was hidden, skulking in the darkness. Gareth, still in his animal form, blood matted in his fur and around his mouth, followed my gaze into the darkness. He raised his head and took a whiff of the air. He started out slowly walking, breathing in the scent, and then he whipped around and went in the other direction. I heard the thud of someone crashing to the ground and a primal roar before someone cried out. It was only a second before the sound was cut off. A shot rang through the air. I felt the searing pain as it entered my body. My senses were still sharp but my magic dulled. I called for it. Nothing but the curdling, painful feeling of magic being restricted. I clawed at the dart and jerked it out of my skin. It was the same type used by the SG to subdue Conner and his crew. They'd tested it on me prior to that. It restricted our magic for six minutes. A potent chemical that was mostly a large dose of iridium pumped into us to decrease our magic.

Sai in hand, I looked in the direction the shot had come from. Just a few feet away stood the unfriendly man who'd interrogated me, aiming the weapon at me again. At least it wasn't a gun. I guess he wanted the satisfaction of killing me the way the Trackers seemed to enjoy: a blade through us as they watched our life drain out. A cruel gratification from wielding the blade that ultimately took a life. Our eyes locked, and I tried to count down the minutes until I had use of my magic. A hard ball hit me in the back—magic hurled by the mage I'd been dealing with earlier. He didn't seem to have the same desire for a blade to end my life. He seemed content to do it with the very thing he hated about me—magic. My body ached as though someone had landed a blow with a heavy stone. My bones groaned at the pain, and my head was pounding from the fae's mind invasion. I rolled on the ground, avoiding another ball of magic. They kept coming rapid fire until the mage was fatigued enough that he needed to stop. I jumped to my feet, sai gripped tightly, ready to engage, when he froze. I heard it, but not soon enough-the cocking of a gun. Several policemen had surrounded us. One of the officers threw the treacherous SG agent face-down on the ground, yanking his arms behind his back before cuffing him.

Another police officer started to approach me, but stopped when several SG SUVs pulled up. A shifter and another high-level mage jumped out. There was no denying he was a strong mage—the magic that wafted off him was stifling.

"We have this," the shifter said. His voice was rough and the shifter ring pulsed in his eyes as he made his territorial claim. His predaceous nature commanded the area, but the human police held.

"This is ours," the police officer said in a gruff voice.

"We can handle this," Gareth said, coming from around the corner. He walked slower than he usually did, but still maintained the grace of a shifter. They looked at him, but I wasn't sure if it was because they recognized him or because he was naked and his face and body were covered in blood.

Gareth repeated himself, and they hesitated, but eventually dropped their guns. As they started to back away, another car drove up and Harrah quickly got out. As usual, she looked innocuous dressed in a simple pair of slacks and a flattering willow print shirt. As she approached the officer, her smile was as dainty and sweet as her mannerisms. Just like all the citizens in the city, the officers seemed enchanted and disarmed by her. I looked at the doorway of the apartment where Savannah stood, her eyes narrowed on Harrah, watching her intently. She'd earned the right to be cautiously skeptical of the fae when she'd watched her walk into a club after an incident occurred and effortlessly manipulate memories.

Harrah was speaking with the police, shaking their hands, holding contact, and for a moment each officer had a glazed look on their face. They looked back at the scene, brows furrowed as if they didn't know why they were there. After they left, she scanned the area, smiling at the neighbors who hadn't had the good sense to duck into their apartments. I suspected that they all would get a visit from either her or another SG agent, because two more cars had pulled up since she had arrived.

I questioned whether it was important to preserve the alliance with humans, given all the horrible things that needed to be done to maintain it. Part of me wanted us to take off the masks and expose ourselves for what we were, warts and all. Humans had their flaws as well. Murder, theft, manipulation, crimes against humanity and decency were constantly done, yet humans didn't go through extremes to guard us against them. If they were trying to minimize our knowledge of such things, someone wasn't very good at their job.

When Harrah approached me, Savannah slipped into the house.

"No one came to the safe house," she informed Gareth, who was striding toward her. He was dressed and some of the blood was gone, but there was so much that just wiping it away wasn't going to be enough. The only way he was going to remove that amount of blood was in a shower.

As she kept speaking with him her voice became lower and lower and it was more than obvious that she didn't want me there. She welcomed me excusing myself.

CHAPTER 5

*T*hings were too quiet. Four days had passed since the Trackers' attack at the apartment, and I expected something—another shattered ward; a visit from Evelyn, Conner's head minion; or even an audience with Conner himself. Nor had the Trackers attacked again. I suspected that between the carnage during Conner's escape and what had happened after they attacked me, their numbers were dwindling. The anticipation of retaliation was making me jumpy and irritable.

"You're in a mood," Savannah said from the passenger side of the car.

"Not a mood, just concerned."

"About?"

"Conner. He should have made an appearance by now to yammer on about his plans for world domination."

"People like him don't respond well to being dominated, and make no mistake, he was. You kicked his ass."

"I just managed not to die; I'm not sure if I kicked his ass." And that was the crux of the matter: I hadn't died. I'd had help from Gareth and the SG, which made me apprehensive about the possibility of facing him alone. The look on his face when he'd been cuffed was anger, melded with a hint of humiliation.

"You kicked it thoroughly and he knows it," she said confidently. "Maybe he decided against it and is just going to scuttle away and live his days in his own little heaven and not have to deal with the likes of us. He can use his magic to make a glorious world. If I were him, that's pretty much all I would do. Speaking of that, we need you to work on your magical construction skills."

"Of all the things I need to learn, that's not one of them."

"Oh come on, you can spruce up the place a little," she teased as I pulled into a parking space on Coven Row where most of the witches had their stores. Savannah didn't possess magic of her own as an *ignesco*, a magic enhancer, but she was overzealous about her newly discovered power and had proclaimed herself my assistant. She seemingly hadn't been advancing quickly enough with on-the-job training alone and was on the hunt for more education. We'd gone through all the books that Blu had loaned us as well as some that Lucas, the Master of the city, had been able to get his hands on. I knew, however, that our day trip was less about Savannah's avid interest in her newfound ability and more about getting my mind off of things.

We browsed a number of shops but managed to bypass the *herba terrae* stores that had become major destinations for many people in the city. It was legal to imbibe cannabis after the witches added a few other herbs, tannins, and salts; an invocation over the concoction; and an authoritative-sounding Latin name. Most of these places were set up like hookah bars or nice restaurants where the entertainment consisted of magic. These acts were nothing more than cruise ship tricks for the entertainment of customers in a *herba terrae* state of bliss who had spent a fortune on the witch weed and the food. The witches could probably make more money if they just served donuts, Cheetos, and Doritos. They were true businesspeople, however, and would never consider serving such things. They even considered themselves too classy to name the places something like Witch's Pot Spot—a suggestion that I'd made on more than one occasion to various restaurants. I thought it had a special ring to it, as opposed to the cutesy names they'd chosen, like Witch's Brew and Shadow.

I wasn't sure if it was my increasingly sullen mood, but Savannah seemed to feel the need to placate me somehow. "It's okay to be anxious about Conner's absence, but don't let it consume you and make you miserable." Her voice was soft and measured as she wrapped her hand around my arm and guided me into an ice-cream parlor. I stopped at the entrance and looked at her suspiciously. I wondered if it was the munchies-inducing aura of the *herba terrae* boites as well as my cloud of anxiety driving her.

"Are you dying?"

She rolled her eyes. "Just because I don't want to completely fill my body with fat and toxins doesn't mean I can't *occasionally* enjoy it. And I just don't think a brownie is an acceptable breakfast."

"I had milk with it, and it was chock-full of nuts. Eggs, milk, nuts, cocoa—it's a superfood," I said.

She dismissed me with a look of derision and ordered a small bowl of vanilla ice cream.

What's the point?

We sat and finished our ice cream as she discussed the plans she had with Lucas that night. Focusing on her as she talked about him was a mediocre distraction: you'd think the experience of dating the Master of the city, who owned two very popular clubs, would be more eventful.

After we'd window-shopped our way down more of Coven Row, Savannah became more absorbed in her hunt for materials to develop and enhance her talent. We'd spent nearly an hour in one shop, and she'd filled her handcart with magic accoutrements that would be useless to her. The store's owner had obviously taken pains to make the store feel magical. The burgundy walls of the store had sigils scrolled over them. I studied them but was convinced that they were nothing more than decoration. The floor space was crowded with rows of books, stones, salts, and herbs. Heavy, dark-colored drapes dimmed the store enough that it seemed gothic and eerie with a hint of an ethereal appeal. Candles complemented the mood, and the air was blanketed with the scent of sandalwood incense. The overall effect made it hard to resist being enchanted by the idea that a person might have some dormant magical ability, and they just needed the right book, stone, herbs, or talisman to awaken it.

We left the store with enough paraphernalia to fill two bags, which warranted a stop by the car to store it so we could continue shopping. A few feet from the car, I sensed it before I saw it. I shoved Savannah out of the way just as Conner's little pet attacked. It was a massive creature with the heads of the three animals it had been created from. It possessed daggerlike teeth; the quick, sinewy movements of a feline; and the powerful build of a wolf. It was a menacing creature and had been hard to defeat the first time I'd encountered it. The serpent head was the wild card. It had a lot more movement than it should have, seeing that it was affixed to a body. Its tongue darted out, tasting the air. Then it struck out, hitting

Savannah, who hadn't gained enough distance from it. It recoiled, ready to strike her again. A strong explosion of my magic sent the creature back several feet, not nearly as far as I wanted. I sent another strong shot of magic in its direction, but the magic rebounded right back with as much force as I'd pushed it outward. I lunged, but couldn't avoid it. A strong thrum slammed into me, and I crashed to the ground.

"Get to the car!" I yelled at Savannah, who seemed shaken but uninjured. "Now!" I commanded when she hesitated. The serpent darted in her direction, nudging her back and keeping her away from me. When I rolled to my feet, I found I wasn't too far from the car. I ran to it, grabbed the twins, and scanned the area. Conner. I knew he'd have to be there. Wherever his pet was, he wasn't too far away.

For a moment I inhaled the air, knowing I wouldn't be able to sense Conner's magic or feel the direction it was coming from as long as the beast in front of me emanated its own brand of odd, overpowering magic. Savannah had come to her feet, slowly backing away from the creature. I focused on the serpent head, whose movements were the most erratic and independent of the body; I knew from experience it was poisonous. I charged the creature, and when it lurched at me, mouth open, I dodged its fangs. Its head whipped back and hit me, throwing me back. Then claws raked across my leg. Pain surged through me as crimson stained my pants. The serpent was snapping its head forward, trying to get me with its fangs. I blocked them with the moto of the sai. I rolled to my knees and plunged one of the sai deep into its side. I had to tug hard to dislodge it. The wolf head howled. Blood spurted. The creature didn't stop moving. It wasn't trying to get away from me, but closer to Savannah. It whipped its serpent head, stretching farther with each movement, trying to clear the distance to get to her. I ignored the crowd that had started to form. There weren't enough lies, enough manipulation of the truth, to conceal this story. Harrah would have to deal with it.

The creature moved faster and more agilely than it should have with the injuries it had sustained. I needed to disable the serpent and hope that if I killed one part of the body the rest would die. But would Conner create a creepy freak creature that could be subdued so easily? I considered trying to roll under the animal, but I didn't want to risk the snake's venom. Timing it as best as I could, I jabbed both sai into it and pulled them out. Blood sprayed from the injury, and the creature retreated. I divided my attention between it and Savannah. *Should I let it go?*

I couldn't. I took off behind it, running to catch up. I barely registered the blurs of faces, the phones videoing everything. As soon as I was within a few feet, I lunged—at air. The creature was behind Conner who was standing a few feet from me.

I looked around the small area. I was boxed into a space Conner had made for me, his beast, and himself. The opaque wall created a fuzzy haze and made it difficult to see anything outside of it; I wondered what others saw. Did it look like a continuation of the background that merged with it and indistinguishable to the naked eye?

"Thank you," he addressed the animal. It nodded and plopped down on its paws, trying to lick at its wounds.

"He will heal soon," Conner informed me.

"I'm sorry, were you under the impression I cared?"

He chortled. "Ah, my Anya, such a witty tongue. I'm often torn between wanting to see how it tastes and ripping it out." His low tone held hints of the ire and wrath he'd directed toward me when he'd finally given in to the idea that I would never be one of his followers and would instead take every chance I had to be an obstacle to him.

He moved closer, and I pointed my sai at him, daring him

to take another step. He smiled and let his gaze rove up my arm, over my face, and up to my hair. "I do hate that color," he snarled at it.

"You touch me, and you will regret it."

Smiling, he took a small step back.

"What do you want?"

"Evelyn is gone, and so are three others of mine." His sorrow-laden voice made it hard not to feel some sympathy for him even though he didn't deserve any. He stepped back again; there wasn't enough room for him to truly pace, but he moved in an easy fluid stride, the gait of a trained and lethal fighter. Although he possessed magic—extraordinary magic—he was a skilled combatant, and I was reminded of it as he moved along the small space afforded to him. He gave me another appraising look along with a flick of anger that I knew was incited by the blood on me from his pet. The last time he'd seemed upset when he'd thought I'd killed it. I thought I had, too, but perhaps this was just one of many he'd created. I wondered if there were any limitations to Vertu magic.

"Perhaps my plans were too ambitious," he admitted. His voice lacked the humility that I'd have expected from someone who had just conceded and admitted to the absurdity of his plan. Instead it was heavy with haughtiness and unwarranted arrogance. "You have been my failure," he continued, giving me another look. His words were tepid as his eyes held mine, a reminder that he believed that I'd betrayed him.

"I'm not your failure, your ridiculous plans were your failure," I said, changing my stance. His position was still casual, relaxed. I couldn't avoid the cold look of betrayal he kept giving me.

He scoffed, a deep, derisive, and throaty sound. "You want us to play nice with the humans. Come out and pretend to be their magical pets incapable of the destruction of the past. We should never be subservient to them." He managed to maintain his composure as he pushed the words through clenched teeth. I drew too much of his attention and it was starting to make me uncomfortable. I gripped the sai tighter, preparing to engage, if needed. I moved back, pressing against the magical wall. The intensity of the strong magic pulsed against my back, rolling over it in waves. The similarities of our magic were overwhelming, but I couldn't ignore the differences either. Legacy were a less powerful version of them, a bastardized rendition rumored to be their creation. I wasn't sure why they didn't loathe our shortcomings the way they did those of other supernaturals.

"You think destroying all magical beings and keeping humans as entertaining pets is better?"

"I have no interest in dealing with them, not even as pets." Indifference was always worse. Indifference evoked no emotions, which made it easier to treat someone callously.

"We can come out and work with them. Are you telling me that their rules and regulations don't have merit? Vampires can no longer compel people. Fae can't use their magic for cognitive manipulation or to change their appearance to anything other than their agreed-upon form. No more glamours." I stopped, studying him with the same interest with which he'd been studying me. "Are you able to do that? Glamour a desired appearance?"

"Of course. But why would I?" He raised a brow, his thin lips slightly kinked into a smirk, entreating a response. I gave him a once-over. For a person who'd been involved in a small war, he looked pretty good—his appearance didn't reflect it. He had narrow, sharp features, and the unique persimmon red hair of Legacy, and Vertu fit his regal appearance. He wouldn't be out of place as part of a royal court. He didn't present the face of a person who would lead a plan that would result in genocide.

Why would I? Someone's very proud of himself. Instead of pointing that out I continued, "Mage and witch magic can't be used for darker arts. What's wrong with that? How can you want to live in an unregulated world when it comes to magic? Your arrogance allows you to consider it unimportant because you don't think you will ever be on the receiving end of the cruelty of it. The system is working." I was taking extreme liberty with the word *working*, but it was better. There would always be rule breakers and those who reminisced about the world of yesteryear when they could do whatever the hell they wanted without consequences, but those days were gone.

"There isn't anything wrong with conceding—" I began.

His loud, taunting laugh interrupted me, and amusement caressed his words. "I'm not conceding by any means. I considered the humans and others; I was too cautious. I will not suffer such foolishness again. I will strike without mercy, and in the end, I will prevail above the rubble and be the victor of this fight."

I rolled my eyes and sighed heavily. "They always have to monologue."

"I'm sorry?"

"Every bad guy *ever* has to monologue. If I were going to be the Lex Luther to Superman, or the Magneto to Xavier, the Loki to Thor, I wouldn't spend precious time ranting about my grand plans. I'd just blow up crap." I rolled my eyes again. "It's a walking 'bad guy' cliché. Please read from another script."

Again, amusement coursed over his features. Deep emotive eyes lay heavily on me, and as the smile wilted, I didn't know what to expect because his features held an indescribable look.

"You amuse me more than you frustrate me," he admitted. It was clearly a bitter revelation for him, and it took several moments before he spoke again. "You know what I am capable of. I've seen your tricks, the games you all played, and it worked once. I wouldn't be confident it will work again."

"Are we done?" I asked.

He shook his head. "Your so-called allies will betray you, don't be naïve enough to think they won't. Now you are a tool, an instrument they will use to find the others. I will give you a safe haven from that and ensure that they will never hurt you. You will be revered in the manner that you deserve."

It was at that moment, when his words were laced with honey and confidence and he presented a caring face, a gentle demeanor, and promises of a better life, that I understood his acolytes. They'd ignored their consciences and shrugged off the maliciousness of the plans made to follow someone who would give them the freedom that their parents had been afforded. They wanted the ability to live without fear that if they performed magic, they would be discovered by a Tracker and their lives would be over. I sympathized ever so briefly with those who had fallen for the charismatic demagogue.

He continued, his tone still as genteel and smooth as it was before. "I don't give an ultimatum without the preparatory thought that it deserves. If you come with me, then I believe I can be *persuaded* into finding another alternative to deal with the undesirables."

I was so confused. Was he implying that in lieu of wreaking havoc, he'd take me? Did he think Stockholm syndrome was going to eventually kick in and I would one day become one of his devout followers instead of his opposition? What exactly were *alternative* ways of dealing with the so-called undesirables? I didn't think for one moment the Cleanse was off the table. It would just be deferred until he felt I was complicit enough to allow it.

"If I surrender to you, then you will pinky swear not to try to murder a bunch of people? How noble of you."

"*Now* our conversation is over." A slight nod of his head, barely a movement, and a flood of magic pushed into me, sending me back through the wall and crashing to the ground, landing hard on my back. I cursed under my breath.

"I knew you were near, your scent cut off here," Gareth said from a few feet away. I was done pointing out how weird it was.

Pulling myself to stand, I looked around.

"She's fine," he said knowing exactly who I was wondering about. Savannah. He gave me a wry grin. "When she sees him again, she's going to 'give him a swift kick where he will remember it.' She's been touting it since we arrived. She is an enthusiastic one, isn't she?"

"That's a nice way of putting it. Is she injured?"

"A few bumps. I think her ego's more wounded than anything." He crossed his arms, taking in my appearance, his frown deepening with each moment. He moved closer. "May I?"

I nodded, and he stepped closer. He knelt down, taking a glimpse of my injuries. He made a sound and I knew the wound from the creature had to be worse than I'd initially thought.

"Let me guess, you're going to heal it, and you don't want to go to the Isles."

"It's like you're psychic!"

He sucked in a sharp breath. My shirt was still raised, so I looked down. Despite the bloodstains, I could still see the puncture marks from the fangs and they looked as angry and painful as they felt.

CHAPTER 6

Two days and I still couldn't get my mind off of Conner's offer. I didn't know if he was an arrogant megalomaniac or a batshit crazy psycho, or worse—a combination of both. I found myself leaning toward the latter of the three options as I kept going through a trunk from our newest find, ignoring the looks that Kalen kept giving me.

"I guess staring at me is more important than clearing this stuff out of the front office," I teased as I searched for whatever magical object in the trunk was giving off the level of energy I sensed. Most of the items weren't of any value, and possibly the magical object or objects wouldn't be, either.

"You're less ornery than usual about having spent most of the day in a dirty attic, why is that?"

"I'm the same as usual, I've just grown tired of complaining about you watching me work while taking shots at my hair." He gave a quick look to the hair piled on top of my head. "My barking about you being lazy and you threatening to take a brush to my hair hasn't worked all these years, so I'm not bothering." I continued rummaging through the trunk sorting things, still aware of his inquisitive gaze on me.

"Have you seen Gareth lately?" he asked with a sly smile before raising his cup of coffee to his lips, taking a seat in the chair next to me. He wasn't even pretending to help anymore.

"Mmmmhmm," I offered. I hadn't looked up from my place on the floor to see his taunting smile. "How are things with Blu, you two had a show or something, right?" Distraction. Distraction. And more distractions. Blu had become the best distraction. I wasn't nearly as interested in his love life as he seemed to be in mine, but there was a small spark of interest in me when it came to her. Kalen was peculiar, and Blu was the first woman he'd shown any interest in. I wondered if there was more than their love of fashion. The more they interacted, the more she seemed to fascinate him.

"Don't insult me with your poorly performed effort to distract me by changing the subject, even if it's about her. It won't work."

He slipped down to the floor and looked out of place among a cordless phone that I had no idea why someone would hold on to, old books of fiction, a small jewelry box that held items that weren't worth much, and several bronze sculptures that might be worth having gone out of the house this morning.

"I've seen Gareth several times."

A small smile peeked through and had fully bloomed within seconds. "Well, this is an interesting turn of events. Do tell." Kalen would fit perfectly on camera, ready to interview whoever decided to sit in the chair next to him. He wasn't dressed for what we did all day: picking up and sorting through mostly junk. As usual he was profession-ally dressed, today in tailored gray slacks and a peach shirt with the top button undone. It was the closest thing to casual I'd seen him wear. But the expensive leather shoes in a deeper gray than his pants didn't necessarily indicate that we were peddlers of used goods and occasional magical objects.

"We are just getting to know each other," I offered dismissively.

"Based on the glow on your face, you seem to be getting to know each other quite well."

"So we aren't going to even pretend this is a place of business and things like that are inappropriate," I scoffed. I was ready to defend my position if only to make the awkward situation go away. When my phone buzzed next to me and Gareth's number flashed, I didn't know if it was a good distraction or would lead to more questions.

I answered.

Gareth barely greeted me. "Are you near a television?" he asked, his voice edged with anger and concern.

"Yes, what's wrong?"

"Just watch it. We couldn't stop this mess from happening."

"What mess? What's going on?"

"It's about the murders of the founder of Humans First and so many Trackers, including the ones that you killed."

I winced when he said it, but that's exactly what I'd done. Killed. The mantra that convinced me that I wasn't a murderer was a distant memory. I tried hard to retrieve it, to remember it, to ingrain it into my very existence. I didn't mind beating a person to a bloody pulp, but I didn't kill—or rather I didn't used to kill. But I wasn't that person anymore. That was it. A chill ran over me.

"Someone else took over."

I wasn't sure why he seemed so stressed by it. "That's not a big deal, people will just consider them another wackadoodle."

"Not really. It's Gordon Lands." It sounded like the words were pushed through gritted teeth.

"The former mayor?"

"Yeah. He's going to do a press conference at twelve. We couldn't find out exactly what he's going to say. Even Harrah couldn't stop this," he admitted. If she couldn't stop it, then the situation was dire. Why wasn't she able to fix it? Did they keep her away from him and the people involved so she couldn't wipe his mind? Were they on to her? Had she performed her little trick one too many times? It wasn't until I exhaled that I realized I had been holding my breath. I inhaled the scent of fresh linen, Kalen's favorite candle fragrance. Most days, I hated it, preferring something with a stronger and fruitier scent, but now I welcomed the cleansing redolence.

"I'll see you later, okay?" I agreed without even considering it and ended the call before standing up.

"What's wrong?" Kalen asked, coming to his feet, his brow furrowed with concern.

"I'm not sure," I said, walking into another room where we had a television. We waited as a few more commercials played, then a midday talk show started for just a few minutes before it was interrupted by breaking news. I wished it was about anyone else but a beloved former mayor who had left office with a wonderful approval rating with the statement that because of "the politics of being in politics" he could do more good as a private citizen. He'd become known for his charity events, large donations to nonprofit organizations, and so many other "good" things that in essence people had elevated him to nobility status. Canonized for his goodwill and contributions, if he was now the head of Humans First, he'd just given them the credibility boost they needed. *Dammit.*

When he spoke, his voice was deep yet soft and notably

conflicted, making his words ring even more sincere. "For years our alliance with the supernaturals was a positive one. It strengthened us as a community, and I still believe to some degree that this is true. It would be unconscionable and irresponsible for me to say that all supernaturals are evil and harmful. Recently I lost a good friend, and although I didn't believe in all his views, I knew his heart was in the right place. He just wanted safety for humans and for history never to repeat itself. I fear that it will. We've lived with the falsehood that the Legacy were all destroyed after the Great War. I have it on great authority that they exist and have been aided by other supernaturals in seeking to cause the Cleanse again. Most of us remember it, have read about it in our history books, or even witnessed the sorrow in our loved ones' eyes as they discuss members of the family who died during it." He stopped, his gentle brown eyes looking over the assembled crowd, entreating and sincere. He took another jagged breath. I listened to him tell us that he would be taking over Humans First and working with the Supernatural Guild to ensure the safety of the people in his city. He'd also be working with federal agencies to ensure that any Legacy that might be out there plotting their nefarious plans would be stopped. Even though he urged people to let appropriate agencies handle things, I knew it wouldn't help. Whether it was an innocent mistake or his intention to incite paranoia and rage, he'd lit the wick that would set off an explosion. My fingers had started to cramp from holding my phone so tightly.

"We are screwed," Kalen said softly.

I squeezed my eyes together, knowing that wasn't the half of it. I'd been the last person to meet with Daniel before Conner and his crew of misguided misfits had shown up and killed him. They'd transported in, and I'd been the only one seen entering the building.

I cursed under my breath remembering the situation. Police had come to arrest me, and it was Gareth who'd convinced them that I was innocent. He'd claimed to have evidence. He'd been bluffing, but it had worked—they'd released me.

Worry had rendered both Kalen and me useless. We went back to the other room and sat on the floor, next to the open trunk. He fiddled with the brass lock on it, a pensive scowl firmly in place, silver eyes resting on me heavily with concern and worry. Although he tried hard to hide it, there was always a noticeable battle, the dichotomy and turmoil he had to feel with me in his life. His affection for me at constant war with his hate for my kind. He'd lost some of his family during the Cleanse. I understood his anger and frustration.

"What do you think is going to happen?" I asked.

"Mr. Lands said for people not to panic and let the government agencies help, so I suspect people are going to panic and do some vigilante justice." He was right, and I was appreciative of him being straight with me.

I looked down at my phone for the third time in fifteen minutes, waiting on Gareth to return one of the three calls I had made or at least answer the four text messages.

Kalen gave me another long, assessing look and then said, "You should go talk to him. If you need to take tomorrow off"—he looked at the unfinished pile of goods and the large trunk that was still unsorted—"maybe I can get Blu to help. She seems pretty interested in this stuff."

Interested in this or you? I wondered but bit back. I wasn't sure what I let out was any better than what I had censored. "What's the deal with you two? There isn't anything that interesting about clothes, shoes, or accessories that would require this much attention."

"I find her interesting."

"Interesting or *interesting?*" I asked, making a kissy face on the latter.

He gave an exaggerated gasp before placing his hands over his mouth in pseudo offense. "Control yourself, young lady, this is a place of business and you will behave yourself in such a manner."

I laughed. I needed some levity, anything that lifted some of the weight of this situation that was getting harder to control.

"We're just hanging out, getting to know each other," he said. "Unlike you and Gareth, we've managed to do it while remaining fully dressed. How about that?"

I flushed, and if he only suspected it, he now knew. The knowing smirk remained on his face as I left.

Kalen was right: telling people not to panic was a surefire way to cause pure panic. The protests didn't take long to form. Outside one of the shops on Coven Row was a small group of protesters, and I slowed my car to take a look. It hadn't seemed to hurt business. Not too many things were going to get between a person and their *herba terrae* or love potions or whatever magical needs they felt they had. Although witches were just as dangerous as mages or fae, they had carved a little niche with their stores, making them the "pleasure supernaturals" and innocuous in the eyes of most. But there were exceptions, and those exceptions were standing outside the door with signs and chanting. At least they didn't have torches, stakes, and pitchforks.

CHAPTER 7

Despite not hearing from Gareth, I decided to go by his office. The Supernatural Guild's large light-gray multistory headquarters always seemed to blend in as just another building on the block. The drapes were drawn on the large picture windows giving an unobstructed view of the streets. Beautifully trimmed hedges surrounded the building, and the lawn was always manicured and so verdant green that it looked like there was more magic involved than landscaping. Usually when I entered the building I was met by agents dressed too casually for their position but that day they had traded their business casual attire for bulletproof vests and military-style weapons. They were never a friendly group, especially the shifters, who seemed to consider smiling a crime in and of itself, but now everyone seemed to be on edge. They watched me carefully as I walked into the front door of the building, something I was sure they were doing to every visitor.

I was surprised to see Beth at the front desk without Avery.

Responding to my look of curiosity, Beth responded in a

dry tone, "Mr. Reynolds sent him home and lifted his punishment."

I looked back at the door: there were guards placed at it, something they hadn't had before. I was sure that having a powerful fae such as Beth at the front desk wasn't a coincidence. She'd manipulated my emotions once, with such ease and deftness that I hadn't realized it until she'd forced me into a state of calm.

"Is Gareth available?"

"I'm sorry, he will not be available for the rest of the day." I scanned the room and hallways, noting that the activity in the building had increased significantly. There were men in suits walking around, and their conversations seemed intense but too low for me to hear.

"Is he here?" I asked.

"Mr. Reynolds isn't available" was her simple monotone response. I'm not sure if that was the generic line she'd been instructed to tell everyone. Uneasiness was there. Was he trying to distance himself from me or was he unavailable to everyone? Was he busy working with Harrah on damage control?

"Will you let him know that Levy—"

"I know who you are." And she treated me to a gentle broad smile. "Levy, don't fret, he tends to be proactive rather than reactive so he's trying to get ahead of things. He's good at his job. But I'm sure you know that."

I could feel the magic creeping near me, like a gentle wave as it eased upon the sand. That cool wave changed the slightly humid air to crisp and refreshing. Light and breezy and she did it effortlessly. I pushed it back with force, and she gasped a breath. I should have been gentler, but I wanted to send a message. *No illegal magic on me.* I felt it ease before it disappeared.

"What's happening?" I took another look out the door at

the police cars in front of the building, the increased number of people walking around, and a few SG people who looked unfamiliar. I knew I didn't know everyone who worked for the SG, but I could tell who did by the assurance, sinewy movement, and subtle lethality to them. It was the hint of severe repercussions if you crossed them. And if that didn't deter you, there were the flashes of magic from the wielders of it and the sharp looks from shapeshifters whose rings glowed ever so lightly, a warning sign.

Things were bad, I just didn't know how bad.

By the next morning, I still hadn't heard from Gareth. The significant changes that had occurred over the past twenty-four hours had me distracted and debating whether to go by SG headquarters before work. If that hadn't been my focus as I walked out of my room, I would have found seeing Lucas, the Master of the city and one of the most powerful vampires in the world, in the Warrior One pose with Savannah a little humorous. He was immortal, stuck in the same state he was in when he'd been turned—perpetually stuck in his midthirties, despite being several hundred years old. His blond hair would forever stay that way without the threat of graying, and his body would be eternally lean and muscular.

"You keep it up Lucas and you'll live to be a thousand," I joked as I walked into the kitchen and grabbed one of the muffins I'd purchased the day before as I watched them. He moved with ease and grace into various poses, mirroring Savannah while wearing a suit. *A suit!*

"I'll give you a dollar if you actually put on yoga pants," I offered once he stopped moving with Savannah and started to approach me.

"I'll give you two to never make that request again," he countered. His tone held humor but not much. He watched Savannah, her svelte body moving fluidly into several more positions. She was art in motion, elegant and beautiful, making each transition look far easier and more fun than it was. It looked like she was executing a dance rather than exercising. We both stood in silence watching her intently, appreciating her beauty of movement for different reasons.

When she finally finished, Lucas looked as though he'd been treated to an award-winning show, his lips wide in appreciation. She strode by me, giving me and my second muffin a disapproving look. She stopped by Lucas to give him a kiss on his cheek.

So, this is really happening. It was the first time I fully conceded to it, preferring to live in a perpetual state of denial and just assume it was far more casual than it was. My room-mate, who was a die-hard vampire groupie, was involved with the vampire of all vampires, the hottest of hot zombies. There wasn't anything I could do about it, and I'd tried it all. Even pointing out that technically he was older than her grandpa.

I wasn't going to ever forget the power he wielded not only as one of the oldest vampires in the area but also as a member of the Magic Council—powerful, wealthy, and feared. But I was happy when he used those qualities to protect Savannah. After recently finding out she was an *ignesco*, I was more concerned than ever: her function as a magic booster was something that people would want to possess for their own benefit. Her dating the hot zombie was a good thing. I'd learned to ignore the light blush of red on her neck and arms from her feeding him.

"I didn't hear you come in this morning," I said. *Okay, maybe I haven't totally conceded to the idea.*

He gave me a sly smile. "That's because I got here last

night," he said in a deep, seductive drawl that seemed to be as natural as my breathing. He just couldn't help himself. The art of seduction was so deeply linked to his existence and innate need to find his next donor that he seemed to have a hard time turning it off—or wasn't aware he'd turned it on. His smoldering dark eyes rested on me. *Hey, turn those things off or at least direct them at my roommate.*

I didn't really want him directing them at Savannah, either. He was too smart and old to be oblivious to the many tactics that I'd used to keep Savannah from him. My failures had amused him; it was aptly displayed by the kink in his thin supple lips and the glint in his midnight-colored eyes.

As I picked at my muffin, I was aware of his gaze lingering on me: an assessment. "Savannah worries about you, and I think rightfully so," he started slowly. He slipped his hands into his pockets as he started to walk around me in a semicircle, making me ever aware of his speed, stealth, and predaciousness. Even dressed in his expensive, tailored suit, he could probably kill me at any given moment if he willed it. I hated that I thought about it. But I did, and him walking so close to me caused me to reflexively reach behind me for the twins, which weren't there.

"Things are getting tense. Last night I even had a group of thugs approach me to tell me I needed to get out of their city." His mirthless, dark laughter drifted throughout the room. "They were quite unhappy to find that I am the city. I was here before they were, and I plan to be standing if this city burns to the ground."

"You wouldn't have happened to tell them this over a nice drink in a less threatening tone?" I asked, with a big cloying smile.

Again, I was treated to his bone-chilling laughter. Hot zombie, I reminded myself. But reducing him to a hot guy with fangs didn't help.

"I told them in a way designed to ensure they won't bother me again. I clearly have better things to do than entertain overzealous xenophobes," he said. In the time it took me to blink my eyes and break off another piece of my muffin, he was on the sofa sitting with his arms outstretched on the back and one leg crossed over the other. Casually dangerous—the worst kind. I liked my danger in your face and a little asshole-ish.

"Has it been like this before?"

"We weren't out like this. Before, we were known, but not really known—feared. After the war, we became a novelty; my clubs are based on that. We're salacious danger: an extreme activity, with the slight chance you might not come out of it alive. Entertaining for others, and I've adapted to it. This is new, and I don't like it." When he inhaled it seemed weird. I had gotten used to him not doing it and each time he made an attempt to seem human, occasionally breathing at an irregular rhythm too infrequently for it to be considered normal or comforting, it freaked me out even more.

He'd delved so far into his thoughts his face had become stoic, but his eyes were dark and a mixture of anger and umbrage shadowed them. "I'm not sure this will end well," he admitted.

Another war? "What do you mean?"

It took him several moments to answer the question and I hoped it wasn't to censor his answers.

He shook his head and frowned. "I heard that Conner has been very busy," he confided. "Last night he broke the wards of the Barathrum." It was where the Magic Council and the SG sent their worst offenders. "So the SG is dealing with that and now the new head of HF. I suspect things will get worse before they get better."

Conner would essentially win. Humans would want the Cleanse to rid them of the supernaturals. Conner's recruiting would be even easier. Even if he couldn't get enough to do a global Cleanse he would have enough to go from state to state, like a traveling virus ridding the humans of supernaturals, leaving only the Vertu and Legacy—leaving things worse off. Humans would not stand a chance once they'd served their purpose.

"This is a mess," I said, frowning. I didn't need to think about it any longer; I needed to see Gareth before I went to work. I headed to my room to get my bag and weapons.

"Levy." Lucas called my name, catching me just a few feet from my room. "I think it will be better if you are not alone."

Okay, this doesn't sound good at all.

"I've decided I will have two of my employees accompanying you until things are better controlled."

"Oh, did you?" And just as I responded, Savannah came out of her room in time to hear my response and tried to slip back in unnoticed. Jabbing my finger in her direction, I stopped her midstep, fixing her with a sharp glare, and then I curled my fingers, beckoning her to come closer. I wasn't fool enough to believe this was *just* Lucas's decision. He wasn't at his home pondering my safety; my little blond roommate was, and he was overly concerned with her and her desires. He'd become one of the many weapons in the arsenal that she used to mother hen me.

Giving me a faint smile, she shrugged, feigning shock over the statement. I kept looking at her. She widened her eyes innocently. "He can be really overprotective. It's weird, isn't it?" I wasn't falling for this doe-eyed look of blamelessness.

I stepped closer to her. "Then it's a good thing he listens to you, isn't it?"

Moving past me, she kept the same smile and quiescent look on her face as if it wasn't her idea at all.

"Lucas," she said in a gentle, pleading voice, "I don't think Levy likes that idea."

"I think it's a good decision, she'll learn to."

She turned and shrugged, giving me a sympathetic smile. "Sorry, I tried."

"Thanks. I saw that you gave it your all. Will he ever recover from that confrontation? It was painful to watch. It was a verbal brawl. One of those takedowns that's implanted in your mind forever. It was a true bloodbath. I didn't think you were going to come out of it unscathed. Are you okay?"

Pursing her lips together, she fought the smile that was threatening to emerge. Instead, she busied herself with playing with the golden ringlets of her hair to avoid meeting my eyes. Then she straightened her shirt and dusted off the invisible dirt and flecks of lint from her pants. "Well, it seems like he's made up his mind. You know how he is. I can't really change his mind. Sorry." Her words were incongruous with the odd twist of her lips and the miscreant gleam in her eyes. I wasn't buying it for one minute.

Savannah was like the cute toy dog you see, adorable and playful. You can't help but smile whenever you see one. And just like a little toy dog, she showed dominance in other ways. She yapped. If you didn't listen she yapped some more, and if you dared to ignore her she'd take a chunk out of your ankle. Afterward, she'd quickly step back and bare a grin of innocence. Pretty much like she was doing now. Apparently, I wasn't being careful enough—or careful enough for her. She'd just taken a chunk out of my ankle. Savannah and I were opposites on many things, but when it came to tenacity I wasn't so sure.

I glared at her for a long time, trying to decide if this was a battle worth the energy it would take to win. Jaw clenched tight, I bit back my words and comments. "Lucas, thank you. Just have them meet me here at ten. That's when I need to leave for work." I wasn't sure if Lucas was staying or going with Savannah, but I had two and half hours to get out of the house and to Gareth before they arrived.

The goal was to get out ahead of the new guards. I didn't want guards. It was bad enough I had Gareth, who tended to get bossy and had a domineering personality. I'd gotten used to it, but if I was going to have to deal with Lucas and whoever he sent to "protect me" every time Savannah over-reacted to a situation, life was going to get even more complicated. Avoiding my guards was going to be harder than I expected. The moment Savannah and Lucas left, they took up position on either side of the door waiting for me to leave. Two unfriendly sentinels—with deadly scowls perma-nently edged across their faces—that no one wanted to mess with. Anyone would think twice before trying to get past them. And I'd twice tried the surly vampires. Deep obsidian eyes narrowed and watched me carefully. They had sharply cut square jaws that made their appearance harsher and deadlier. Anyone landing a punch on one of those mugs would probably be hurt more than the intended receiver. They moved with predatory alertness. One of the pair was tall, nearly six foot eight with auburn hair, and except for the scowl, his appearance was pleasant. The other guy was a little shorter by maybe four inches.

As with anyone that surrounded Lucas, they were dressed in suits, designer suits. Which made the whole situ-ation even more obnoxious. Being followed around by men in suits seemed pretentious, and I had pointed that out several times to Lucas, who seemed to have an entourage most of the time he left his home. When he visited Savan-nah, he usually came without them. But in his clubs, they were there. When he went out, they were present. It made me wonder what in his past required him to have guards all the time. Was he the only Master of the city who had them or did he have enough enemies that they were warranted?

I blew out an irritated breath and gave them my hardest stare, complete with the eyebrow raise that profoundly said I wasn't one to mess with. A look that didn't faze them.

"I'm relieving you of your duties," I said as I attempted to move past the body barricade they'd put in front of me.

"That can only be done by Mr. Westin," said one of the guards. And that wasn't likely to happen.

They held identical looks of frustration when I attempted to go out the back door only to find them waiting for me. Their eyes were onyx abysses. We were deadlocked, and they returned the same hard glare I gave them tenfold. Even when they finally broke their rigid scowls to smile when they caught me trying to leave out the back for the second time, it was a lethally amused look—cats playing with a mouse.

I accepted that I wasn't going to get rid of these guys. Once we were on the curb they took one look at my Ford Focus and frowned. Even if the drive to Kalen's was only forty-five minutes it was going to be an uncomfortable one for them. Even with my height I found it difficult to get the legroom I needed.

"You can follow me," I offered.

They looked at each other for a brief moment, their eyes narrowed in suspicion as they looked at the car and then to the SUV that was parked behind me.

"Look, I understand this is going to happen. Why should you be uncomfortable? It's not like you don't know where I'm going. I'm going to stop by SG headquarters first, then I'm going to head to work. I have no doubts that you know where both of those places are, and if you need to you can track me in the city." I wasn't sure if they could track me, something that Gareth could do which I found simultane-ously intriguing and creepy.

It didn't take very long for them to decide to drive the SUV. And even if I had assumed I was going to get away from them, they tailed me so closely it was impossible to do. Since my run-in with the Trackers I'd begun taking a different route, one that had more traffic, but at least I didn't have to worry about another orchestrated attack.

Four blocks away from SG headquarters, panicked screams rang so loudly I could hear them over the music I'd been blaring. Now people were running by, arms flailing, and I heard a roaring sound. Some idiots had cameras in hand, swiftly walking backward while still trying to take pictures. I stopped my car abruptly, the guards stopping short to keep from slamming into the back of it. I put the car in park and grabbed my sai before jumping out. I had only made it a couple of feet before one of them grabbed me. I snatched my arm away. "Either you help me or stay in the car but you're not going to stop me."

"You don't even know what they're running from," he said in a rough voice, scanning the area. He inhaled, and then made a face. The roar, deep and aggressive, reverberated and skipped off the buildings and pavement, echoing off in the distance. I winced. Moments later I saw the source of the panic, a monstrosity of a griffin. No, those had the body of a lion and the head and wings of an eagle. This thing had many features of a griffin but also a dinosaur-looking tail that moved wildly throughout the crowd. Instead of fur, the tawny hide was rough, thick, and seemingly impenetrable. My sai might not break on it, but how much force would I need to get through it? The heaviness of the skin and the massive body made me question the purpose of the wings. How powerful would they have to be in order to make flight possible? I couldn't decide which was more overwhelming:

the monstrosity of the creature or the heavy magic that wafted off of it. Swiping people out of its way, its tail slammed into cars, collapsing the metal. Each step it took pounded into the ground, making it shake, and it seemed to be looking to destroy anything in its path. People ran away in terror, screaming; the ones who weren't victims of its tail were crushed under its massive feet or picked up by its beak and tossed several long feet away. Bones crunching from impact, metal bending, ragged gurgled wet noises from people crushed made up the brutal, pain-filled din, punctuated by the heavy raspy breathing of the creature as it ravaged the area.

I saw SG cars, and behind them three mages stood; embers of purple covered their hands before large balls of magic formed in them. They readied themselves for the strike. When they tossed them at the creature, they hit hard. And then nothing. Nothing. The animal wasn't even fazed as the powerful balls hit its body and spread along it. A light glow covered the creature, engulfing it before dissipating into the air as though it never existed. They lobbed more, stronger and harder. I could feel the magic coating the air. A blanket of it lingered, but they were unsuccessful. *Fuck, this thing is a shifter.* Its thirst for destruction was probably why it had been put away in the Barathrum. I could taste my anger and frustration and tried to quell them before they became distracting. The SG had allowed this creature- immune to magic, with an appetite for destruction- to exist, yet they were okay with Trackers being unleashed on Legacy without any repercussions.

I focused on the task at hand. I'd address the Legacy hunt situation later. Shots were fired from shotguns by the officers standing at my right. The bullets that hit the armored scales didn't penetrate. The creature turned, plucking up one of the officers as if it was grabbing a worm and slinging him out of the way. Before it could grab the other one, I let magic flow through me, strong and powerful, and pushed it out, hitting the creature. It stumbled back, but only a few inches. I blasted another ball of magic straight into its chest, sending it moving back farther. It lost its footing, stumbling to the side. The officers shot at it again. They must have used different bullets because these penetrated. Blood spilled and the creature let out an angry sound. Then the massive wings expanded with one big flap and a swoosh of air. The animal didn't take flight, but nearly everyone within a five-foot radius had been tossed to the ground. It spun around, its tail clearing the area and smacking into bodies. Another string of screams split the air as more bones broke, metal groaned under the impact, and panic reached a crescendo. Terrified people bumped into me as they made their escape.

I stepped a little bit closer, and when one of my guards cupped my shoulder I shrugged his hand off. "I'll be careful" was the only thing I could offer him. Sai gripped in my hands, I approached the creature. It stopped for a moment. I wondered if it could sense the difference in my magic or if it didn't even care. The keen eyes homed in on me. Up close I could see the sharp points of its beak, which could easily puncture me without much effort.

Animancy was one of the skills we possessed. I didn't have experience with it and assumed it was nothing more than manipulating the mind of the animal as opposed to that of a supernatural, which I'd done before. I hoped the aberration had enough animal characteristics to be controlled in this way. I connected with the creature, trying to get through the barriers of its mind. Bile crept up my throat. This felt different, leaving a dank taste in my mouth and what felt like a needle plucking at my mind.

Sit.

Its head tilted slightly, hearing the command but fighting

it. I delivered the command again more forcefully, pushing, trying to delve into its needs and thoughts. Deeper than survival, there was a lust for carnage and violence. I gave the command again, making it a need. *You need to sit down.* Its will was stronger than that of any other mind that I'd ever attempted to manipulate—too primal to control, too driven by violence. Magic rolled through me, another blast of it hit the creature, and it stumbled back. Several bullets hit it, and it stopped moving. Its massive body collapsed in the middle of the street.

For a moment there was calm, relief, but it didn't last long. People started to stare at me. I'd used magic—magic that had subdued the monster when others couldn't. I wondered how many of them knew that there were only certain people who could use magic against shapeshifters. They'd witnessed how ineffectual the magic from the mages had been. I gripped my sai even tighter, but the cautious curiosity quickly disappeared. Eyes that were focused on me became glazed over before they flickered with anger. I felt a familiar magic coursing through the air, along with the panic, anger, and frustration that it instilled. Within moments people had turned on one another and were shoving, punching, and clawing while screaming obscenities.

The Maxwells, I thought angrily. What was Conner's endgame? I didn't have to think about it long; I knew what it was. He was going to cause enough chaos, panic, and fear that people wouldn't consider the Legacy bad. The Cleanse would no longer be considered a deplorable act. Humans would consider it a rational decision to get rid of the supernaturals who were destroying their world. They'd forget about the alliance, the camaraderie, and the things that they enjoyed about the supernaturals. That would become nothing more than history, the yammering tales of their parents' and grandparents' years of yore. I backed away, bumping into a woman beside me; angered, she attempted to punch me. One of my guards stopped her, grabbing her fist and pushing her against the car as she lurched and resisted.

"Get your hands off of her!" a police officer demanded, aiming his firearm at my vampire guard. A flash of movement and the other vampire was behind the cop, disarming him. The vampire's knee was on the officer's back while he pressed him against the ground, securing him there.

I ran, following the lingering bands of magic that would lead me to the chaos mages. I knew the Maxwells would be close and I wanted to secure them in this location instead of allowing them to migrate farther out and cause more havoc. So much magic was in the air from the effort to subdue the creature that it was hard to detect the nuance that was exclusively theirs. But I got a hint of its dank smell, the ominous aura, and I felt it: the rage, paranoia, and violence that coiled in me demanding to be released. It was overpowering, coaxing a response.

I inhaled and pushed magic from me, erecting a shield as I ran through the city, ignoring the fighting and violence that was taking place. Perfect timing: morning, when most people were on their way to work or appointments. Create a nightmare with the creature and then end it with a brawl of people hopped up on fear and anger-induced adrenaline, now ready to pummel and accost anyone in sight.

I only had to stop one of the chaos triplets. Their power was linked—wound one and the rest became magically neutered.

I knew they wouldn't be out in the open, instead choosing to skulk in the shadows as they caused trouble. The area near the SG was mostly buildings: a technical college, small banks, law offices, and several restaurants. The majority of the buildings were close together, separated by just garbage bins and minimal space for moving between them. Just enough space for three bodies to hide. I walked past several of the openings, peeking in trying to get a look. The triplets' strawberry hair wouldn't be hard to miss, and one of them was extremely tall. Each alleyway reeked mostly of garbage more than anything else, overpowering my senses; I had to rely on the feel, the prickle of magic as it moved over my skin, causing the hairs on my arms to stand up.

Their chartreuse eyes shone as bright at the sun. I advanced toward them, ready to attack. Before I could reach them, something or someone grabbed my legs and yanked them from under me. I crashed to the ground face-first. My assailant maintained their tight grip on my legs as they dragged me back toward them with another hard jerk. I was too far from the Maxwells but they were distracted by fear of my attack, which was good. They couldn't do magic if they were distracted. I turned and found the assailant, his eyes black lava, his body stout, solid—a troll. His massive tree trunk arms were big, but slow. His torso was larger than his stumpy legs, making it a perfect target for my sai.

I slung a ball of magic, but before it could reach the troll, a wall rose up in front of him, sending it back at me. I dodged to the right and my own missile barely missed me as it crashed into the ground, creating cracks in the pavement.

"Tsk tsk," Conner's voice whispered in the air. I turned to find him there and the Maxwells gone. He smiled. "Now, little warrior, we'll have none of that cheating, will we?" I lunged at him. He disappeared, and I spun to find him standing in front of the troll. "I want a fair fight. If for no other reason than to entertain me."

I wanted to entertain him all right. "Why don't we play a nice game of tag and whoever gets the blade through their chest, loses," I suggested, sneering at him.

He tossed his head back, laughing. "You are always a delight."

Anticipating my intention, which was to start the game then, he disappeared. The troll's large arms swung in my direction; I twisted around, plunging one blade into an arm. The other I jammed into his foot. He used his other hand to lay into my side; my ribs groaned under the pressure and then yielded, breaking. I cursed before sucking in a rough breath. I winced as I moved to block his arm from coming in for another strike. A sharp pain shot through me, and I saw colors, different from those of magic. It was agonizing taking each breath, and I hoped I wouldn't black out from the pain.

I was able to get a few glimpses around me, trying to find Conner.

"I'm still here, love," he said from behind me, his tone an amused taunt. I could easily picture his haughty look of satisfaction. I yanked the sai out of the troll's foot and then jammed it into his neck just as he landed another blow into the side of my head. I stumbled but ignored the pain, blurred vision, and swimming of my head. I was able to see the troll step back and drop to the ground with a thud. I took in another painful breath and then called the magic, stronger than anything I'd used today, and pushed it into the direction Conner's voice came from. His laughter floated in the air in the opposite direction.

"You fight even to the bitter end, such an admirable trait."

Narrowing his eyes on me with interest, he disappeared. Magic was still a heavy dense shawl that curled around the air, a combination of the Maxwells', mine, and Conner's. I lifted my eyes to look at the troll, wondering if he was one of the things that had been kept in the special prison of Barathrum or another one of Conner's little pets. I was in too much pain to really care. I rested back, placing my hand over my ribs, chanting, the magic wrapping around me, a gentle warmth that shadowed the throbbing pain. A gentle cradle of it surrounded me as it healed, but it was not without consequences. I was exhausted and knew I wasn't in a position to fight anyone again.

"You shouldn't have left," barked the shorter vampire guard, the other taking up a position next to him, blocking out the sun, casting a nebulous shadow over me.

"What should I have done, nothing?"

They both made sounds that gave me the distinct impression that that was exactly what they'd expected. I knew how humans felt about the tenuous and frail relationship that existed between them and supernaturals, but I'd never considered the impact the arrangement had upon the supernaturals. Supernaturals were predators by nature and in earlier times had preyed upon humans. Now they were forced to walk the fine line between being guardians to humans and losing themselves. Vampires needed humans for food, but they were restricted by rules of engagement. They couldn't compel anyone, it was illegal. They now had to rely on skills of seduction and appeal to humans. Shapeshifters traditionally didn't prey on humans, but it was obvious they would rather not deal with them. They seemed to have limited patience with other shapeshifters. The magics of fae and mages were restricted by numerous laws to protect humans.

A fragile relationship was being fractured by Conner.

My vampire guards gave me some time to regain the ability to walk back to the car. I stood and stumbled, and like moments before, they were ready to pick me up and carry me. I sighed. "Only in the movies do women want people sweeping them up and carrying them places," I advised. Based on the blank looks they gave me, they didn't know that and were reluctant to believe it.

CHAPTER 8

*I*n the mirror the raspberry coloring wrapped around my torso looked a lot more painful than it actually was. I'd healed the broken ribs, and it felt good to breathe without the overwhelming pain. My thoughts were the things giving me the most concern now. Conner was an enigma, a psycho with chaotic plans that were going to work. He'd killed Daniel, the founder and leader of Humans First, which had led to another director, a credible one. The group was no longer seen as a conglomeration of rabid, crazy conspiracy theorists spouting separation between the supernaturals and humans. They were about to become a political force.

Conner was breaking out the most dangerous supernaturals and unleashing them on society just to cause havoc and feed people's fears. He'd demonstrated that the Legacy were alive and real. Perhaps if he caused enough chaos, HF would approach him and encourage him to do the Cleanse. Ignorant fear would lead to their demise.

The room felt stuffy despite having the window open; the crisp air wafted into my room, but it wasn't cleansing enough. I needed to be out there allowing the wind to gently brush against my face, inhaling all the scents of the city, feeling the ground pounding against my feet during a good run, and figuring out how to fix this mess. I wished I'd heard something from Gareth. At least if I knew what the SG and the Magic Council planned to do, I had a direction. I didn't like being unfocused.

I tried to clear my head as I laced up my running shoes and went out the door. I had taken just a few steps when the guardian Suits flanked me, running alongside and making it painfully obvious that my speed was just a fraction of theirs. It was the best I could do because my ribs were still sore.

As I sped up, so did they. My babysitters. *Are you freaking kidding me?*

I stopped abruptly, just about a block from my apartment, aware that I wasn't going to be able to think with them following me and pushing me into a state of high alert, which was a place I wasn't too far from on my own. I decided just to return home. When I got back to the apartment, I found Lucas standing just outside the doorway, dressed more casually than usual in just a simple shirt and slacks.

I shook my head at the little smile that lifted his lip just a bit too high, showing the edges of his fangs.

"No," I said quietly. I knew he'd heard it.

He inclined his head, letting the word linger, studying it as if it was foreign to him. A word he wasn't familiar with as a command. His dark eyes narrowed, and the halo of light that framed his body from the rising sun made him look more ethereal than dangerous. It was enough to make me forget I was dealing with the Master of the city and consider him just my roommate's boyfriend. Well, I tried to make it seem like that was what he was, but he wasn't just some random guy that my roommate was sleeping with. He owned the most successful clubs in the city, had a place on the Magic Council, and with just a simple command had two imposing men following me around like I was an influential political figure who needed a security detail.

"I don't want or need guards," I complained.

"They were helpful yesterday, am I not correct?"

"They were helpful to the SG, not me."

I raised my hand, exposing the band around it. His brow lifted in inquiry. I closed my hand, and metal claws shot out.

"How clever," he observed.

It was something I'd started carrying with me after my last Tracker attack. I would always carry a knife with me, but I could keep this in my palm: one squeeze and I had claws that were sharp as hell.

He looked at the Suits, back to me, and then into the apartment. Fighting the laugh, I clenched my teeth together ignoring the fact that he seemed to be taking his orders from Savannah. She and I definitely had to have a talk. Seemingly overnight she had become a force to reckon with, her place with the Shifter Council and relationship with Lucas giving her access to power that comforted me for her sake but was quickly becoming a pain in my ass because she was using it against me.

For several moments I commanded a great deal of Lucas's attention. Then he inclined his head in the Suits' direction. "Thank you, I think she will be fine."

"For good," I added. "No more guards, I don't need them."

An amused smile nestled on his lips. "Have a good run, Levy" was his only response, and I figured it was the only one I would get. I didn't push it. I decided to pick my battles with him as needed.

Seconds later I was running, clearing my head, my thumb running along the metal bar warmed by my hand. The troll was dead, gone to whatever hell the other creatures had gone to. A streak of anger ran along my face. The SG gave full rein to the Trackers to put us down like animals, but they let things like that continue to exist. I pushed the thoughts out of my head as a car crept up beside me. I did what I typically did, ignored it. I wasn't sure what it was about a woman running and sweating that made men think she wanted to be hit on.

The car kept creeping along and I was about to tell the driver where to go, how to get there, and what route he needed to take, when I recognized Gareth's AMG.

I stopped. "First, Lucas and now you."

His brow furrowed. "Lucas."

"Yep, he gave me my own personal detail. I tell you, a couple of people try to kill you and everyone overreacts."

Gareth laughed and leaned over to open the passenger side door for me. I considered continuing on my route, but I needed to talk to him more than I wanted to run.

As soon as I got into the car, I asked, "How big of a mess is it?"

He exhaled heavily, running his hands through his hair, mussing it. "Last night, we apprehended the Maxwells." I didn't ask more questions. Something in his tone led me to believe that they'd been apprehended, but may not have lived through it. I was curious if it was a political move or something that had happened during the process. I studied his face but it didn't betray any emotions.

"What about Gordon Lands?" I asked as he pulled into a parking space in front of my building. Once again, his face didn't give much away as he followed me through the door. As usual, he and Lucas studied each other. There wasn't any animosity, just the tendency to check the boundaries of their dominance in an odd predatorial display. The first time they'd done it, I'd found it odd; now it seemed normal. Or as normal as weird crap like that could be. I felt a bit better when Gareth followed me into my room and I'd shut the door.

"I don't know what to think about him. We met with him yesterday and he seems to want HF to be a human rights advocacy group." He shrugged.

"And you don't believe it?" I asked, plopping on the bed.

"No, but he believes it. However, I have a feeling there is a fragile line between it being what he wants and what the original founder wanted, and yesterday didn't make things better."

"You're not confident that if Conner approached him, he wouldn't try to cut a deal."

"Exactly." I understood the strained look on his face. Conner didn't need HF: the Necro-spears had been confiscated, so they didn't have anything tangible that he wanted. But they could be instrumental in severing the alliance between the humans and supernaturals and planting more seeds of discord. The weighted look that marked Gareth's appearance was understandable. This situation was getting complicated.

"Harrah still would like you to come out."

I shook my head. "I don't want to do that." I'm not sure why it was a big deal; technically I'd revealed myself yesterday.

"Are you willing to meet Lands?"

"What am I, your show pony? The well-behaved Legacy that represents us all? Do I get to perform for him? What persona would you like me to display?" Frustration made my voice sharper than I wanted.

He didn't seem too bothered by it and kept the half-grin on his face. "Well, Anya, when you aren't babbling about your comic book heroes and seeing if your next sentence can be snarkier than the last"—he moved closer, his lips just inches from mine—"you can be charming. So yes, he will see that there really isn't anything to fear and there aren't supernaturals lurking in the dark, ready to do an apocalyptic spell that will wipe out a bunch of people." He kissed me lightly, allowing his lips to rest there for a few moments before pulling away. "After all, you charmed *my* pants right off." He returned to his seat across from me.

I rolled my eyes. "I'm sure I could have done that by just saying, 'Hey you, take off your pants.'"

He chuckled, a deep rumbling sound that leveled the tension in the room. "I'm not that easy." Then he grew quiet.

"At least meet Lands, okay?"

I nodded.

ordon Lands had settled into his position as the head of HF quite nicely. He'd traded one cliché for another. Instead of men in black t-shirts and pants, sporting stern, hostile looks and an air of badassery, the membership was now represented by men in slacks with guns holstered at their sides, grimaces in place, and eyes narrowed in scrutiny. I was sure if I checked their pockets I would have found each had a pair of sunglasses. They stood on either side of him.

He had changed a lot about the office. The executive desk had been replaced with something smaller. There was a computer monitor placed on each end, and two comfortable-looking leather chairs were in front of it. I didn't remember the bookcases being there before. They held a collection of mythology, law, and history books. I didn't doubt for one minute he'd been studying up on the Cleanse and the war, and the various supernaturals that existed, and their gifts and weaknesses. Hanging behind him was a framed copy of the HF mission statement.

I looked at my phone. I was on time, but Harrah, who was

sitting in one of the leather chairs, her legs crossed and bouncing, looked as though she'd been there for a while. Lands leaned forward from behind his desk the moment I walked in. His slate gray eyes stayed fixed on me, watching me carefully with avid curiosity and perhaps antipathy. He definitely didn't like me.

"Have a seat," he offered in an even voice. My attention moved between the men standing at his side and Harrah, and I wished I hadn't decided against bringing in my sai. This was supposed to be an amicable meeting, but there wasn't anything about it that seemed like it was. I ushered a gentle smile on my face before sliding into the chair, sitting with the two politicians. I wasn't under any illusions that Harrah wasn't just that, a politician.

She spoke, her voice melodious and satiny smooth. "I'm very happy you decided to meet with us." I remembered her touch that made the police officers' eyes glaze over and what Savannah said she'd done at the club. She looked at me and gave me a sharp look, perhaps sensing the shield I'd put up. If this meeting didn't go well I wasn't confident that she wouldn't change the outcome.

"Of course." Lands leaned over, opened his drawer, and pulled out two thick iron manacles. "No offense, but I will feel better having this discussion knowing that magic won't be used to influence the results."

Harrah kept the pleasant smile on her face as she leaned forward and took one off the desk. She held his gaze as she snapped it around her arm.

He looked at the remaining one and then my wrist, a subtle way of telling me to put it on. He'd studied, but not well enough—iron didn't affect my magic. Instead of correcting him, I snapped it around my wrist, content to have at least one weapon at my disposal.

After several moments of tense silence, Harrah spoke. "I

wanted you to meet Levy. You're probably familiar with her face for her courageous intervention the other day. I doubt things would have gone as well if not for her involvement."

Lands relaxed back against his chair, his fingers steepled, waiting patiently for her to continue. After he didn't say anything, she continued, "She is a Legacy." She waited for him to react—something he didn't do. Even the grimace that he had on his face earlier had disappeared and his face was a mask of stoicism.

"The reason I wanted to have this meeting is because I do not think Humans First's existence is a good thing. It will only show strife between humans and supernaturals. And you as head provide a legitimacy to the separatism that this group promotes; it will compromise everything we've worked for."

He nodded slowly. "Of course, Harrah." His tone was just as genteel and pleasant as hers. And then he flashed her a smile, one I'm sure he'd used many times on the political trail. "Please understand that the reemergence of Humans First has nothing to do with us no longer wanting a working relationship between the two groups. However, over the past months, I've watched the Supernatural Guild and the Magic Council, and you fail. Can you not agree that things have become more chaotic and tumultuous? And although I appreciate the visit, I don't think trotting out your little murderer is going to help things." With that his voice dropped and his sharp gaze fixed on me.

He turned his monitor toward us and clicked on a few things on his keyboard until an image popped up. Not just any image … an image of me going into the Humans First office and moments later running out. I remembered that incident as though it was yesterday. I'd been invited to a meeting with the head of HF and one of his recruits. They were supposed to convince me to help Conner perform the Cleanse, which I'd refused to do. But they had a Necro-spear, which they planned to use to perform their own Cleanse. They had made a deal with Conner in hopes of getting rid of supernaturals, unaware of the disadvantages and the predicament they were putting themselves in.

His gaze remained fastened on me, as did those of the two other men. They didn't see a Legacy, a potential murderer, but Levy, an actual murderer.

"I didn't kill your friend," I asserted.

"Do you mind explaining this?"

"That was handled," Harrah offered. And from *handled* I assumed it had been cleaned up, explained away with a nice story, and put in a tidy little box with a pretty little bow and presented to the world. But it hadn't been handled, and we were looking at the results of that. It wasn't tidy. It wasn't cleaned up.

"I know it was handled in your way—explained away with a web of lies." His attempt to appear pleasant was becoming more difficult.

"I want to know what really happened to my friend."

"Your friend," I started, trying to hold my voice steady and prevent anger from tinting my words, "made a deal with Conner. If you don't know who Conner is maybe you should look that up as well. He's a Legacy." I wasn't sure if he knew about Vertu and I didn't want to explain it. As far as everyone was concerned we were one and the same anyway. "He was so disgusted with supernaturals he was willing to make a deal with this man to do a Cleanse and kill us off. Us. All. Off. I'm sorry you lost your friend, but he wasn't as innocent as you would like to believe. His betrayal had consequences. I didn't kill your friend; the person he made his deal with did."

"Then why were you there?" he asked.

"Daniel invited me. They were trying to convince me to help them do this. I understand your sorrow, but in essence your friend was trying to kill me and my friends because of his hate. And reviving this hate group isn't going to make things better."

He shifted in his chair. I wasn't sure if he was even considering my words and the idea that his friend had so much hate for supernaturals that he would do such a deplorable thing; I wasn't in a mood to care. Whatever he was thinking about had consumed his thoughts and a frown was etched over his appearance. After long moments of silence ticked by and the tension in the room became palpable, he finally spoke. "I don't necessarily believe in what my friend did." He started off slowly and perhaps it was sorrow or anger or a combination of both, but his voice dropped, cool and darkly ominous. "Sometimes we have to do what we perceive as the greater good. Magic is unexplainable, chaotic, and messy. There are so many ways to circumvent the rules constraining it, and I'm sure we both have seen instances of that. Perhaps what he wanted was cruel to some, but I don't believe it was wrong. I appreciate you all coming here, but I have not changed my mind. The direction of Humans First isn't known at this time, but I will not dismantle it."

He rose slowly, keeping a steady eye on me as he did, the mistrust apparent. The more his keen gaze stayed on me, the more it jabbed at my anger. At this point, things had become a clusterfuck of all clusterfucks, and I was ready to rain flames on it and walk away. I'd fought, been injured, attempted to do everything I could to resolve things, and now I watched as any chance of reconciliation slipped through my fingers.

I stood. "Your friend is dead not because of what *I* did but because of what *he* did. He made a fool's bargain with someone unscrupulous. And in case you read the Cliffs

Notes version of the Cleanse, let me give you the real version. A group of very powerful magical beings who make the magic that you are used to looking like a magician's at a child's party decided they wanted to be the *only* magical beings that existed. The other supernaturals' crime for such a vile sentence? Having inferior magic. If they consider people who can shift into animals, make magic their bitch, and take down people with a flick of their hands, manipulate minds, and cause glamours that are so real they aren't distinguishable"—I glanced at Harrah. As powerful as I thought she was, I doubted she was a match for Conner—"inferior to them, unworthy of living, what do you think they think of you? And what do you think will happen when they lose interest in you?"

He crossed his arms over his chest but continued to listen to me intently, the stone-cold look easing but not by much. Barely moving into his nod, he urged me to continue. "The Great War was won because supernaturals and humans worked together. I know history tends to make us lose perspective. You can't on this. I'm sorry about your friend, I really am. He and his misguided Justice League were zealots."

He made a face. "Justice League."

"Sorry, they had the whole mean mug, fitted T-shirt, and 'I'm the ultimate badass look' going on. It annoyed me." I recovered my train of thought. "I've had losses, too. That very hate you are instilling by reviving the Humans First agenda is the same view that a group stalking and trying to kill us has."

"Trackers?" he asked.

I nodded. Studying him, I was trying to make a snap decision about whether I was getting to him or if his mind was already made up and he was just entertaining my little spiel to get more information. "How do you know about them?"

He glanced at the pile of papers on his desk. *For fuck's sake is HF working with the Trackers?* It was now clear to me that HF aligned themselves with anyone who could do the most damage. They were loyal to none. They'd aligned themselves with Conner to get rid of the supernaturals and the Trackers to get rid of the Legacy. What were their plans to kill off the Trackers? They were more devious than I'd given them credit for.

The men to the side of Lands hadn't moved. Their appearance was still stern, cool with indifference, which was probably the worst thing a person could feel. They didn't care whether I lived or died.

"Thank you, Levy, for taking this meeting with me." And with that he dismissed us with a sweeping look as his eyes brushed over us and went to the exit he was kindly asking us to use.

Harrah had settled into a gentle professional smile as she waited for the manacles to be removed.

"That was informative and something he needed to hear from you," Harrah commented after we'd exited the building.

"What are your plans?" I asked, turning to look at her.

Several moments passed before she spoke. "Surely, you've discussed it with Gareth," she said.

"No."

"You two don't talk between your amorous activities?"

Heat brushed my cheeks, but I ignored it. I wasn't going to fall for her distraction techniques.

"We don't talk about work."

"Of course." She flashed a smile. "We have no desire to be at odds with the Legacy. The Necro-spears have been destroyed. From my understanding, the number of Legacy that exist is too small to do anything like the Cleanse again. I'd like to enlist you in helping us find the others before the Trackers get to them. We go from there."

"No one will be hurt?"

"Of course not."

It was the best option. If everyone was out, the Trackers couldn't work in secrecy anymore. Trackers who killed would be handled within the system. Better-case scenario: they'd be handled by a Legacy, and it would be self-defense.

CHAPTER 10

 spent two days considering looking for the
Legacy, and with access to a private plane and SG
funds, my search for them had become more ambitious than
was feasible. Gareth's furrowed brow and constant questioning had quickly reminded me how unreasonable it was.
The massive global search I'd planned had been reduced to
the city next to us and its environs. Which was why I was
sitting next to him in the passenger seat of his car as we
made the three-hour drive to Indiana.

I scrutinized the information in the Trackers' dossier. My
fingers slid over the paper as I inspected the details in it. The
particulars: the family tree, last spotting, jobs, and even some
details of the daily routine. All this information just so they
could track us down and kill us. And I was driving down a
winding road, looking at the passing poplar trees, appreciating the azure sky as it faded to an indigo blue as the sun
set, sitting next to a Tracker. A *former* one, I had to keep
reminding myself. I had to get past it, and most of the time I
could, but the dossier in my hand was a reminder of his association with the Trackers. With effort I pushed the thoughts

aside and considered the positive things that came out of it; between the dossier, which was a result of his affiliation with the Trackers, and my ability to locate my own kind through magic, we shouldn't have any problems finding the other Legacy.

The silence between us for most of the drive was comfortable, or at least I thought it was until after two hours of driving Gareth turned down the radio. "What's the matter?" he asked, taking his eyes off the road to look at me.

Shaking my head, I refocused on the dossier.

"Do I have to go over the whole spiel about how I can detect changes in your vitals? I'll remind you if you want me to, but it's getting a little redundant."

I looked up to find his gaze attentively focused on my face. The humor in his voice wasn't there—he was concerned about me.

For several moments I chewed on my bottom lip. "I know I should let it go and I realize you aren't the person you were when you joined them, but I can't help but think that person is lingering in the shadows holding all of us accountable for something other people did. If I were old enough, I wouldn't have had anything to do with it. And I'm sure that others wouldn't have."

"I wish I could give you an answer that would make you feel better and able to drop the subject. We were taught you were monsters, cruel people who killed thousands. Make no mistake, the Cleanse killed a lot of people." He turned into the parking lot of the hotel where we were staying. He parked and turned to face me. "I'm not proud of it. I assure you, as you know, I'm good at a lot of things"—a smile curled his lips—"but changing the past is beyond my control."

"Yes, you are good at everything, including humility. I'm in awe. You should write a book or something," I said, getting out of the car.

Shapeshifter speed was just as off-putting as a vampire's and hiding it was hard to do when he met me at the trunk of the car and started taking out our bags.

We were headed toward the hotel entrance when he cleared his throat.

"The woman who has a problem with being *damseled* doesn't seem to have a problem with someone carrying her oversized overnight bag."

I rolled my eyes and ignored his sardonic remark and the slanted look that he gave me while I waited for the doorman to open the door for us.

"In the past four days I've been attacked, had my ribs broken, been accosted by one of Conner's strange creatures, and had an uncomfortable meeting with the ex-mayor of the city, whom I suspect hates me. I need a break, don't judge me."

His dark chuckle floated throughout the large lobby as he went to the desk to check in. I looked around the posh hotel. I definitely would have chosen something less extravagant since we were only using it to sleep for the night. While he checked in, I took a seat in one of the tan square-shaped leather seats and fought the urge to put my feet on a table that was made up of interlocking dark brown circles. Muted tan walls were decorated with similarly eclectic art in various hues of brown, cream, and green. The restaurant off to the right of me already had people sitting at the bar, drinks in hand, lilting music drifting out along with the scent of food. I wasn't hungry, but a drink or maybe even two, three, or four would have been nice. I wished we had arrived early, and that I hadn't practiced my speech over and over to the point that it didn't sound authentic but as rehearsed as it was. It was compelling—or at least I thought it was. How did you tell someone they were probably going to be approached by a magical zealot who looked innocuous and like royalty and it would be hard to decline him because he seemed to have the extraordinary ability to charm people into doing ludicrous things and his goal was to do the Cleanse again?

I winced, imagining if I'd been approached the same way. How would I have responded? How would I have responded to Conner before? Could I have been lured into following him blindly in hopes of a different future where I didn't have to hide or fear for my life? I pushed it all aside, far out of my mind. Conner was a problem, a big problem, but HF was going to be a bigger one.

"What's with the face?" Gareth asked as he approached my chair. When I stood, I pasted on a placid smile, but it didn't fool him: his unwavering frown remained. I stayed silent until we were in the elevator and the door was closed.

"We tell them about Conner, then what?"

Gareth's tongue rolled over his lips as he considered the question, and I really tried to focus on the furrow of his brow, the dark cast that overshadowed his eyes despite the bright unforgiving lights, but my gaze kept slipping to the delineation of the muscles of his chest and arms as they stretched his t-shirt.

"Focus," he said in a low rumble.

"What?"

Fixing me with a miscreant grin, he shouldered my overnight bag. "Stop undressing me with your eyes and focus on the issue at hand."

Ugh, this guy.

His deep throaty laugh filled the elevator, and I was happy when the doors opened and I could increase the distance between Mr. Arrogance and me.

"I think you all should come out. Every one of you will be under the protection of the SG. Living in the shadows is what makes you vulnerable. You live in anonymity with fake names, identities, and very few ties to people. So, when the body of a Legacy is found, most of the time you are just Jane or John Doe. Very few of you have identification, and if you do, it doesn't take a great deal of resources to discover you aren't the person you say you are. Isn't that right, Anya?"

The same tightness that I got when I thought of my real name and my former life grabbed me. Anya Kismet was the name I'd been given at birth, and part of me wanted to take that name again and don my persimmon red hair with pride as opposed to shame.

He continued, "If you're not being hunted by everyone, Conner has no power over you all."

"With HF recruitment at an all-time high we still might be at risk—so might all supernaturals."

"Lands isn't a zealot, he can be reasoned with."

I didn't think he was a zealot, but he wasn't totally innocuous, either. He had the charisma and magnetism of a politician. That type tends to be dangerous.

Our spacious room had a large TV on the wall and rich mahogany furniture. Off to the right was a sitting area complete with desk and what I assumed was a sofa bed.

Most of my attention stayed on the bed, or rather the beds: *two queen-size beds.*

He sidled in close to me, his breath hot against my neck as he spoke. "You seem disappointed."

He stepped back, and I took my focus off the beds and turned it to the taunting expression on his face that made the ignominy of my response even more humbling. Warmth crept up my cheeks.

"I didn't want to be presumptuous. That's not my nature." The smirk he gave me didn't reflect those words.

"You do realize we haven't just met, right?"

Again, I was treated to a laugh that started deep in his chest, very feline, nearly a purr. It drifted throughout the room as he took off his shirt and walked toward the bathroom, leaving me watching him as he walked away.

His leaving to take a shower was a good distraction, but not enough of one so I turned on the TV to a comedy and tried to allow it to divert my thoughts. Gareth was right: if we came out of the closet it would remove Conner's power. But there was too much history behind it, and I wondered if I could be convincing enough for the others to listen to me. I lay back on the bed, my hands clasped behind my head, and closed my eyes trying to think of the pros and cons of the situation.

I thought I would drift off to sleep, but I didn't. Instead, my mind became an erratic backdrop of images from over the past few days: the creatures, the fights, the blood, the murder of the Trackers, and what it must have looked like when Conner annihilated the other Trackers. Those weren't productive thoughts. We needed to be out, living among the supernaturals, with the rules and restrictions that they lived by. I was comfortable with doing that. I felt pretty sure they were going to require that we wear something to limit our magic. Maybe a small iridium bracelet. Depending on the size, it would limit but not totally restrict it. It didn't seem like a terrible trade-off. We had betrayed humanity. Well, our predecessors had betrayed humanity, but we had to live with the consequences.

Once I gave in to the idea, sleep came easier than I expected. I was woken up by lips lightly brushing against my cheek. Gareth's tongue slipped out, laving. I turned my head to meet his lips and our tongues entwined. He explored my lips, my neck, and my shoulder before abruptly pulling away, a teasing grin tugging at his lips. He stepped back, giving me a full view of him in just a towel: the well-defined muscles of his chest, the sculpted lines that ran along his abdominals and stopped at the crest of his hips.

One tug and he would be naked. I considered doing just that. Instead, I jumped up from the bed, sliding past him, my fingers running along his stomach as I made my way to the bathroom. I returned his smile before slipping off my shirt and pants and allowing him to watch me as I went into the shower. I should've taken a cold one, because that's exactly what I needed. I was petty enough not to want him to know how I responded to him. When I came out, Gareth was still in a towel, standing in front of a tray of food with a bottle of wine, and the smile from earlier hadn't faltered.

He handed me a glass of red wine. "I figured you could use this." I took a couple of sips. I was a whisky type of gal, but I did enjoy a good wine. Gareth could pick the best. I took a long sip, enjoying the deep currant flavors.

"Have you decided what you're going to do?" he asked, his voice still low, a sultry, deep rumble. He stepped closer and brought his fingers up to trace along my cheek, down my jaw, along the curves of my neck, and over my collarbone. Gentle, languid movements.

"I think you're right. But meeting them and warning them about Conner is going to be easier than convincing them to come out."

Gareth was so close, I could feel the warmth of his body. Stepping closer, I put my hand on his side, my thumb resting on his stomach. He kissed me softly at first and then trailed kisses along my jaw until he got to my ear and whispered, "I wasn't talking about that. Have you considered the sleeping arrangement?"

"Is this a business trip?" I teased.

He made another deep rumbling sound, and it made me laugh, remembering the first time he'd asked me if I wanted to hear him purr. I actually had, and it was a very sensual, throaty sound that I wanted to hear over and over again.

His hands were gentle and commanding as they moved

along my body caressing my curves, kneading into the towel. They moved down farther, slipping under the towel and running along my butt. Strong, expert fingers roved lightly over my body, and then he pulled off my towel. He took a step back, appreciating the form in front of him. He walked me back to the bed and I stretched out on it.

He resumed the gentle travel along my body. His fingers ran along the top of my breast before cupping it and taking it into his mouth. The warmth of his lips and the softness of his touch made me shudder. Then he delivered the same treatment to the other breast. I tugged at his towel and tossed it aside. I pulled him closer to me and kissed him hungrily. His kisses became more fevered and ravenous before moving from my lips and exploring the rest of my body—down my breast, my stomach, and between my thighs before he nestled himself between them; tasting me. He began to make lazy circles with his tongue and then brought me to pleasure. I writhed, clawing at the sheets. It wasn't enough to sate me, I wanted more—I wanted him, and it was obvious that he wanted me, too.

He ran his hands along my legs before lifting them and securing them around his waist. Sheathing himself in me, he moved carefully, slowly, his hips setting a leisurely rhythm. I stroked his back, but as his movements became more rapacious my fingers dug in, pulling him closer to me, needing him to quench the desire that was burning in me. He moved harder, more aggressively, commanding my body and coaxing an erotic pleasure that caused me to wilt into the bed, my fingers still curled into his back, my legs wrapped around him. We stayed in that position for several moments and then untangled from it. He didn't move far from my side. He pulled me into him and held me there, periodically pressing his lips against my neck and shoulders.

Our amorous activities throughout the night didn't allow

for a lot of rest. It was nearly three o'clock before we finally went to sleep.

I hated doing magic with an audience, especially locating spells, because it seemed so intimate. Even if this was the second time he'd seen me do it, I still felt like Gareth was encroaching on something that had been just mine for so many years. The blood welled once the knife cut across my hand. He stood across the room watching me with acute interest, occasionally looking as though he wanted to get closer, to feel it like everyone else— the thrum of magic, even if it was used against them. It was a peculiar curiosity that I didn't understand.

The magic blossomed, spreading in front of me: reds, orange, purples, and deep blues merged, coiled around each other before pulling away to form a unique tapestry of the city. I lifted my eyes to meet his and saw fascination there— an avid interest in magic that he wasn't immune to, that was just as detrimental to him as anyone else.

"This intrigues you, doesn't it?" I asked softly.

He shook his head. "We are able to track people when we have their blood, but it never looks like this. This is art, beautiful, making what others do seem so pedantic."

The smile on his face didn't belie the slight edge to his voice and the look that flashed just for a moment, apprehension and concern. He quickly mastered them, sweeping the emotions away, but not before I saw them.

The colors pranced around, swirls forming a whirling kaleidoscope. Speckles of color spread over the unique map that emerged. I stared at the map with the same intensity as Gareth, feeling that familiar bond, that connection that was specific to us and no other supernatural. The link allowed us to find one another.

Gareth stepped closer, his narrowed eyes homing in on the map.

The list wasn't as long as I'd wished, just three Legacy in the area. The first one was about fifteen miles from the hotel.

After we'd driven there, I hesitated before getting out of the car. The quaint home didn't make me consider turning around, but it felt as if I was there to disrupt a piece of normalcy the owner had carved out. A soft yellow house with a white fence that enclosed it off from the world. The lawn was neatly trimmed and verdant. Strong magic strummed through the air, intense and bleak; it was foreign to me. I leaned in, getting a feel of it as it coiled around me.

"Stop," Gareth commanded, taking hold of my arm. He went ahead of me and then leaned forward, inhaling the air, and his frown changed to a thin rigid line.

"Blood," he said.

My heart dropped to the pit of my stomach. I inhaled a breath knowing it wouldn't be as relaxing as I needed it to be. I didn't smell blood, but the magic rode the air hard, tickled my nose. Maybe it was from an injury.

Optimism prevailed when I noticed that the locks were in place, but then I took one look at Gareth's face. His expression faltered into a deep frown. We stood in a moment of frozen silence. His eyes burnished to a deeper shade, anguished and disconsolate. Had he smelled death or just the blood that told him that death was inevitable?

He shoved into the door until it gave. Shards of wood splattered at the entrance. The body lay faceup on the kitchen floor, eyes open in shock, lips parted in dismay. Hair splayed in a halo around her. I knelt and reached out to her. The skin was pallid but still warm. The room was uninterrupted and everything seemed to be in place. It looked like the typical home, a few dishes in the sink, flowers I assumed were from her garden in a vase on the counter. In the next room, the television was on; the sofa, chairs, and knick-knacks were all in place. There wasn't a sign of a fight, or even a poorly executed struggle. How could there not have been a struggle? Even the most inept magic wielder could put up some sort of fight.

I looked at her fingers: there wasn't any bruising around them or blood where she'd attempted to claw her way to freedom. Nothing. There was more than *nothing*. There was the magic, an odd mélange that felt cold, strong, strident, and oddly venerable as if it predated anything I'd ever encountered. I feared it although I had no reason to. I didn't like the feeling it invoked in me—fear verging on terror.

Redirecting my attention, I refocused on the body. One mark through her chest. Not a bullet or a knife wound. I couldn't pinpoint what it was. Gareth examined it. It was pinky-sized in diameter and over her heart.

We both scanned the scene, although there was nothing to take in. Gareth beside me, I walked through the house sensing the magic and committing it to memory. I wanted to be able to identify it when I encountered it again. After a long moment of consideration, he pulled out his phone and spoke to someone for several minutes. When he hung up he said, "The local SG will be here."

"How are they going to handle this?" I asked. I just couldn't believe the scene, undisturbed, as if the person had seen it coming and hadn't done anything. The lack of any magic other than the foreign magic bothered me. My brand of magic should have inundated the air, unwavering and strong. There wasn't any, as if she hadn't made one effort to defend herself.

"Do they know about us as well?" I asked, a hint of irritation filling my voice. I thought I could temper my words, but they were frosty and angry.

"We haven't discussed it with any other agency but our

own, and it is on a need-to-know basis. But since your meeting with Mr. Lands, I doubt the existence of Legacy isn't widely known or still considered a fable or conspiracy theory. He said in his press conference that you all exist."

"What are you going to tell them?"

He frowned, crossing his arms over his chest, and I wondered if he was having the same disconcerting feeling I was. It took him too long to answer. "We share information with other agencies, and this isn't something that we would keep from them."

I didn't want to wait for the SG to come—I felt that we were on borrowed time to get to the others—but Gareth urged me to stay. Ten minutes later, they swept into the house, dressed similarly to the agents at home: slacks and shirts, and nothing more than a badge to identify them. They moved in a practiced and strategic way, looking for prints, taking pictures of the room, the victim. Just as I did, they looked perplexed by the scene and the lack of evidence of the woman defending herself.

A tall, tawny-colored brunette, who moved with the same stealth and grace as most shapeshifters, eventually walked in. I suspected she was a werewolf. After surveying the area, her light hazel eyes, dark brown shifter ring encircling them, landed on Gareth. The ring roiled and glowed ever so slightly when she directed her attention to me. Her lips pulled into a taut line, and she redirected her attention to Gareth.

He nodded his head in greeting. "Tina."

"Gareth, thank you for calling me," she offered in a cool professional tone, whetted with suspicion and curiosity. "What brings you here?"

Dammit, the shifter will be able to detect a lie. I was about to respond, hoping she wasn't as good as Gareth at detecting them, but he spoke. "We were here to visit her friend."

The female shifter's brows came together and her lips twisted to the side as she looked at him with a hint of doubt. She made no attempt to mask it. "So you and your . . ."

She waited patiently for him to offer more explanation of who I was. He didn't give her anything more and instead simply reiterated what he had said before.

"Witch?" she asked.

Gareth hesitated before he spoke. "Put down witch for now," he said in a way that left no room for more questioning. After a few minutes of silence her eyes narrowed on him, trying to read a face that was blank, devoid of anything.

"I will be able to give you more information later, but at this time I must act under extreme caution. So just put her down as a witch, and if you find any information, I hope that you will be open to sharing it with my department."

A wry smile settled on her face, apprehensive and suspicious. "As long as you are forthcoming with what she really is. I've been around a lot of witches, and I don't think this is one." Shifters might be able to scent magic, but they couldn't sense it the way I could. All they knew was that this was magic. Most people seemed to default to *witch* because there were more of them, and since I was a female, that was probably the first assumption. Although there were male witches, there were far more female ones.

The existing magic was so strong and powerful, I wondered if it masked our magic, if in fact the victim had fought at all. It was concerning. What type of magic could render us powerless and put this person in a state of terror where she was paralyzed and unable to fight, forcing her to succumb to whatever it was that took her life.

It looked as if the agent was preparing to pepper us with more questions when I touched Gareth's arm. "We really should go." I laced my voice with enough sorrow to make the officer think that I couldn't bear to be there any longer. Part of that was true—I couldn't bear to be around the body. I also needed to get to the others. This wasn't a coincidence and I needed to make sure they were going to be safe. I wondered how this was going to be handled. Did they have their own version of Harrah who would manage to clean this up, or would they call her in? There was nothing like the original.

The next location was just thirty minutes away, similar to the other home we had just left. It was a little larger but not by much, a ranch house that wasn't as neatly cared for as the other. But it was nice and quiet, and so was the neighborhood. The inhabitants lived closer to their neighbors, something that most Legacy didn't do. But staying in smaller cities was something we all tended to do. Not too small that people would know who we were, but big enough to disappear, usually in suburbs outside of a larger city.

When we walked up to the house Gareth put his fingers to his lips to silence me. He pressed his ear to the door and after a few minutes he knocked. There was an answer. "Someone's in here," he informed me. I took out my sai and assumed the defensive position. He put his hand on his firearm; it was the first time I'd seen him carry one, let alone consider it an option.

He knocked again, and then we both heard footsteps and sobbing. A young woman in her mid- to late twenties answered the door. Her jasper eyes were red from crying, her tawny skin flushed, her nose ruddy, the latter, I assumed, from wiping it aggressively.

"You're not the police." She sobbed harder. Her shoulders sagged and she looked as though she was going to fold into herself. Gareth caught her before she hit the floor and helped her to the sofa, briefly looking at the body in the middle of the floor.

He showed her his ID. I don't think she cared whether or

not he was the police or any other official. She just wanted to talk to get it off her chest.

She looked at the body again as tears streamed down her face. It was doubtful I'd soon get that image or those of the two dead Legacy out of my head anytime soon.

"He just looked past me," she said between gulps of air.

"Who?" I asked. Her gaze fixed on the sai, and she started to tremble. I sheathed them quickly and softened my voice when I asked again.

It was harder to look over at the victim—he was younger. Probably in his late teens or early twenties, and like the other victims, his face was frozen in a state of somnolent awe. There weren't any defensive wounds, and once again no trace of his magic—our magic. He was in the living room, just inches from the TV, a game controller near him and nothing more.

The woman took several controlled breaths before closing her eyes, but opened them again quite quickly; I assumed the images were too much to bear. She looked at the body again and then returned her focus to us.

Her voice shook as she spoke. "I come over here on Saturday mornings and we play games. There wasn't an answer at the door, but I have a key so I used it. I saw this man standing over him. At the sound of my steps, I think it was a sound or probably screaming, no, I didn't do that until after he left." She closed her eyes again, this time for longer, recounting the events. "No, I didn't scream. I gasped; then he looked up. But he didn't … he peered at me. He looked through me almost like he couldn't see me."

Gareth asked, "What did he look like?"

"Tall. Really tall. Possibly six ten or taller. His skin pale, almost translucent-looking. And his eyes weren't right. They were gray, all gray, and I thought it was my imagination until he wasn't able to see me." She took a moment before she spoke again. "Maybe he was blind," she said half-heartedly, as if she didn't want to commit to the ridiculousness of the idea. I understood why; I was also having a hard time accepting that we might be dealing with a blind magical assassin. I wondered how he'd paralyzed the victims with fear so they wouldn't react and what instrument was being used to inflict the same identical wound over the heart.

We questioned her longer but didn't get much more than we had in the first few minutes. She walked in on a tall gentleman wearing a white tunic and slacks, pale skin, gray eyes—not much descriptive appearance, except she said his nose was broad and flared. Then he disappeared.

"And then you called the police?" I asked.

She shook her head. "I called the police and then the other police."

"Which other police?" I asked.

"The one for supernaturals."

My heart skipped, and I wondered if she knew what the victim was.

"Why did you do that?" Gareth asked.

"The man disappeared. That's not normal. What the hell are the police going to do?" Her tone was harder and it seemed like anger had replaced her grief. I could identify with that; I was starting to feel my own anger and was struggling to subdue it enough to be of any use. I looked over at Gareth. I didn't want to leave her alone. When there was a knock on the door I was prepared to leave her with the SG officers. We were met by the same brunette, her eyes now laden with suspicion, and rightfully so.

"Gareth, I'm trying not to be cynical, but it's awfully peculiar that you have been the first person on the scene at two murders today."

"You have every right to feel skeptical, but it's not warranted." His eyes moved over the scene again, and his frown deepened. "I can assure you that I have nothing to do with this and will do everything I can to find out who did." His words came out in a growl—his anger was blistering— and the muscles of his neck were taut.

He looked back at the witness: her face was still flushed. As the agents questioned her she brushed away the tears streaming down her face. He returned his attention to Tina. "Do you need anything else from us?" he asked in a tight voice.

The expression on Tina's face changed; no longer skeptical, she seemed to possess a hint of fear and apprehension as she assessed Gareth. He wasn't as reserved and emotionally controlled as usual. I wasn't sure if his emotions were mirroring mine or a result of the magic that inundated the room. It was stifling, and I hated the way it evoked fear and dread. My fight or flight response had kicked in, but I had no idea who I needed to fight or be wary of.

Tina interviewed us for a few more minutes, asking for details of what had happened. Gareth filled her in on most of it. I interjected if I had anything to offer but I was distracted, once again committing the magic to memory. If I ever felt it again I hoped it wouldn't elicit the same feelings of fear but instead make me want to fight like hell and kill whoever was responsible for this.

I'd suspected this was going to be how the day ended—in an SG office—after we discovered a third body, this time not in a house, but in the woods. She was alone in a bosky area among the foliage, in the same faceup position as the others. Long blond hair feathered out around her, her mouth and face resting in death's confusion. The same pinky-sized wound through the heart. Three deaths. Three Legacy deaths. In one day. I wasn't sure which feeling was more overwhelming, anger, frustration, or rage.

At least we weren't in an interrogation room but, in Tina's office, which was very similar to Gareth's. Her arms were crossed and she leaned against her desk. Gareth and I assumed similar positions, standing next to each other after declining to sit down in the chairs that she offered. She stared at us, her lips pressed into a defiant moue, as she waited for us to give her something we didn't have.

"And you have no idea who is behind this?" she asked in disbelief. We'd been there for over twenty minutes, and although we weren't in an interrogation room, we were definitely being interrogated.

"No, we don't," Gareth said.

"Then at least can you tell me what brought you all here?" she asked.

Perhaps it was the fatigue from the day, or the overwhelming feeling of helplessness, or the desperation that came with being hunted by the unknown, but I didn't feel like I had a lot to lose. I wanted to confess, but the words didn't come as easily as I thought they would and remained trapped behind my firmly pressed-together lips. Gareth looked at me as if he sensed my hesitation, but I couldn't tell whether or not he was okay with it or was telling me not to talk. I suspected that he was leaving it up to me.

"We came here to look for Legacy," I confessed softly.

She didn't look as surprised as I'd expected her to. Instead, she took a long breath and then regarded me for a long moment. "Is it because you are one?" she asked in a quiet voice.

My head barely moved into the nod.

Again, there were several beats of silence before she spoke again. Her voice was flat, and her position changed slightly: she assumed something defensive as though she felt the need to protect herself. To protect herself from me and what she'd heard I was and what my kind were capable of.

Why are you looking for them? I didn't need to speculate—I knew what she was wondering. Was I like Conner, trying to gather enough to do a Cleanse again? Did I have some nefarious plan?

I hesitated, and before I could speak, Gareth placed his hand on the small of my back for reassurance. "Have you kept up with what's been going on in our department lately?" he asked in a confident and familiar way as if he was used to them doing that. Was his the department that others looked up to in order to pattern themselves after, or were they the ones that had the greatest incidents that other ones could learn from?

She nodded her head. "You all seem to have had a lot of *events*. Events that seem odd. I thought most of it could be attributed to the fact that the Maxwells had gotten out. But I can't help but think that maybe there is more to it."

Gareth ran his fingers through his hair, mussing it more than it was from the many times he had done it as we followed them to the precinct. He took a long time to consider his words, which didn't seem to bother Tina. It was my assumption that she would've been just as careful with her own words.

He told her more than I expected: including the information about the Necro-spears and the betrayal by one of their own from the Magic Council, and Conner's past transgressions of letting the Maxwells out of Barathrum twice. Continuing with the listing of Conner's acts, he told her about him killing the founder of Humans First. It was the first time she had shown any reaction to the new information. She stood up taller, squaring her shoulders, and her eyes widened as she sucked in an audible breath. Seconds later she'd regained control over her demeanor. The mask of professional stoicism had returned. Gareth disclosed everything except for the leak they had in their department, and I suspected it had less to do with his "need-to-know" policy and more to do with the embarrassment associated with such betrayal in the department.

"You do seem to have your hands full. How is Harrah dealing with it?"

So everyone knew about it. Gareth shrugged. "You know she can spin anything; we aren't getting a lot of pushback and hostility."

"*Yet*," Tina added. Looking concerned, she mulled over the new information. "Camden is handling the situation with the three murders. It's going to be hard to keep down the panic." She gave me a faint smile. "Witches will be up in arms, fearful that they are under attack. Three murdered witches is a pattern. We'll do what we can to quell their concerns. Camden is as good at his job as Harrah," she offered.

Was there a special "spin" school that they went to where they learned to be "good" at their job? Did everyone go to lie-your-ass-off university, but only the top graduates got those jobs?

"Thank you for sharing this with me," Tina offered. "For now, I think it best that this conversation stays between the three of us. I'm not in a hurry to have the Federal Supernatural Reinforcement snooping around, and the moment they consider things aren't in our control, they will be there."

I didn't know much about the FSR, because our city rarely had cause for them to intervene, but they were equivalent to the FBI and dealt with things in the supernatural world. Going by the similar scowl the mention of their intervention brought to Gareth's face, he didn't want to deal with them, either.

CHAPTER 11

*I*didn't want to stay another night in the city where three Legacy had been killed within hours of each other by a blind assailant who'd been able to render them paralyzed. Whether he did it by magic or fear, they'd been unable to fight. The dense, dark, shadowy magic inundated the air, or perhaps it just lingered in my mind because I'd forced myself to commit it to memory. I just didn't know what I would do once I encountered it. Would I run or stay and fight?

I finally crawled out of my bed close to noon, and I was glad that Gareth was okay with me sleeping alone and hadn't stayed. The day before had been trying, and I was left with so many questions. There was an assassin coming after Legacy and it wasn't Trackers. Every time I thought about the murders one thing left me perplexed: why the hell did they not fight back?

Showered and dressed, I went into the kitchen ready for the onslaught of questions that I would get from Savannah. She deserved answers, but by the time we'd gotten to the house late last night I couldn't give her any. I still hadn't sorted out things, and I'd felt like everything was spiraling out of control and I was just grasping for something. The only comfort I had was at this point Gareth didn't want to err on the side of caution—he was going to bring the Trackers in. Every last one of them. This didn't stop the most immediate danger but at least they wouldn't add to the situation.

Savannah's face was absent her typical gleeful morning smile, instead it was somber, concerned, and perhaps a little angry.

"Things are getting bad, aren't they?" she said softly.

"It'll be fine," I offered, putting more confidence in my words than I felt. But she didn't start with questions about what had happened the day before. Instead, she poured us both a cup of coffee and pulled out a box of donuts. If it were any other day, I probably would have had a nice little quip about it, especially when she bit into one and didn't have a look as though she had committed the most wrongful act and sin imaginable.

"Lucas won't *let* me come to Devour anymore."

Savannah must have agreed, because she wasn't big on anyone *letting* her do anything and didn't have any problem telling whomever it was what they could do with their "let." She continued, "He said it's not safe. Fear is making people impulsive and violent. Someone came to his club last night and the night before and attempted to attack vampires. I don't know if it was hate that made people stupid, but it didn't necessarily make them smart. You go to the oldest vampire bar to start trouble?" She made a face, and I didn't blame her. It wasn't easy to kill a vampire, and it was hell of a lot harder doing so when they had the home advantage. Without prying eyes, they were able to use their magic to compel. It definitely wasn't a wise decision.

"Do you think that had anything to do with the terrible triplets?" she asked.

"It's not the Maxwells, the SG has them." I really hoped they had them separated from each other so there wasn't any chance of all three of them escaping or being broken out again. Without the power of three they were harmless.

She sighed and grabbed another donut, and that was worse than knowing that assassins were after us. Someone might as well have told me there was about to be an apocalypse and we were going to be forced into a dystopian world. Her second donut was my apocalypse.

"Things are going to be fine, Savannah," I offered in a low, comforting voice, giving her a sympathetic smile.

Her voice broke when she spoke and that was the most heartbreaking thing, "I don't think they are, Levy." I was sure she was concerned about many of the same things that I was —most importantly Conner. He was out there causing havoc.

It looked like she couldn't take any more news, and I wasn't prepared to deliver it. She kept talking and told me how Mr. Lands had made another appearance asking for people to be calm and to adhere to the alliance. He was reasonable; I took some solace in that. But I suspected his calm would lead to another branch of HF becoming radicalized, and there wasn't anything a voice of reason could do about it. But that wasn't the most pressing thing: I needed to find out who was targeting the Legacy and what type of magic they possessed that rendered us helpless.

After several moments of weighted silence, Savannah split her attention between the television and the various stories popping up on her Facebook feed and alerts. She grabbed the remote and changed the television to a comedy and silenced her phone before turning it facedown. The heaviness of her feelings was displayed on her face: her eyes darkened and her smile was forced and strained.

"What happened yesterday with the other Legacy, were you able to speak with them?" she asked.

I shook my head, deciding to tell her the information later.

"Don't," she ordered softly. "Don't hide things from me. We are in this together."

There weren't many truer words. Her life had changed, too, but she had the benefit of living in the shadows, her skills nothing more than a blip on the spectrum. However, if Conner were successful with the Cleanse, she, too, would die.

Savannah had mastered the placid look she held on to, an unwavering mask that didn't show shock or disgust at what I was telling her. Her tone remained level and flat when she asked her questions. "Do you think it was a spell?"

"That's possible, but it didn't look like the victims made an attempt to defend themselves. That's the most troubling thing."

When someone knocked on the door, she looked at it appreciatively—a reprieve. She jumped up to answer it. Looking out of the peephole, she smiled, and I didn't have to guess who it was. She pulled open the door, and Lucas stepped in and leaned down, quite a bit, the eight inches he had on her proving to be a disadvantage. He pressed his lips to hers, giving her a slow, lingering kiss. His fingers intertwined in her hair, his other hand wrapped around her waist, and I looked away. When I returned my attention to them they were still kissing, seemingly forgetting I was there or caring very little that I was.

I cleared my throat. They both looked in my direction. "Oh, good morning, Levy." He stepped into the apartment, his hands resting on the small of her back. With the halation of the sun behind him, his skin was slightly paler than Savannah's. His tall, svelte physique closely mirrored my roommate's. His short sandy blond hair was just a few shades darker than her blond hair. He was dressed in what was probably his Sunday "casual" attire, a pair of gray slacks, matching vest, and white shirt. My roomie was dressed similarly to the way I was: a t-shirt and a pair of yoga pants, yet she didn't look out of place standing next to him.

"Did I interrupt anything?"

I shook my head; it wasn't as if he'd turn around and leave if he had.

"Were things bad last night?" I asked.

Dragging his fingers through his hair, he made a sound, then bared his fangs, something I figured he'd had to do quite a bit last night. And he was only doing it now in response to my question. I felt sure they looked more menacing when displayed as a warning. His eyes narrowed and the muscles around his neck corded and bunched. "I do grow tired of the delicate fashion with which we must deal with humans now. Very different than the way it used to be. So much so that they've forgotten that we are a bigger threat to them than they are to us."

"Devour was pretty bad last night?" I asked, going for my third donut.

He shook his head. "No, Crimson," he grumbled. "Devour is more selective but ..." He sighed again. Devour was the club the older vamps frequented, a den of hedonism and seduction. Crimson was where the younger vampires dwelled. Taking their cue from every modern vampire noir, they surrounded themselves with fanboys and fangirls while they donned broodiness and angst like they were part of their uniform. Often you'd find older vampires in the club, monitoring them because laws prevented vampires from compelling people to feed, and some had a difficult time adhering to it. Since the laws stipulated that sires were responsible for the sired, older vampires took an interest to make sure the youngsters behaved. Just like some of them lacked the discipline not to retaliate when provoked.

"Did you spend the evening making sure the children behaved?" It was odd referring to people who had decades on me as children, although their appearance wouldn't imply that they were older.

He nodded once. "Diplomacy is something honed with age. For most vampires it takes centuries not decades. When they are confronted, they respond with force. Temperament and patience for humans' bad behavior are becoming low and the desire to maintain an alliance and play nice is strained." Lucas rolled his eyes, irritated, and it was clear that he didn't appreciate having to deal with either.

When I shoved another donut in my mouth, he gave me a disapproving look. *I don't need that from you. You drink blood, or did you forget that?*

"What did *you* eat this morning?" I asked with a smirk, goading him. A reminder that my delicious donut was a far better alternative than his meal.

He laughed. "Perhaps we should have brunch."

It seemed odd going to brunch with a vampire knowing that I wasn't on the menu. But the way he coveted Savannah's neck, the delicate way he stroked along the pulse of her wrist, and the salacious and inappropriate kisses he gave her, led to a reminder that I was still there in the backseat of his car.

"I haven't forgotten you are there; if your presence ever became missed or unnoticed then the scowl you have on your face each time I look in the rearview mirror serves as a reminder. *And* if I dare miss that, those groans are a quick prompt," he joked. A couple of times I caught his eyes fixed on my neck; I didn't think he could help himself.

He slowed as we drove down Coven Row. He stopped and glared at a group of four men dressed in camouflage pants and green shirts with Human Rights Alliance printed on them, guns at their sides, who were heading into one of the shops. They stopped when two men dressed in uniforms stepped out. I recognized the badges but I wasn't used to seeing the bearers in uniforms—perhaps they were for appearances to demonstrate a united front because the style was similar to the human uniforms, but they were definitely not human police. One was a shifter, and his pale brown eyes pierced into the men, the dark shifter ring glowing in defiance, the predaceous confidence and lethality apparent. The mage next to him made a show of playing with a glowing ball of magic that was a burnt orange and reminded me of fire. The humans tensed and scanned the immediate area, seeing similarly dressed supernaturals posted outside of each business.

I speculated how much of this was Conner's doing and when he would make his grand appearance to ally himself with whoever would help him with his agenda. He'd dispose of them when he was finished, of course.

Frowning, I felt pulled in so many directions, and none led to a solution. The Maxwells weren't the problem; Humans First was a minor and insignificant problem. The Human Rights Alliance, although agitators, still weren't the problem. It was Conner, and it had to end. I didn't feel any guilt or remorse when I wished the thing that had killed the other Legacy had set its sights on him. But I was quickly burdened with the thought that maybe Conner was responsible for it. Had he approached them and they declined and that was the penalty? Anger flittered through me, starting off as a little prick. By the time our food had arrived at the little French café we'd decided on, it was a roaring inferno and difficult to tamp down.

Lucas proved to be a good distraction for Savannah; once we returned home, they immediately went to her room. I didn't want to consider for what—for sex, feeding, or both—I pretended none of them were an option even though both of them were probably on the menu. It allowed me to slip out of the house unnoticed by Savannah.

Dressed in running clothes, I blended in with the people in the area, most of them running along the trail. I veered off the trail and trekked through the woods to my special spot. My cave. It was pointless and unnecessary now, but I still found comfort in the solitude that it offered. It was my little place where I could perform magic, hidden from the world, a ghost. I wasn't a ghost anymore. I was known and outed—but this was still where I'd always felt safe.

The comfort was there as I dropped down through the small manhole.

"What took you so long?" I adjusted to the darkness and focused on Gareth, his eyes dulled by dusk. His voice carried in the empty space, and a small echo of his teasing reverberated off the walls. He moved closer, flashing me a smile.

"Let me guess, you were feeling a little stalker-y and decided to do something about it."

"When did you suspect that Conner might be behind whatever killed the others?" he asked. My eyes narrowed on him, and I had an eerie feeling that he could get in my head. My heartbeat increased at the very thought. Had we all underestimated the skills of shapeshifters? If someone had told me he could track me in the city, I would have balked at the absurdity of it. But there we were in my cave, with Mr. Arrogance fighting a smirk.

I opened my mouth but the words didn't come out immediately due to fear of broaching something that I might not want the answer to.

"I can't read your thoughts, Levy, but I am excellent at reading your expressions. What's going through your mind about me that has you so afraid of me knowing it?" He moved closer, just inches from me. I could see the miscreant expression in his eyes. "After all, you've seen me naked plenty of times, and we've had enough *encounters* that you clearly can't have more things to fantasize about me."

"Good." I made a face. "I'm glad you don't know all the names I call you—it might hurt your feelings."

"If that's what you want me to believe, but I think what goes through your mind might be a little more salacious than a few names."

"Mr. Humility, can we get back to work?"

"Of course," he said, but the taunting curve in his lips remained. "Let's find Conner."

I strode to the wall of the cave and slid the knife over my hand, hissing at the pain. It wasn't any easier, nor did it hurt any less, no matter how often I did it. Blood welled from the cut and I let it drop, chanting the spell. As crimson spread, the area darkened, and the edges of the city revealed themselves, the lines and structures giving me a very broad map. I looked over it, watching for that flicker of light that would locate Conner and the others. The map remained blank, just the landmarks and nothing else. I felt nothing but the overwhelming feeling of the unknown. Had they been killed by the pale creature? If so, was it an act of betrayal against Conner? If not, who was really responsible for the other murders?

I chanted the spell again and waited for something more to reveal itself to me. The same map, unchanged from before, was presented to me.

"He's probably dead," Gareth asserted, but there was a

hint of doubt. Usually when Conner used magic, there was at least a flick, not long enough for me to get a location. But before he'd been playing a puerile game of cat and mouse. After everything he'd done and everything that had transpired, he was no longer playing with me. Perhaps he was taking his ill intent to another level. Gareth was waiting for me to give him the confirmation he needed, but it wasn't there.

"We should look for him," was the last thing I said before exiting my little hideaway. Gareth followed me and wasn't too enthusiastic about my plans.

"A blind search seems like a good plan to you." He kept in step with me as I went through the woods where I'd found Conner before. Large oak trees populated the area, and instead of magic remnants lacing the air, it was overwhelmed by the scent of lavender and grass. I walked past a stump, the remainder of a tree that I'd destroyed when I'd first encountered Conner and powerful magic had consumed me, demanding to be released.

Magic was nowhere to be found in any of the places I'd run into Conner. There wasn't any evidence of his existence in any of the places where we had battled.

I was reluctant to let myself give fully in to the idea until I'd searched a few more places.

They all came up empty. "Conner is dead," I said quietly. Uncertainty clung to my words, but I said them aloud as if for some reason that confirmed my belief.

Gareth was just as reluctant to accept it. "I need to see the body," he said.

CHAPTER 12

Kalen and I moved around the office, pretending that life was normal. It had been three days since I'd seen those murdered Legacy and just a day since I'd had enough evidence to believe that Conner was dead, but things were still off. Someone had killed the Legacy, and there were so many questions unanswered. My curiosity was second only to my thirst for revenge on whoever had killed them. It was becoming increasingly frustrating dealing with the feelings of fear and helplessness that managed to wiggle their way into my mind—two emotions that I detested. Instead of succumbing to them, I immersed myself in trying to find out who the blind assassin could be. I'd spent most of Sunday evening going through any spell book, mythology, or history book I could get my hands on.

I knew my silence was bothering Kalen as I typed away at the computer. I'd never been silent during inventory reconciliation. It was an easy job, just making sure what we claimed to have matched up with what we actually had and then determining what could be sold and what needed to be offered to different sects prior to selling. If we had spell books, we offered them to the witches first, most recently Blu. If it had anything to do with vampire, mage, or fae then it was dealt with through the appropriate liaison. Kalen handled that, because, until recently, I'd made it a habit to stay away from supernaturals. Oh, except for occasionally being dragged by Savannah to a vamp bar to canoodle with hot zombies.

Concerned silver eyes peered at me from the other side of the room and then immediately went to the twins next to me, hilts placed in my direction within reaching distance, ready to engage. In fact, the slightest movement and sound had me reaching for them.

"Are you going to sit there and continue looking broody and lethally silent, or do you plan to tell me what the hell is going on?" he finally said. I glanced at the clock: it had taken him twenty-two minutes, a record for him—ten minutes of silence between the two of us and he'd get twitchy.

"But I'm nailing the whole dark, lethal, and broody thing," I teased.

His laugh was tight and tense. "Seriously, what's going on?"

I told him everything, and like Savannah, when faced with the information he made great efforts to hide his emotions. Occasionally, the facade would drop and I could see his concern, but he quickly reasserted it. I even told him that Tina now knew about me.

"I don't think it's that big of a deal that she knows," he said. "The moment Gordon Lands took over HF and said that they believed Legacy existed, you all were outed anyway. He wasn't just some wacko spewing nonsense and conspiracy theories. He's a well-respected man in the community. Most people wouldn't expect him to take such an interest if he didn't believe it was true."

I knew he was right. "The witness said the killer was

blind. Each victim looked like they didn't fight, and there weren't any remnants of their magic in the air, and no signs of struggle."

"And you don't think it was a fae?" he asked.

"I've been around your magic, Harrah's, and that of the fae at the SG. I'm familiar with it. It doesn't feel ominous and dark. Even Harrah's doesn't feel that way. I just feel power when she's around—strong, controlled, overwhelming power."

Kalen came to his feet, crossing his arms as one hand drummed against his bicep. He finally let his emotions show, and his fear and frustration made things even worse. As he slowly paced the length of the room, I watched him as he did a mental inventory of everything he knew about the various supernaturals that populated this world. There were so many subspecies and those that we thought were extinct. I nearly laughed at the contradiction of it; I'd been considered extinct for a long time.

"What did she say he looked like?"

"She said he was tall, pale skin, and gray eyes—totally gray."

"But he was able to find each Legacy without sight, which means he's tracking you by your magical aura or blood the way shapeshifters track by scent. Tracking an aura is very difficult to do. I don't know of any supernatural who can do that."

Blood was the source of who we were and was our fingerprint. The very thing that bound us to others. If you had the blood of a supernatural, you could track that individual. Possession of my blood would allow someone to be able to track any Legacy. I recounted every battle I'd had, every fight, every time I'd spilled blood and never considered cleaning it up. *Damn. Stupid. Stupid. Stupid.* But when you were fighting for your life, it was hard to think about a cleanup job afterward. In the last big battle I'd had with Conner, I'd lost a significant amount of blood. It couldn't be easily cleaned with a wipe or a napkin.

"But that doesn't explain why the others didn't fight back," I said, eying my sai, moving them closer. Kalen stopped pacing and regarded me for a long time and whatever he saw brought a frown to his face. He was the King of Useless Information, and I lovingly called him KUI because of it. It was hard to deny that most of his information was rather useless, because most people didn't care about how the notebook came about or the history of the coffee press. But he was also the source of a lot of valuable information, and the fact that he didn't have any information on this weighed heavily on me. It ripped away the very tenuous grasp I had on the situation.

"I've never seen you nervous before," he said in a level voice. His handsome and stately features were overtaken by a scowl. He moved with grace and elegance across the room and went to the closet and pulled out a sword. Slowly, he drew it from a brass scabbard that had swirls of intricate designs covering it. The same art covered the hilt of the sword. Light gleamed across the blade. It looked like something you'd see in a martial arts film. He turned it with a surprisingly skilled technique. He lunged with it, cutting through the air, causing a slicing sound with each movement. His stance reminded me more of someone who only practiced in a class, and, based on Kalen's lifestyle, I assumed a fencing class. But his strikes, even through the air, without an opponent, were precise and proficient. At least in presentation. I never forgot how a fight against an imaginary assailant was always different than one in real life, when skills were the difference between life and death.

"You look dangerous with that thing. Do you know how to use it?" I asked.

He took a few more swings where he handled the weapon with the skill of a marksman. He struck, parried, and moved to block and attack his imaginary opponent.

"If he comes for you, he comes for me." Even impeccably dressed in slim-fitting dark blue slacks and a white French cuff shirt, with cuff links that would pay my bills for the month, he looked menacing, a formidable opponent.

"I guess the next time I have to wade through a sewer and fight off a troll, you got it, right?"

He scoffed, allowing a crooked smile to lift his lips. "I said I would save you from death, not sewage. Priorities woman —get your priorities straight."

I suddenly heard a soothing lilt, a tranquil melody that embraced my mind, ushering me into a somnolent state the words that rode it willed. I heard them, mesmeric and commanding. My gaze went to Kalen: his eyes were widened, blank. His face was expressionless, and he swayed gently for several moments before collapsing to the ground. Other than the gentle rise of his chest from breathing, he wasn't moving. The words continued, just as entreating and soft, yet the command was stronger. I pulled magic, erecting a shield as I fought hard to ignore the enchanting sound of a spell that meant nothing to me but fought to control my mind and body. The scent of a stronger magic was there. That magic I'd felt at the other Legacy houses. It struck hard against the shield and eventually infiltrated it. Bile rose as pain gripped my body. I fought harder. I needed noise to drown it out. *Drown the sound out. iPod!* Like my phone, I always kept it close to me on my desk. I turned it on, jammed the buds in my ears, and increased the volume to high, shoved the iPod in the waistband of my pants, to keep it close to me. Music blasted from them but I could still hear sound. Each movement was a struggle. He appeared, the person who'd been described as being at the male Legacy's home, and the witness hadn't done him justice. His presence over-powered the room despite the delicate look of his long, slender limbs and coltish body. He seemed overwhelming. Nearly seven feet tall, he had over a foot and a half on me. I grabbed my sai, expelling a breath of relief when I didn't see any weapons on him; he had just his words. Words that I couldn't block out. His eyes fixed on me, or rather in my direction. The witness was right, they were gray—everything including what should have been white. He moved slowly, I assumed trying to determine where I was. Stepping back, I made sure not to make a sound. The magic came harder, not nearly as somber as before, rough and forceful as he attempted to take over my mind.

"Anya." The pattern of words changed as if they had been manipulated just for me. My joints ached as I moved, and my body slowly betrayed me. I held the twins closer to me, ready to defend myself. They felt like they weighed a ton; my muscles quivered as I tried to hold them. I made them rigid. Squaring my shoulders, I forced up stronger shields that he seemed to find small openings in, getting through. My head pounded. Faster and stronger his spells came, countering anything that I used to defend myself. He moved like a fluid wave of threat, stepping over Kalen's still body as though it was inconsequential.

Through the spells he cast he whispered my name—no, *cooed* it. That indecipherable draw I felt to listen came harder. Drawing more magic than I had, I blasted it into him with force. It hit then flowed over him, taking on a solid form before shattering into pieces. He lifted his hand and waved his fingers, taunting me, and the nails extended to points. Each was a dagger, the same size as the wounds found on the murdered Legacy. I forced myself to action, every movement painful as my body rejected the most minor motion. Moving just enough to go into a defensive stance, I waited until he was closer. He inched toward me, his weird eyes focused on me, the chanting in my head becoming louder trying to drown out the music. I focused on the words of the songs coming from the earbuds, the bass, the variations of the melodies. Anything to keep me from being lulled into submission.

I struck when he was close, moving slower than I was used to, my muscles groaning under the resistance. A blade slid into him, and he moved farther on it, getting closer to me. The look on his face was the same impassive one that he'd had before, unfazed by the pain.

Reaching out, the dagger-clawed hand sliced over my stomach; the searing pain was overshadowed by the shock of my legs folding under me, collapsing me to the ground. I couldn't move them and I only knew they were still there because I could see them as I unsuccessfully willed them to move. He slid back off the sai, and his blood spilled for only a moment before it ceased. With a wave of his hand, the tear in his shirt closed, and I suspected the wound did as well. I kept a firm grip on each sai, aware that I was limited in movement and only had a few opportunities to strike. He was biding his time, pushing his spell through the shield that was wavering, trying to drown out the music.

Just get closer. I needed him closer. I closed my eyes for a moment, mastering my panic so I could focus. If nothing else I'd fight his spell, keep him from subduing me with his magic. He wouldn't get his claws near my heart to paralyze it. So much noise in the room, in my head, I couldn't hear him move, but his imposing body cast a shadow over me as he knelt down. One strike was probably all I had in me. Timing it as best as I could the moment he was close enough, I jammed one sai into his left eye, and then the other into the right. While dropping my shields I used magic to push him back, pin him to the wall. He struggled. I held. He struggled more. Bile crept up my throat, and my muscles screamed for relief that would not come until he was dead—or so I hoped. The spell would be lifted but I wasn't sure about the paralysis. It was probably a poison. I would need an antivenin.

"Levy." Harrah's voice rose over the music, the spell no longer raging in my head, just music. I never thought I'd be happy to see her, but I was.

"This is a mess," she said as she moved around me to turn off the iPod. I heard her draw a ragged breath before making her way to the creature that was struggling, trying to hold on to life that would soon no longer be his. I propped up on my elbows, watching her as she looked at it.

"Do you know what it is?" I asked.

She nodded, slowly. "A Mors. A very dangerous and old sorcerer, who can only be summoned. A great deal of magic is required to do it, beyond anything that any one individual possesses." She turned, a slight smile working its way onto her lips. The same placid, gentle eyes reflected back at me, innocuous and kind, but behind them lurked something more.

I focused on her as she walked slowly around the room and knelt next to Kalen. "He's alive," she said. "Once the Mors dies, the spell that has enchanted him will be released." It was hard to ignore how undisturbed she was about the Mors pinned against the wall slowly dying, as if it was something she was used to or she didn't have it in her to be bothered by it. Why wouldn't she just kill him, release him from his pain?

She took off her suit jacket, folded it, and placed it under my head. "People are paranoid when it comes to your kind. I thought it would be an easy transition, but it doesn't seem like it will be." Her tone was so soothing and melodious that I closed my eyes, allowing her reassurance to wash over me. "It's not your fault. I wish they could see what I do. Do you know our history? The fae weren't much better. Glamours and the manipulation of the mind are great powers, and it's so easy to give in to the illusion of omnipotent power. But we are always just one iron dagger away from being subjugated. You all were much stronger. People fear the idea that a small army is necessary to subdue just one person, but that's what it takes to do that with you all. Out there, you reinforced their fears: the monsters, the people with godlike power. I'm sure it is a burden for someone your age."

"I think people will come around," I said softly.

"You've seen so much and yet you hold on to a beautiful innocence. Those thoughts are comforting. Hold on to them." I felt it. Her. Hard, forcing her way in, fighting to control me, seducing me into a quiescent state. Nothing good happened in that state. I pushed back, and she gasped. I wasn't as weak as I looked. She tensed next to me.

"Sleep, dear child," she commanded. It seemed odd coming from a person who might be just fifteen years older than I was. I fought the good sleep, the somnolent state she was trying to seduce me into. While I fought it, I missed the blade she sliced across my throat.

Then she sat there for a moment gingerly stroking my hair. How cruel she had to be to do this to someone and sit and wait until they died.

I wrapped my hands around my neck, blood seeping from the cut and covering them. My breaths became labored. The pain overshadowed it all. I ignored the fatigue—it was the pain and the light-headedness that were threatening to take over. I needed to get through this. I remembered her light fingers stroking through my hair, her gentle words, her hollow explanation. Did she even care?

I needed to survive. I willed myself to fight through the exhaustion. Pulling in magic, I attempted to use it. My hands warmed, colors bouncing and swirling around them. Not nearly as vibrant or strong as usual, but the magic served its purpose. I just needed to heal, but blackness came, subduing my perseverance and will. I directed my magic to my neck. The warmth nicked at it, wrapping around it.

She came to her feet and spoke, her voice seeming to come from a distance.

"The Mors are unique beings. Bloodhounds, you can call them. Wonderful assassins. All they need is a little drop of blood and they can track your magical aura. But you of all people know that, don't you, Anya?" Her light, wispy voice floated through the air like a gentle melody, as kind as it always was. "For someone as dangerous as you are, you aren't careful with where you bleed. You should be more careful, a handkerchief, a spot in the soil, a discarded shirt after a fight can all be used. Your blood could be used by him to find the others. Too bad he failed. I told him to leave you for last—I'm not wrong often." She paused. "Just as I wasn't wrong when I told the other members on the Magic Council that you would cause Gareth's fall and potentially that of the Council."

I wondered if she had done something to Gareth.

I felt it, her pushing into my mind, not nearly as much as the Mors had, just a gentle probe. Her smile widened. "You want to stop me, don't you? But can you keep the Mors there, heal your wounds, and stop me? Can you?" She leaned over me. A dark cast drifted over her delicate features. Although she knelt before me with the cherubic face that had fooled so many before, I saw her as what she was, a monster.

"You have quite the task, don't you? Let him go and he'll finish you," she taunted.

I pressed my hands to my neck, trying to stop the bleeding. I struggled to hold the Mors, stop the bleeding, and keep her from doing whatever she was trying to do in my head. Everything was hazy.

I vaguely saw her figure as she strode over to him, slowly

and languidly. Her voice dropped. "You failed. If you fail again, then I will send you back without the payment we promised." With a quick tug she pulled out my sai and tossed them aside. There was a thud as my magic wavered, and he fell to the ground. I wondered what it took to kill him; a sai through the eyes should have done it. He shouldn't have lingered so long. I focused my magic on trying to slow the bleeding. I kept fading in and out, but I saw the Mors rise to his feet. I dug my elbows into the floor and scooted back, pulling the dead weight of my legs with me. I couldn't let him get near me. It was his final mark—the kill strike of his poisonous claw piercing the heart. Deadly information that I stored for the future—if in fact I had a future.

Harrah left to allow him to finish the job. If Kalen were to wake, he'd only see my body and never know that Harrah had been there.

Once again the soft timbre of the spell filled the air as it tried to shepherd me into complacency. Weak, tired, and barely clinging on, I had to decide whether to use magic to try to heal my injury or to fight him. Neither one was a good option because both led to death. Without the music from the iPod, denying that sound became harder and harder. My eyes were heavy—so heavy. Keeping them open became more of a chore than anything. I leaned my head back, allowing the sound to take over so I could rest. Peace—that liminal place between life and death where I felt as though I was lingering.

My eyes popped open at a shrill noise that burst through the room. If I hadn't known better I would've thought it was a banshee, but the sound was different: not as high, but enough to distort that lulling, beautiful sound that was threatening to overtake me. That *had* overtaken me. Fighting the weight of my heavy lids, I opened my eyes just enough to form little slits; Conner was standing there, but his mouth wasn't open. A diaphanous ball waved around his fingers, as if reacting to the chant. That shrill sound cut through the air, dominated it, and prevented me from hearing the spell any longer. The Mors stood up and directed his attention to Conner. The sound became louder. The shrieking noise that in any other case I would've hated was the most beautiful and welcome thing I'd ever heard because it stopped the spell.

The Mors was just inches from Conner when the paralyzing chanting stopped. I struggled to keep my eyes open and my hands over my wound, magic coursing through them trying to heal, but it wasn't enough. It eased the pain but didn't heal it. Then a sword manifested in Conner's hand, and with one strike the Mors's head fell from his body. He collapsed to his knees, blood painting the walls and the front of Conner's shirt. Droplets of it landed on my pants. I tried to move my legs—still nothing. The sorcerer was dead, so I should've been able to move them. I collapsed back just as Conner knelt down next to me, his fingers gentle on my chin as he turned my head to look at my injury.

"Do you want me to help you?"

I had a snarky response ready for him, but I didn't have it in me to deliver. I wanted him to help me. I didn't want to die.

"Please," I said in a faint voice.

"As you wish." I heard Kalen call my name off in the distance, then there was nothing. Absolutely nothing. I didn't know if I had passed out or if Conner was moving me to a different location.

CHAPTER 13

I knew I was only experiencing darkness because I didn't have the strength to open my eyes, look at my surroundings, and see who else was around me. I didn't care as long as it wasn't the Mors. I felt the warmth of someone's body next to mine. Then a face was close to me, and gentle hands cradled my face. I moved my head; a sharp pain in my neck caused me to raise my hands to it. I pulled them back and saw red. How much blood had I lost? How much more could I afford to lose?

I wanted to speak but even swallowing hurt. Conner's voice was gentle, a soothing whisper, a murmuring oceanic sound. It might not have been that beautiful; perhaps I was just happy not to be so close to death or at least be given the illusion that death wasn't imminent.

"My magic can heal you. Make you whole. Anya, would you like me to help you?" His words were more than an offer of assistance; if I accepted I'd be making a tacit agreement of allegiance to him and his agenda.

I fought through the darkness. My blood-drenched hands felt like lead and my head was becoming lighter as the seconds ticked away. The cloud of darkness came and I attempted to fight it off.

When I didn't respond immediately, he continued, "You are mine. I will protect you. Heal you."

I mumbled a weak "no." It was a feeble but defiant rebuttal. I needed Conner's help, but I would not be indebted to him. He would not take me and try to use my weakened state to convince me to be by his side. He ignored me—the weak magic that pushed off me wasn't enough to do damage. I swallowed more of my defiant words, the metaphorical act was just as painful as if I'd actually done it.

I awoke in a large room, the soft bed a welcome change from the floor that I remembered. I pressed my hand to my neck—my unmarked and unscarred neck. No physical reminder of Harrah's betrayal, just the anger that raged in me. It took great effort for me not to jump out of the bed to find her. I pushed away the covers, revealing my naked body. I was clean, uninjured, and unmarked, and I had Conner to thank for it. He'd probably respond with his rhetoric about wanting to live in a world separated from the humans with just us. I was so happy to be healed and alive I'd half listen out of courtesy because my anger toward Harrah and thirst for revenge had left me depleted. Listening to stories of an ideal world where people like her would be killed by a spell seemed more palatable than it had been before.

I looked around the grand room, far more spectacular than needed for convalescence. The pale yellow walls were enhanced by ornate molding. A small, exotic plant in the corner was different than anything I'd seen before. Its blooms produced a delicate scent of lilac and honeysuckle. Hardwood floors were adorned by elegant, expensive plush rugs. The large windows were open and pale moonlight streamed in. I wondered if it was as artificial as everything in the room. I tried not to think about the level of power Conner must possess to make these things and maintain them.

Each time the thought of the debt I'd incurred popped in my head, I pushed it aside. I refused to think about the nonsense and rhetoric I'd be treated to, or the fact that I would probably have to try to escape because his plan most likely involved me and some variation of Stockholm syndrome. I slipped deeper under the silk sheets that felt light and cool against my naked body and tugged the top one even tighter around me.

"You are as you were," Conner said, his tone even, devoid of any emotion. His appearance mirrored his voice. His lips were a thin even line. I stared at him, holding his gray gaze. He was dressed in slacks and a pale green shirt that did little to flatter his natural persimmon red hair color, which he'd reverted back to. I sat up, making sure to keep the sheet tightly wrapped around me. His approach was slow but had the same confidence and assurance that he always displayed. After he'd sat on the edge of the bed, he lightly placed his hand on my chin and tilted my head to the side and assessed my neck. I assumed he was making sure it was completely absent of any reminders of Harrah's attack.

"The very people you've aligned yourself with against me are the ones that did this to you," he said softly, dropping his hand to my shoulder.

I swallowed—a reminder I could now do it without pain. I looked down at my hands. There was a hint of a glow, probably a result of the light that filtered in, but they weren't stained with blood.

His thumb stroked my throat where there should have been a scar. His tentative, gentle touch moved across the skin as though it was still injured and needed to be handled with care.

"Thank you," I said, my tone as low as his.

"No thanks needed. You were injured, it was my pleasure to help."

I shifted my gaze from his because I didn't want my gratitude to cloud my judgment. I wanted to see who he really was and not the one he wanted me to see. The face that he presented to me was that of a charismatic demagogue who enthralled people with his kindness, mesmerized them with his words, and seduced them into doing foolish things. I was given, again, a glimpse of the man that people were willing to follow over a cliff. They'd become embroiled in an unwinnable battle, facing down a tank with only their hands as weapons. This was the man whose words obscured the line between right and wrong as he deluded people into accepting his lie that there was hope in the most desperate situation.

He stared at me for even longer and there was something different about the way he looked at me, a longing that I'd seen when he'd claimed me as his consort. He leaned into me, and I rushed to my feet, cinching the sheet tighter around me. "No," I said firmly.

Pulling his lip into a sneer, he narrowed his eyes on me. "I've saved your life, when you've given me no reason to ever do so. How cruel it is to be so dismissive of my act of benevolence."

It's not really benevolence if you keep bragging about it.

"I owe you gratitude, not *me*."

After several moments of silence, he nodded then came to his feet. "Let me get you something to eat." His fingers whirled, the gentle rhythmic sound of water falling caressed the air, and off in the distance birds sang. He was laying it on pretty thick, giving me a taste of the utopia that my mother had spoken of. A land where Legacy were surrounded by elegance and beauty as a result of extraordinary magic.

"How long have I been here?" I asked before he left.

"Five days. I kept you in a state of sleep so that you could heal and only woke you to feed you."

What a glorious way of telling me you slipped me a magical roofie.

He inhaled, and moments later he was standing close, too close. I fought the urge to cringe as he reached forward to touch my cheek. "You were injured badly, left for dead and required a great deal of magic to heal. Let me assure you that it isn't without consequence. It took a great deal out of me as well…"

"Thank you, again." Our gazes locked, but he kept an indecipherable look on his face. Eventually his lips curled into a plaintive smile.

"Conner, I cannot express how much I appreciate you. I would have died without your assistance. But it would be cruel to lead you on, to make you think that a couple days here in this striking and beautiful place will change my mind, when it will not. We aren't on the same team. We are by all intents and purposes adversaries. You will not change my mind, and I won't change yours." I kept my voice light and gentle. I appreciated him saving my life, but I was aware his intentions were anything but altruistic.

As he rose to leave, he pointed to the right. "The bathroom is that way; there are clothes for you in there as well."

I headed for the bathroom and stopped. "I would like to go home after I shower."

"Where will you go, back to those who betrayed you? The person who slashed your throat, like a coward when you were at your weakest, and left you to die—do you even know if she was acting on her own or if it was a group plan? Will you continue to serve them while they lie in wait to strike again when you are in another weakened state? The next time I might be unavailable to help. Please know that of those you've encountered, I am the only one willing to extend kindness and mercy to you."

He rolled his shoulders back, stood taller, and shrugged off the persona he'd donned for the sake of getting me to drop my defenses and skepticism.

I realized he was right. I didn't know what I was going back to. Was it just Harrah acting alone, or had the attack been an orchestrated act? Thinking about it made me sick. The very person who'd sent his strange creature after me and Savannah, locked me in another realm with the same animal, and vowed to allow me to die like I lived—which was an expression I was still trying to figure out—was the person who had saved me.

He'd mastered his anger, his face once again gentle and welcoming. "You will need to eat. Shower, and then you can evaluate what you want to do. I suspect being here with me will not seem like such a reprehensible option."

Showering didn't give me the clarity that I needed. I stood under the running water, my fingers gliding over the area where the knife wound had been. Then I let them trail to my stomach, another place where an injury should have been. I wondered about Gareth and Savannah. Were they looking for me? Did Gareth know what Harrah had done?

The large bathroom, the size of my room in my apartment, made me feel more at home than the massive bedroom I'd been in. Between the blue-gray walls that reminded me of the sky after a heavy rain, the glass-enclosed shower, waterfall shower head, stone tile, and gentle crooning of the birds from the bedroom I felt like I was showering outside.

I stepped out of the shower onto the cool marble floor. It felt good against my bare feet. The sensation was more relaxing than the shower, and I wasn't sure why. Was the hard floor a reminder that I needed to be resilient throughout this, deal with it, and not be overtaken by the plush carpet situation? If I allowed things to overwhelm me then I wouldn't think strategically.

As I dressed in the clothes that I found in a closet in the bathroom, I cursed Conner for the use of the word *clothes*, which for me would have been jeans or a pair of jogging pants and a shirt. Instead, I slipped on a long satin dress that conformed to my body, molding to my curves. I definitely would have liked underwear or at the very least a bra, but the fabric was thick enough that I didn't feel completely naked. But I felt utterly ridiculous slipping into the thong sandals placed in the corner. I looked like I should be walking on the beach on a private island.

Conner smiled when I stepped into the dining area. His languid gaze slowly trailed over me, taking in my appearance. Once several minutes had passed it was harder to ignore it. *Cleanse.* I imprinted that word on my mind, made sure I didn't forget who he was and what he wanted.

"You look beautiful," he said softly.

I looked down, doing anything to avoid his lingering gaze. "I'm overdressed for pancakes, don't you think?" It wasn't really breakfast; it was only three in the morning.

He extended his hand to a chair pulled out for me. "Please, join me."

I slipped into the chair in silence.

"I'm glad you are here with me."

I wanted to tell him that this wasn't a date. He'd saved my life, I reminded myself, but I had a feeling he would keep revealing things to me that would chip away at my gratitude.

He maintained the smile, and I focused on the table with more food than two people could eat, even with my appetite. He served me fruit, an assortment of cheeses, meat that looked like lamb with an odd gravy, and French toast. It was an odd breakfast, but since it was still the middle of the night I supposed we could eat whatever the hell we wished.

We ate in silence for several moments, and ignoring his unwavering attention was getting harder. I gave him a half-smile; he returned it in kind, baring his perfectly aligned white teeth.

He had only eaten a few bites before he wiped his mouth with the napkin and tossed it in his plate of half-eaten food.

"Your skills are abecedarian and amateurish and in great need of refinement."

I didn't point out that my "abecedarian" and "amateurish" skills had kicked his ass on several occasions.

I simply smiled, plaintively. "It has served my purpose over the years and I do believe allowed me to get away from you on many occasions."

"I didn't say you were incompetent, just that your magic isn't as honed as it should be. You don't have the skills one of your strength should have. How odd that your parents sent you out in this world defenseless."

"They prepared me just fine," I snapped. Him talking about my parents seemed blasphemous, knowing how hard they'd tried to teach me in forced secrecy. Our magic meant death, a horrible thing for a child to know, to grasp. I'd been reluctant, and when I wasn't being an unwilling participant in my lessons, I'd been careless. It wasn't until several accidents with magic, where we'd been nearly discovered, that I'd learned to be more cautious, and so had my parents. Admittedly, I didn't learn as much as others had learned. I wished I knew how to teleport and do glamours.

Conner studied me with interest, his eyes inquisitive, seemingly discovering something that he hadn't seen before —perhaps a weakness he could exploit.

His tone was as gentle and smooth as the finest silk and laden with a sympathy that I'd expect from a friend, not a psychopath with draconian plans. "Our lives have been quite difficult, haven't they? I guess our parents dealt with it differently. You see us as very different, and perhaps we are. But can you at least agree that we are bound by a unique and perhaps tragic childhood? I lost my parents as well. The wounds are still there."

I ate, ignoring his stares and most of his conversation, which had devolved to banalities. I saw the trap before me and didn't doubt it was intentional.

After sliding my plate to the middle of the table, I stood. His eyes trailed my movements. "I would like to go home."

"To what? What you are going back to will not be what you have known. The veils of dishonesty that the supernaturals had in place have been lifted. The city is in chaos. At least stay here, as a reprieve." How did he know that? Was he just making it up? What could have happened in the days that I'd been gone?

His words were delivered in such an entrancing tone, denying him was getting harder. "Stay, let me teach you and hone your skills. Make you the true warrior that I know you can be."

My brow furrowed. Each moment I stayed with him the more confused I would become, and the lines between our differences would blur. Emotions didn't always align with logic. "Even if the things that you teach me will be used against you in the future? You'd do this knowing that the very things you show me may be what I use to stop you, perhaps even kill you? I will not be swayed," I offered in challenge.

A smile settled casually on his face, as though I'd whispered words of adoration and love to him instead of my plans to kill him. He couldn't let a little thing like a threat on his life be of any concern to him.

He nodded once. "I'll teach you in hopes that you will remember this and never use it against me."

I felt the burden of the debt that I could not bear. I shook my head and said softly, "No. I want to go home." I turned and started out of the room. I felt like an ingrate, but Conner and I were on opposing teams, and it was ridiculous to accept a gift from him without the expectation that the repayment would be so high that I'd regret it.

"I could have let you die; do you know why I didn't?"

Curiosity got the best of me. "A moment of mental clarity," I offered with a hint of humor.

He threw his head back in laughter, louder and more robust than the hackneyed joke deserved. "I couldn't kill you any of the times I've tried. Despite your novice magic and amateurish delivery." He rested back, magic lacing around his fingers, vibrant colors of blue, yellow, and red, putting on a light show for me. He caused it to perform for him in a spectacular display of control and skill. The magic smothered the air, a reminder of his strength and power.

He continued, "I couldn't kill you. For a moment as you bucked against my control, denied my offerings, and rejected me, I considered you a fool unworthy of me. But you survived. Only someone truly deserving of me would have. It was a sign."

I blew out a hard breath that made my lips rumble. *Welcome back, Conner.* He'd picked up his first-class ticket to Arrogance-ville. I prepared for him to yammer on about me being his consort and how I was going to be used as his broodmare and would push out his superpowerful magical babies who would be revered like gods.

He didn't do any of it; instead his gaze rested on me. His eyes traveled along my face, down the curve of my neck, and then to my breasts. Then they lazily lifted to my mouth again. "I'd like to kiss you," he said quietly.

My tone was just as soft and gentle as his. "I'd like for you to do that, too—so that you'll be close enough for me to punch you."

He threw back his head in a boisterous laugh. "I find our banter amusing."

"Really? My threat of violence is amusing to you? You must have been in a state of bliss the times I stabbed you."

I sat down again and leaned back in my chair, and he did the same, mirroring my posture. It was an intentional act that would make it seem as though we were operating as one.

He waited patiently for me to continue, and no matter how I tried I couldn't temper my words. "Perhaps me foiling your plans and trying to kill you was too subtle. Let me not mince words here. I'm not interested in you. Period. There isn't anything you can do to change that. You saved my life—I am grateful—but my opinion of you remains firm."

His expression didn't change, as though he was trying to decide whether or not to take me seriously.

"You think what I want is selfish and cruel. I think what you are willing to concede to is just as egregious. Tell me, Anya, how would you like to see the world and our place in it? Throw out caution and everything you think is impossible and tell me." His tone struck me as genuine curiosity. It was easy to feel this was sincere and not an effort to usher me into complicity and willing acceptance of his dogma.

"I can't do it, because no matter how powerful you are, you can't change time. We all live with the consequences of others' actions. Why do you think we have laws, rules, and regulations? At some point, someone screwed up so terribly rules had to be put in place. Our predecessors screwed up." I took a breath. "I don't want to hide anymore or fear I will be hunted like some animal because of something I couldn't control and had nothing to do with." I admitted it and immediately regretted it as his eyes softened, along with the edges of his scowl.

"Let me make that happen for you."

He rose, approaching me slowly, and his features softened. The magic that played over his fingers performed for him, a clear demonstration of his power and an indication of how much I could learn from him. Before he could close the distance between us, I stood, moved away from him, and put several feet between us.

"I'm going home." I looked around for my things. I figured he'd tossed my clothes but not my weapons. I looked around for my sai. I guess it would have been too much to ask him to give them to me.

"Your weapons?" he asked.

I nodded.

He considered it as he watched the magic in his hand in a state of newfound wonder as if it was his first time seeing it. At his command, the magic was smothered to nothing. In silence, he went to the closet and pulled the twins out. The blades gleamed as the light hit them. The blood from my last fight was absent.

I took them from him and started to back out of the house, surprised when he didn't make an attempt to stop me. Instead, he followed me slowly. Still nothing. His passivity made me more nervous than if he'd attacked me. I looked around the area surrounding the home. Three houses just as grand as the one he'd had me in. Vast trees, with thick florets of lush leaves, were intermingled with fragrant flowering bushes. The grass so green that it looked fake, which it probably was. The air, just enough of a breeze that it gently caressed the dress against my skin. My eyes narrowed on him. When he spoke, his voice had a gentle timbre, laced with his brand of confidence.

"Iridium is a funny thing. I hate it. I wish the lesser beings never discovered it was our weakness. Our only defense is that it takes so much of it to really subdue us. But you know that, don't you? So much that you helped that group test it before that spectacular ambush. I will admit we were ill-prepared for it—for you. But there you were, my consort, my chosen, leading the cadre of agitators. Your diminutive little resistance."

I pressed my lips tightly together fighting the urge to tell him that resistance had taken down most of his group and captured him. His bitter look of defeat was imprinted in my memory. It was the first time his confidence and arrogance had faltered.

"I wonder how they discovered melting it and putting it in a dart. It was quite effective, but short-lived. *But* I'm sure if they could have gotten us to ingest it, it would have lasted longer. And you hardly can detect it. Mix it with fruit, sauces on meat, or even just add a dusting of it to French toast—syrup nearly overwhelms the taste. I never understood why people would ruin the taste of a perfectly delicious dish by putting that overly sweet mess on it. But they do. I guess it was lucky that you do—and hunger had made you ravenous. Did you even taste your food, or did you scarf it down without a care for the taste?"

He disappeared and reappeared, just inches from me. "Of course you did the latter, because you were too busy ignoring me and rebuffing me as though I'm just some common peddler of magic as you've done before. If only I wasn't so—"

He'd poisoned me! All the kindness and words had been a distraction as he tricked me into eating iridium.

He jumped back just in time to miss my strike with one of the twins. I wouldn't miss again. I lunged; he moved. I swiped his leg, and when he hit the ground, I dropped to one knee and tossed one sai aside so I could use all my force to impale him with the other. It slid into his arm, like butter, and blood gushed. He hissed. The golden ball that formed in his hand hit me in the chest, sending me back several feet. I hit the ground and another jolt slammed into me. His face contorted in pain, he winced as he pulled out my weapon. He came to his feet, his shirt crimson, trails of blood running down his arm. I glanced at the discarded sai that was just a few feet from him. He stared at the one he'd pulled out of his arm before tossing it to the ground next to the other.

My breathing quickened as others came out of their houses. Just three of his crew were left. So small now. Weak. They were all probably just as rooted in their plans as they were before. Whether there were three or three hundred and three, they wouldn't be dissuaded.

"If I stay here, you will never sleep, because the moment you do, I will try to kill you," I warned. As he flashed me an amused smile, I again found myself wondering what type of person I was dealing with, demagogue or psycho. Well, I got my answer: he was a psycho with a side order of lunacy.

He bared his teeth in a wider smile. "How can I not be drawn to that passion?"

"Believe me, your murder won't be a crime of passion. It will be calculated and strategically executed." I glared at him, becoming even more irritated. My threats meant nothing to him. He expected to get what he wanted.

He'd drugged me. My magic paled in comparison to his and he'd still weakened it and me. The more I thought of his plotting to drug me and render me helpless in case I didn't fall for his insincere altruism, the angrier I became. It made me more violent than I'd ever felt.

"That's hate," he said, staring into my eyes. His hands roved over his arms, and the blood slowly receded until it was just a little spot. He used magic to pluck it from the shirt and allowed the red rivulet to linger in the air before it fell to the ground. Then he made a show of pulling back his sleeve and exposing the injury. With a wave of his hand, the skin meshed together, leaving the fawn-colored skin as unmarked as it was before.

The others came closer, but he held a hand up to stop their advance. "This is between us. We are just having a spat. It will probably be one of many. She is quite feisty." He kept a cautious eye on me as he addressed them. I called on my magic, pulling it from the recesses where it was strongest, hoping to draw enough that it would override anything he'd put in my system. But it sat like a boulder in me, inert. The heaviness of magic that couldn't be used left me feeling even more agitated and angry.

When Conner spoke, although his tone hadn't changed much, I felt like he was taunting me. *Asshole.* "I thought kindness could convince her, but you all were correct. She's so far gone, under the finger of the humans. Their little pet: she will do so much to serve her masters just at the mere smidgen of hope that they would absolve her of a past she had nothing to do with. It's rather pitiful."

His eyes flicked in their direction. "If you all were nearly as hard as her to convince, I do believe I'd be too exhausted to be of any good." He looked at the only man present. "But you see why I've taken more time with her. My warrior, my consort, my future bride.

"You all please hold while we continue our little quarrel." His voice was as light and breezy as the little flicker of his lips. He opened his hands, and a sword materialized. The same one he'd used before. He bowed to me. I inched toward my sai with apprehension. "I will not cheat. You win, and you get to leave. You fail and—well, you know what happens then."

I ran to get the twins. I stabbed one through the front of my dress and ran it up the fabric, ripping it to give me room to move my legs. I didn't care that I was indecent in front of strangers. I lunged; he spun out of reach. I twisted and rammed the butt of the sai hard into his skull. Dazed, he stumbled back. Strike. Parry. Strike. I advanced toward him aggressively, moving around him striking and retreating to gain the advantage. One hard jab caught him in the side, and blood seeped through his shirt. I caught his sword overhead in the moto of one sai. I dropped to my knees and jammed the other into his thigh. I yanked it out quickly and in one swift move jammed the handle into his throat. He choked but held on to his sword that was locked on the sai. Jerking it with enough force, I urged the sword out of his hand. I grabbed it and rolled closer to the observers. They didn't see it coming. Two of the three bodies dropped to the ground seconds before their heads. I grabbed the other one by her hair, refusing to give her the chance to disappear.

Eyes red, Conner was able to grab a few breaths as he looked at the carnage and more of his people fallen by my hand.

His lips parted, anger-stricken. Torrential waves of magic came off him as he clenched his hands at his sides, seething.

"Let me out," I demanded, pressing the sword to his acolyte's throat and swallowing the bile that had crept up as I considered what I'd done. The rules of war were different, I knew that, and I had no illusions this wasn't one.

Weighted silence ticked by and he finally closed his mouth. His voice was a whisper. "I am sorry." It wasn't directed to me, but to my hostage. As the words fell from his lips, the air became coated with a dark and dangerous magic. His eyes were intense, hard, cold as marble. He moved, faster than I'd ever seen him, jabbing my sai into the woman's chest. It went in just enough to puncture her—my enchanted weapon was prevented from being used to injure me. She slumped against me, her blood moistening my dress and mixing with the blood that already stained it.

I stepped back and let the body fall. Conner and I stood just feet away from each other. I readied the sword to engage again, and he raised his hand. "You've proven to be a worthy adversary. I've had two failures, and behind each one is only one common denominator—you. You've seen the lengths I will go through to keep you. Shall we fight daily until you concede, or will you do it now? Understand those are the only options. It's just us now..." He looked at the three remaining bodies, his anger flashed, and I wondered how much control it took not to retaliate.

"I'll never concede. You'll be miserable with me here." It wasn't a statement but a promise, and the arrogance that he'd allowed to falter so infrequently reasserted itself. Although he was watching his established plans wither away, he didn't seem desolated. I wanted him to feel hopeless, because that would cause him to abandon his plans.

I lunged at him, swinging the sword. He disappeared and reappeared nearly fifteen feet away. He waved his hand, and magic struck me hard. A symbolic smack across the face displaying his displeasure. My bones groaned as I smashed into a tree. The bark bit into my skin as he left me fastened to it. Only then did he move closer. He studied me with great interest before he gathered the weapons and strolled to his house, where he stayed. I expected to be released—but I remained, fixed to the tree.

The iridium darts that the SG used had a six-minute effect, then our magic was restored. How long would it take for ingested iridium to be out of my system?

I tried to think of every book I'd read, everything Blu had shown me, the things that Kalen had told me. I tried to devise an escape plan, but nothing would work if I didn't have magic to break the ward.

I wasn't sure how many hours had passed when he finally released me. I looked at the bodies that lay at my feet, preferring to look at them rather than him. I doubted I could see his face without wanting to claw out his eyes. That's what I was reduced to. However, I believed in using whatever was available to succeed, including kicking Conner in the groin, which had become a priority.

He waited for me at the entrance of the house. I crept slowly toward it, hoping that each moment would allow me to devise a plan to get away from him. In silence he beckoned me to follow him to the dining room. Once there he pointed to the chair where I'd sat earlier. My jaws were clenched so tightly that they started to ache. I glared at the food on the table but didn't make an effort to reach for it.

With a heavy sigh, he moved and clamped a wide iridium manacle on my arm. He returned to his seat then slid a plate in front of me. I looked at him but didn't respond; I wouldn't give him the pleasure of even a scowl. I looked straight ahead, expressionless, occasionally looking at the manacle on my arm. He looked at me several times, finally sat back, and smiled. "You can decline eating but eventually you will have to. You are stubborn but not foolish enough to starve yourself to death."

I remained silent, emotionless, knowing that would bother him more than me talking. In his world where the psycho demagogues roamed and wielded their delusions of grandeur like measuring sticks, venomous words from one they had their eyes on were probably equivalent to a sweet sonnet or words of adulation. Ignoring him was my best weapon. I'm sure it was hard for him to deal with his unrequited ... well, it wasn't even love or lust, it was a peculiar fondness based on whatever odd list of attributes he found desirable in a mate.

"You look lovely." I didn't bother to look at the new dress that a wave of his hand had placed me in. It was similar to the first, except it was emerald green and complemented my eyes and the persimmon red hair that he'd seen fit to crown me with. I kept a sharp hateful eye on him as he wiped away the blood from my hands and arms. I needed a shower; just putting me in a pretty dress wasn't going to make me look "lovely" by any standards.

"The food is fine." He took several bites out of his as proof.

He didn't even wince when I stabbed my fork into his steak, put it in on the napkin, and started to eat it.

"You are behaving like a savage."

"Says the man who poisoned me and killed his own in order to keep me hostage in his pathetic little world."

"Do you know how long I've been working on this? Nearly eight years. Do you think you can outlast me? I find it distasteful to control your mind to get you to concede, but if you don't leave me any other option, I will," he chided.

I didn't doubt *controlling* me was of lascivious intent. I hated the way he looked at me. His eyes trailed over my lips, the curve of my neck, and my breasts, where they remained too long. He moistened his lips, igniting a rage in me that made choosing death rather than remaining another day with him an easy choice.

I grabbed the vegetables and potatoes off his plate and slowly ate them. A smile had settled on his face, easy and quietly amused by me. A trite look of pleasure.

I finished it all in silence, and then he stood to clear the table. A blistering windstorm suddenly thrashed through the air. Magic—strong, and so many variations of it, I couldn't pinpoint the source. Witch, fae, mage, it was all melded together into a conglomeration of virulent, dominating power.

Conner rose, indignation covering his face. Magic twined around his hand. He'd never looked so truly affronted before. His ward had been broken, by people he'd considered beneath him, without my help.

Then came the deafening sound of a roar reverberating off the walls. Conner's eyes fixed on the entrance of the house, and he gritted his teeth and started for it. I used his distraction to my advantage and jumped up, allowing the cuff to slip toward the heel of my hand. The odd angle of the hit and the impact of the strike weren't likely to leave my wrist unscathed, but I didn't care. I smashed hard, leveraging the position of my body to get more power. The strike jerked his head back, I hit him again, feeling the bones of my wrist and hand groan under the impact. The excruciating pain brought tears to my eyes, but I couldn't stop. I grabbed a plate, thrashing him in the face with it. He stumbled back again, blinking. A pulse of blindly hurled magic shot through me. I grabbed his shirt and we went back together, landing a foot from the table with him on top of me. I pushed Conner to the side just as the lion dug its claws into his back, pulling him off me and onto the ground. It swiped across his throat and then mauled his chest and body until there was nothing but gore left. Conner's death was far more barbaric than I'd expected for him. It didn't involve magic or my sai.

CHAPTER 14

"I'm fine," I said, exasperated after twenty minutes of Savannah's, Gareth's, and Lucas's attention. I didn't want soup, my legs propped up as if I was injured, or to lie down. I had a small fracture in my wrist, something that the mage doctor at the Isles diagnosed and fixed within minutes. I wasn't injured—just magicless.

I wasn't sure how long it would take for the iridium to pass through my body and finally be gone. Being without magic made me feel vulnerable—even when I didn't use it at least I had access to it. Now I felt like I had lost one of my senses, like a part of me was gone.

I concentrated on my rage, and I had plenty of it. It was unfettered, borderline dangerous. These feelings of vengeance and ire were indeed lethal—and scary even to me. Never had I plotted and desired to rip someone apart more than I wanted to do to Harrah. Her betrayal tasted bitter in my mouth and her conniving ways made my skin crawl. I wanted to kill her and bring her back to life just so I could do it again.

"How did you find me?" I asked, letting my gaze skate

over each of their faces, refusing to focus on them. I knew they would be twisted in various versions of concern.

"Finding you wasn't the difficult part." Gareth's voice held some humor but not enough to belie the anger and frustration in it. "Getting through the veil was the problem. I owe Tina a lot of favors since she agreed to use her team to help us. Otherwise, we wouldn't have had the manpower to do it even with using the Hearth Stones."

No one had to say it because we were all thinking it—we were glad Conner was dead.

"How long was I gone?" That was the only question I could slip in between theirs. I gathered that Kalen had come to just in time to see Conner whisk me away, and they had been looking for me ever since. I can only imagine the scene that Kalen had woken to: the severed head of the Mors and its body. A blood-painted room. Pools of more blood where I'd lain. Stifling magic that inundated the air.

"Five days," Savannah said, anger and sorrow low and heavy in her voice as she growled the words.

Five days. My hand ran along the imaginary scar, the skin now smooth and unmarred, of the wound that would have killed me or at the very least left me scarred if it weren't for strong magic.

"I need to find Harrah," I said in an even tone. Thirst for her blood was so deeply embedded that it was part of who I was at that moment. It didn't change the modulation of my voice, the cadence of my words, or even rile my emotions as it once did. It just existed, and I felt like I existed because of it.

"Levy," Gareth said, regarding me for a few moments and then frowning. "You can't retaliate—" I was about to voice my objection and had an excellent rebuttal stating why I had every right to retaliate, but he held up his hand to stop me. "Not now. The narrative that you were attacked and so were other supernaturals has been established. They attributed the crimes to Trackers. The ones that weren't killed by Conner are now in custody." He said it like it was tied up with a nice pretty bow. I didn't care about politics or narratives.

"And she just gets away with it? She summoned some weird assassin for the sole purpose of killing me and my kind. For what? I wasn't a danger. If she wanted to go after Conner, fine. But she came after me without cause."

Gareth sighed. When he spoke it was barely audible. I leaned forward in the chair to hear him better. "You have to let it go for now."

I had a hard time looking at him: I didn't want to hear his logic, didn't care about reason. The idea of even entertaining his suggestion made me nauseous. I wanted my revenge. I got up from the couch, went to my room, and threw myself on the bed. I heard Savannah advise him to give me a few minutes, and that was all he seemed capable of. Moments later he was there with me. I sat up from my position on the bed and glared at him. He worked hard at ignoring it, biting his lips to keep back his words. He stepped closer to me, tentative. It was the first time he'd ever displayed anything other than extreme confidence.

"You're angry with me, aren't you?" he asked.

I wasn't angry with him, just upset with the situation. "No, but I'm not necessarily happy with you. I'm tired. I'm tired of being the person trying to take the high road. I'm tired of being the person trying to do the right thing and constantly being betrayed because of it. I could have done the Cleanse. I would've been safe. I could've had Savannah, Kalen, and you behind the veil of protection with me without any problem. I would never have given in to Conner, and yet I was rewarded with a knife slashing across my throat. Tell me, exactly how should I feel? How should I respond?"

"You have every right to your anger and even your

revenge. I hope you get it. If you do it now you get revenge and also death. I'd rather you just get the former. So think about this and do it strategically. Don't respond out of blind rage and get yourself in a situation you can't get out of."

That was the reason people shouldn't respond or act when they were enraged: they didn't think about strategies. They became consumed with quenching the thirst for retribution. I was thirsty to the point of dehydration. Gareth moved closer to me, and when he was at arm's length, he reached out, stroking his hand against my cheek.

"I'm glad you're okay," he said. I could hear the hint of relief and sorrow in his tone. I looked down; I didn't know what to say. Everything seemed so confusing, and I couldn't have anything more than a physical relationship with Gareth. Things were just too complicated to have anything more. I wasn't ready to have an emotionally intimate relationship with him, and part of me had always thought he wasn't the type of person who would want one. For several moments we just stared at each other in uncomfortable silence. He leaned forward and kissed me lightly. His lips coursed over mine, his tongue sliding against my bottom lip before parting them and kissing me harder, more urgently.

He pressed me back onto the bed. His thumb stroked my cheek before he gently kissed me again. This time it was a feather touch. I wrapped my arms around him, pulling him closer and feeling the warmth and security of his body against mine. I wished I didn't want it so much, but I did. I needed it, and that's where we stayed, his body a heavy cloak of warmth over me. Periodically his lips brushed lightly against mine. Eventually, I drifted off to sleep.

While I was sleeping, Gareth was devising a plan, and the

first step was to find out how Harrah had summoned the Mors and make sure she wasn't able to do it again. Early the next morning we were headed to see Blu.

She answered the door as soon as we knocked, stepped aside, and waved us in. It was the first time I'd been to her home after often meeting her at her coven's home. Her apartment was definitely what I'd imagined, based on what she'd told me about her parents. They were jazz musicians and their profession had an influence not only on her name but also on her style. Throughout her house she had eclectic pieces of canvas art of people playing instruments. Several clay figurines of women singing in various positions were placed around her home: one seated at a piano, another standing at a microphone, a set of three women with their arms positioned differently. The light-colored walls were accentuated by various artistic depictions of musical notes. There was a guitar placed in one corner. She didn't strike me as a guitarist, but there were a lot of things very atypical about her, like the fact that she always had some variation of blue in her hair. I'd expected her home to be the very same way, but she seemed to have a penchant for earth tones of light brown, pale yellow, burnt orange, and burgundy. Her oversized sofa was dark brown, with burnt orange and beige accent pillows. A large table ottoman sat in front of the sofa and on top of it were stacks and stacks of books. The small armchairs in the corner were burnt orange; the pillows that belonged on them were tossed to the side, and on top of them and the sofa were more books. In the opposite corner she'd placed a brown decorative trunk that was open, and I could see several medallions, stones, and globes inside. Her apartment wasn't very large, a little bit smaller than the one I shared with Savannah. I assumed she had to find creative ways of storing things.

Blu's normally kind demeanor seemed weighed down by

the seriousness of the matter.

She directed her attention to Gareth. "Someone summoned a Mors?" she asked, taking a seat on the edge of one of the chairs leaving the sofa for the two of us.

I wasn't going to beat around the bush, or be coy in any manner. "It was Harrah."

Her brows furrowed together and her scowl deepened. "There is no way Harrah could do that. Not even a high-level mage or powerful witch could do that. Summoning one requires a great deal of power. Strong power. I can't even summon one using a Hearth Stone, and that allows me to channel magic from my ancestors." Then her face blanched. "I think I'm responsible for this." Her voice was ragged, low. She jumped up and started pacing back and forth, mumbling loud enough for us to hear her castigate herself. "I thought I was doing the right thing. The last Hearth Stone you all sold me was too strong for anyone to have. I didn't want to risk losing it or it falling into the hands of someone who would misuse it. I turned it over to the Magic Council."

"When did you do this?" Gareth asked.

"About fifteen days ago," she said. Her eyes and her shoulders dropped. "I'm sorry."

"You have nothing to be sorry about. That is the protocol if you thought it was too strong to be in anyone's hands and that it should be guarded. You did the right thing. That wasn't an act done out of malice."

It didn't seem to unburden her from her guilt; she continued to walk the length of the room twirling tight coils of her hair around her finger. "A witch with a Hearth Stone, a mage—a powerful one—with something equivalent, or a fae with a Broven crystal together could do it, but performing such a summoning is so dangerous."

"How many Mors are there? Is this a one-shot deal, and he's the only one we have to worry about?" I asked.

She shrugged. "I'm not sure how many Mors there are, but it's not as though people are calling them frequently. It's difficult, and they are called for a specific job."

I frowned. "Are the stones destroyed during the spell?" I remembered some stronger spells I'd read about in one of the books she'd given me in which the sacrifice was the object being used.

"Based on what I know about that type of spell, the stones would be given as tribute or an offering of some kind."

"Then there probably isn't a chance to do it again," I said with hope. I just needed something to go right. Let this never be repeated.

When she started to chew on her lips, hope quickly dwindled.

She exhaled the breath she'd been holding for several seconds. "There are many objects that can be used like the stones, any number of which might be in their possession. Since the war, supernaturals are more cautious, and they have every right to be. It was a reminder of how fragile our existence is. One spell and life as we know it disappears." To maintain that illusion of safety, they handed magical items over to the people who were appointed to ensure that it wouldn't happen. She looked at Gareth, her gaze soft but entreating. "Gar, how many people have access to items once they are turned over?"

They all blindly followed the Magic Council, expecting them to have their best interests at heart. Based on the way Blu looked, it was going to be a harder endeavor to trust them in the future. Her frustration-laden gaze remained on him as she waited for an answer. I focused on him, brushing off the twinge of anger that sparked in me. The Magic Council had been given unchecked power, because along with the individual councils and the Supernatural Guild, they maintained safety in the community and the alliance with humans. They were the faces and integrity of it. Harrah and her accomplices had violated that blind trust.

Gareth started slowly, carefully choosing his words, which made the situation worse. People only chose their words carefully when they had something to hide. Brought to the forefront of my mind were the Magic Council's and Supernatural Guild's magical collusions—the times they broke the law, circumvented it, or rather, ignored it for the greater good. How many minds had Harrah erased? New memories implanted. I wasn't sure if she could do the latter, but I knew she could compromise memories and do glamours.

"Most items we destroyed, but everything is subjected to a vote."

"And the Necro-spears?" I asked, suspicious. The threat of another Cleanse was minimal, but I still didn't want there to be any chance for it to happen. For every Conner who was destroyed or stopped another could rise. A chill ran up my spine at the thought that one could already be in the making. How many people had he discussed this with? How many Legacy lived with the superiority complex that they should be revered and live in their segregated society with magically enhanced homes, greenery, and lives, adored and feared by those that saw them as the magical elite? Reviled by those that they considered common, spurious examples of magic, basic, and nothing more than people to look down their noses at.

"To my knowledge, they were all destroyed," he offered. Doubt tinged his words, but he held eye contact with me, which had to be difficult because I was glaring at him. I blinked a couple of times to try to get a handle on my misdirected anger. They could have done a lot of things, but I had a feeling the others followed Harrah as blindly as the average citizens. If she said to keep objects of great magical power "just in case," I'm sure they were easily convinced. This time the "just in case" was summoning an assassin.

"I'm sorry," Blu said again, and I hated that she was carrying a burden that wasn't hers. I owed her a great deal: the books she loaned me and her instructions had helped me improve my magical skills. Unless she was the actual person who summoned the Mors I wasn't holding her accountable.

"Do you think it was the entire Magic Council who planned this assassination attempt or did Harrah just recruit some random person to help?" I asked Gareth, whose eyes became slits at the harshness of my tone. I wasn't doing a very good job of tempering my anger.

"Summoning Mors is very difficult, but the use of the stones or objects similar to them would give enough of a boost that there would only need to be a few, maybe three or four powerful and skilled supernaturals," Blu offered.

"Harrah told the Mors that if he failed, she would invalidate the contract. What do they offer?" I asked.

Blu thought about it for a long time, returning to slowly pacing the room and twirling her tresses around her finger, delving deep into her thoughts. She looked like she was trying to remember history or separate the tales from what was true. Finally, she stopped pacing and left the room, returning with three large books. We watched in silence as she perused them. Fingers ran over the pages, and it was apparent why she and Kalen got along so well. He was truly enthralled by her and it extended beyond her love of fashion to the adoration she had for knowledge. Each time she looked up from the pages, considering the words and what she was reading, there was a spark of interest.

"There is a blood contract," she started. "If the assassin succeeds, then he is allowed to stay."

"I saw the thing, he wouldn't necessarily go unnoticed," I said.

"He doesn't stay in that body. There just has to be a recently deceased body around and he can take it."

I cursed under my breath, happy that Conner had killed him. I also wondered how many others could be summoned. The only way to ensure that it wouldn't happen again was to destroy all objects that could be used to summon one. I was ready to set the Magic Council's building ablaze and destroy everything in it. I felt like I'd experienced the ultimate betrayal.

Blu was still allowing guilt to sully her mood when I rose. "Thank you so much." I smiled. "Please"—I jerked my head in the books' direction—"if you can share this information with Kalen, do so."

She grinned. "I'm seeing him tonight."

Of course you are because you two are now joined at the hip. Midwest Barbie and Ken.

The ride back from Blu's wasn't as uncomfortable as I thought it would be, but it was getting harder and harder to ignore the furtive glances from Gareth. My anger and frustration were so blistering it was getting hard to suppress them. It was misdirected, and unfortunately some of it went in his direction. "How could you just blindly follow them!" I barked.

"I didn't blindly follow anyone," he snapped right back, his tone frosty and so deep it sounded like a growl. I was sure he was just as upset by Harrah's betrayal as I was. It wasn't just Harrah's, it was attributable to all of those on the Magic Council, with the only possible exception being Lucas. Secret meetings, collusions, and hidden agreements just so they could kill the Legacy. I had traded one enemy for another. One with better resources. The Trackers were just considered crazy conspiracy theorists yapping about a nonexistent group of people that everyone believed was extinct. The Magic Council didn't have any restrictions or limiting labels. They knew I existed, and Harrah had wanted me to be the poster girl for us all to come out. I'd initially gone along with her intentions thinking they were pure. I'd suspected that eventually it was going to be problematic and had decided against it. I was tired of giving people the benefit of the doubt when they could not extend the same courtesy to me. I was not a murderer. I didn't have a desire to do the Cleanse again or feel the need to be revered by others or separated. I just didn't want to live in secret, hiding what I was. I understood my powers scared people. I would've agreed to wear an iridium bracelet to restrict my magic just so I wouldn't have to live in hiding. That wasn't enough for Harrah—for them. I remembered seeing the platitude that the only good Legacy was a dead one. Fury rolled over my skin, raising the hairs on my arms.

"If I knew this was their intention, do you think I wouldn't have told you? Wouldn't have stopped them?" Gareth asked.

"I never would have thought you would have been a Tracker, either, and I turned out to be wrong." I wasn't sure why I was being a total bitch to him. Before I could stop, the words were flying out; I just wanted to be angry at anyone available and he was there.

"I'm sorry," I said softly. "I feel betrayed. Not by you; by them. I'm tired of trying to prove myself. I've done everything I could."

I looked out the window at the trees that we passed, the clear turquoise sky, and eventually the buildings. They didn't call me the way they should have, instead inciting a new memory of trees I had destroyed because I had too much magic in me that had to be released. The clear blue sky of the fake world that Conner had taken me to. The buildings where I'd tracked down the other Legacy and Conner's acolytes, and even the Maxwells.

"I can't let this go unchecked." I breathed out.

Silence stretched for long moments, and before I knew it, ten minutes had passed. When Gareth looked at me his eyes shone with a clear understanding. Behind them I saw the same fury and frustration that I had felt. "I know."

More silence. The muscles in his forearms bulged from gripping the steering wheel so tightly. "I know you hate when I bring up the politics of things, but you can't discuss the harmony that exists between the humans and us without addressing it. If you go in there and destroy everything and them, what happens? How do you explain that away? It's easy to explain one person dying or stepping down from their position. But the entire Magic Council with the exception of Lucas and me, the only two people who do not possess magic? You think people won't put one plus one together?"

"Honestly? I don't give a damn." But that was the furthest thing from the truth. I cared. I gave a lot of damns. Because at the end of the day when the fires had been set and the buildings were ablaze, the bodies lay dead, my revenge was sated, and I felt a sense of vindication, I still would have to answer for my actions. Gareth would have to answer for allowing me to do it, and then it had to be explained away. The humans had to know the reason it had been allowed. I wondered if the narrative would be that those members of the Magic Council were the few people able to stop me, so I had killed them and destroyed the objects so that I would be unstoppable.

"The Unstoppable Juggernaut," I mumbled.

Gareth's head jerked in my direction and his brow furrowed. "What?"

"He's a super villain—Cain Marko, he's the Juggernaut. An unstoppable villain," I explained.

His eyes were limpid as he looked at me, and confusion marked his face. Then a small smile blossomed and quickly became a grin. "Don't give that narrative, which will not work in your favor." He shook his head. "In fact, let go of all the superhero references. Don't talk about the Avengers, X-Men, Suicide Squad, or any of that. You are a very odd woman, Levy."

"I'm the odd one?" I teased. "I'm the one who knows who the Unstoppable Juggernaut is, along with millions of other people. I think *you* are the odd one. You're not very hot right now."

"I'm pretty sure I'm going to have to do more than not know a few comic book characters for that to be true."

Hello, Mr. Arrogant. "Well, at least we know your super-power isn't humility."

"Should it be?" he asked, his smile widening.

I wanted to continue my banter with him, flirt and tease him some more, and for a few seconds it was what I needed —a break. People had been trying to kill me since I was a child; for once I just needed a break. That wouldn't happen anytime soon, though; I needed to deal with the Magic Council in some way. I wasn't naïve enough to think this would be their only attempt.

I let the silence fall and did nothing about it when it remained, although I'd have preferred the chatter to continue. When I had to answer questions, I didn't think about the problems I had to deal with. And maybe if I didn't think about it so hard, the desire to storm in there and take out anyone in sight would eventually vanish. I knew that was impossible. All it took to rekindle the rage was thinking about me lying on the floor, my neck slashed, and the bodies of the others killed by the Mors.

When Gareth followed me into my apartment instead of just dropping me off, I was relieved. I was acting on emotions—dangerous dark emotions—and he was the voice of reason. I hated that some of it was rooted in politics, but he didn't have a lot of choices, he had a responsibility that extended further than mine. For hours, the conversation was banal; we didn't even broach the topics of HF, Harrah, Conner, the magical objects, or the Mors. We both needed a reprieve. Dinner was filled with more frivolous conversation, but as the time ticked by, we couldn't pretend that things were fine and normal because they weren't. Ignoring it wasn't going to prevent the slaughter from happening again, or get Harrah and the others.

"What's going on with Humans First?" I asked, taking a seat on the sofa after dinner. He remained standing, taking up a position next to the wall, his arms crossed over his chest, his eyes glued on me. He considered my question for a long time, and I wondered if he was assessing me and trying to figure out if I had abandoned my ideas of revenge. Did he consider himself the only roadblock preventing another scene with bodies fallen as a result of my anger?

"They're a problem but more to themselves than any of us. It's as it was before—" He stopped abruptly, taking in a ragged breath in lieu of saying "before you were nearly killed by Harrah and abducted by Conner." He continued, "Before things happened with you. They are going to destroy one another from within. The radical members are being controlled by the more reasonable members, and they seem to be spending too much of their time fighting one another to be of any concern to us. I suspect the more radical ones will split off. We'll watch them once they do and hopefully deal with them."

"Would it be such a bad idea for supernaturals to separate from the world?" I couldn't believe I'd said it, but for a brief moment, it seemed like the simplest option. "Think of everything that you all do: the efforts put into establishing these narratives that make us palatable to the humans, dealing with groups who will never accept us, and having to live under all these restrictions."

Gareth's eyes narrowed, studying me as if he was seeing someone different and was trying to figure them out. "What did Conner do to you?"

"Nothing that would have made me feel this way. I'm not looking to have a world like Conner's, but just one free of all this BS." My mind went to the dead Legacy, the Mors, and my finger traced along the line where my throat was cut.

"You of all people know you can't change history, it makes us who we are. HF doesn't even have a hundred members." He let his words linger for a moment. "In a city with the population that we have, those are the only people who are willing to be part of it. Even with Mr. Lands over it. What does that tell you?"

Logic, he was the voice of it, and I needed it. Gareth watched me carefully as I kept playing with the handle of my sai. I kept them close to me—too close. If they were just a few feet from me, they seemed too far away. I wondered if they were my security blanket. He made a face, I'm sure remembering how I got out of bed the night before to put them next to me. Each time I'd tossed and squirmed in his arms I'd been waiting for the Mors' magical chant that would render me paralyzed. I swallowed, trying to push it all down. I was better than this.

He tentatively approached me. He knelt down, placed his finger under my chin and lifted it until my eyes met his, and kissed me softly on the lips. Then he pressed his lips to my cheek.

"Let's go," he said coming to his feet.

"What?"

"Your heart rate has increased, your respirations are too high, and you're tense. This isn't you, and I don't want you to be this way. Screw the politics behind it. Let's go destroy some things." He winked.

I was slow to move although I'd gotten to my feet the moment he'd mentioned destroying the objects. "I don't want you to lose your job or your position on the Magic Council for me."

"And I don't plan to. You were right. They broke the rules —that will be the narrative. And if anything, it should demonstrate that we will do anything to preserve the trust people have and our dedication to following the oath we took. Harrah is a liar and I've always known it. I just never knew how despicable she could be. I understand her position, but I also realize that there are lines of ethics and even laws that she has crossed. That can't go unchallenged, nor can she be given the impression that she can do whatever she wants without consequences. There will be penalties."

Was he considering "consequences" her being put in the Haven? My idea of consequences was to put her six feet under. Perhaps knowing what it felt like to have her throat cut as well. But I would settle on destroying the objects that allowed her to murder.

I was on Gareth's heels, sai sheathed and placed on my back as we headed for the door.

"There shouldn't be anyone there except for the sentry and the guards," he offered. Having been in the Haven, I knew that could be enough of an impedance. Anyone who worked for the Haven wasn't exactly the weakest link in the supernatural world. Quite the contrary; like the agents at the SG, they were the strongest and most skilled. Since the Cleanse, there weren't a lot of weak supernaturals. It had wiped them out first. Even the weakest now were still pretty strong from a historical standpoint.

We drove up toward the entrance. A guard was at the gate; Gareth gave him his credentials as well as his badge, although the man waved him forward without giving them a good look. He eyed me for a few seconds, and then his gaze went back to Gareth, but he didn't say anything.

"You bring people here often?" I said with a little amusement.

"If he doesn't know who you are he probably thinks I'm giving you a tour."

"A tour at eleven o'clock at night?" I was skeptical.

He shrugged. "Maybe he thinks I'm trying to impress you with my position. You look like the type of woman who requires a lot more to woo. I'm sure most men don't look at you and think they have a chance. And they damn sure don't know that the way to your heart is to start talking endlessly about comic books and superheroes," he said, shooting me a look before his lip lifted slightly in derision.

"Well, pray tell, which is the best way *to your* heart?

"I find myself strangely drawn to tetchy brunettes who talk incessantly about super villains and the Suicide Squad, call me kitty, and have roommates who don't have any boundaries." He parked and got out of the car.

I followed and fell in step with him. "A woman like that seems pretty hot to me."

He gave me a half-grin, and I knew he had a smart response that he held.

He used his badge to enter from an entrance other than the one I'd used when I'd been arrested for murder. The illumination above the door offered a little more light than the muted ones surrounding the building. I'd expected them to be brighter so they could see if someone dared to break out, but being seen was the least of an escapee's worries. Since no one could teleport, except Legacy and Vertu, getting down the ten-foot high walls would prove to be difficult. If a prisoner attempted to climb down them, the flowers that laced up them, which I was sure were poisonous or magically enhanced, would stop them better than a bright light shining on them. If all that failed, the shifters on guard and their immunity to magic and predaceous nature would ensure that you weren't getting too far. *Ok, so they don't need lights.*

From the outside, the building didn't look so scary and overwhelming. Inside it was a different thing altogether. Magic stifled the air, and even though there were sigils in many of the rooms to prevent it, it inundated the halls like a dense shawl. So much of it and so many variations that picking out the nuances was difficult. Not impossible, but difficult. Fae, mage, and witch magic all intermingled in the rooms.

It was hard to ignore the memories of my time here faced with magical beings who hadn't done a great job making me feel welcome—but why should they have? If a magic wielder was there, they'd been accused of something pretty bad that put the alliance between humans and supernaturals in jeopardy.

I followed Gareth down the long halls. I slowed, drawing magic from within and letting it travel down my arms until sparks of it danced along my fingers, making sure that I had access to it. And Gareth, as he did each time I performed magic, stopped to look at it briefly, enchanted by it for so many reasons. I'd come to the conclusion that he was humbled by it in a peculiar way. The only magic that he didn't possess immunity to. For most it was a source of disdain, but not him. Or perhaps it was and he was better at hiding it.

We passed several rooms that were locked; others had keypads. I stopped for another moment to look into the room where I'd first encountered the Magic Council. Rows of chairs, large opulent desks on a dais elevating them to the point they could look down upon the accused. The fear of knowing that your life could be changed by seven people.

There weren't any juries, who might have some sympathy or understanding. I vividly remembered them questioning me. It was the first time I'd met Harrah and Lucas, not to mention Jonathan, who'd eventually betrayed the others and been killed. I almost laughed at the absurdity of it. They'd killed him because they felt he'd betrayed them by siding with Conner just to curry favor with the Vertu and be part of a world where he would be considered one of the elite by association. Clearly I didn't understand that desire to be revered, to long for power and be willing to sacrifice whatever and whoever to have it. I understood revenge. It bothered me that I did, but the desire to achieve it at all costs was something I now knew.

Backing out of the room, I had to increase my speed to catch up with Gareth. He took me down another hall. The lights were dim, and the walls were a plain white, unlike the others, which had been painted rich colors and had some decorations. It was as if someone didn't want this pathway to catch anyone's attention. It was a space they didn't want other people to know about—where they held the illegal and powerful objects deemed too dangerous to be out in the general public.

How did the Council establish such a list? The history of magic had so many embellishments—how did they extrapolate the truth from fantastical revisions? Even when I read books about the Cleanse, some of the tales were entirely different. Revisionist history, I supposed. The same could be true about all these objects that were deemed so hazardous. Some could be innocuous, but based on one person's retelling of their history and attributes, they were shelved in this room with the other powerful and dangerous objects.

Gareth punched his code in and then pressed his finger to a reader before opening a door.

"They will know you were in here," I said, following him into the room.

"I showed my badge at the door." He shrugged. "There is no way the others won't find out I did this." He seemed awfully casual about participating in something that might cause him to lose his job, or worse, be convicted of a felony. But if he wasn't afraid, I wasn't going to be, either.

"I don't want to indiscriminately destroy things in here," he said, turning on the lights and revealing a massive space. I focused on the sigils that lined the upper edges of the walls. If one didn't know what they were they would have considered them beautiful decorations of interlocking loops, curves, and twirls of red clay-colored symbols that wrapped around the room. A couple of white circles with black dots within them looked like eyes. I had no idea if they even meant anything or were just subtle ways of letting whoever entered know they were being watched. I scanned the room again looking for cameras. There weren't any, so once you bypassed the locks and the fingerprint security you were free to do whatever the hell you wanted. Whatever the hell they wanted was exactly what they did. I wanted to make sure I could use my magic. I opened my hand and let a small glow expand; it pulsed and then vanished.

Once I'd confirmed I could do magic, I directed my attention to the rows of shelves along the walls. In the far right corner were three bookshelves filled with books. Some were old and weathered-looking, with brown or dark blue leather binding. The others looked like books I would expect to find on display in a magic shop to present a fantastical look. Their spines had ornate designs in swirls of gold or bronze, some titles English, but most in Latin. A few were in languages I couldn't identify. This was where forbidden treasures were kept, and I was sure the books fell in the same category. They were probably filled with forbidden spells. Low glass-fronted cabinets were massed in the center of the room, and the magic coming from within them was undeniable.

There was just enough floor space remaining for a small black desk that held a desktop computer and a large monitor. The leather chair looked comfortable enough for hours of sitting and reviewing.

I started opening cabinets. I had no idea what I was looking at. I saw a staff, markings curving around it. I couldn't make them out. It seemed like a bad plan, destroying these things without knowing their capabilities, which might be beneficial in the future. I was faced with the same double-edged sword that the Magic Council had come up against. Destroy them and know that they could never be used for evil or keep them in the event that you needed to use them.

I held the staff in my hand, running my fingers over it and feeling the power, the strength in it, wondering what it was for. "We should look this up and see what it does."

"You will want to destroy that," Gareth said, looking over his shoulder from the computer desk. He looked at a picture of it on the screen and then the description. "It's worse than the Hearth Stones."

I cracked the staff over my leg and winced at the pain. It was sturdier than it looked. Another attempt coaxed a curse out of me. Grinning, Gareth walked over and snapped it into pieces. Using the handle of my sai, I smashed them into smaller shards. Breaking something shouldn't have felt so good, but it did.

Back at the desk, Gareth went through the catalogues on the computer. "There are six more Hearth Stones." He studied the screen again and then moved to a cabinet on the far right. "These should be destroyed as well."

The contradictory feelings were weighing on me. I

wanted to get rid of them, but there was that nagging feeling of "what if." Gareth gave me a tight half-smile. I had heard the hardness in his voice and the anger from the betrayal, and I felt it, too. But I also hated the idea of leaving people defenseless. They weren't totally defenseless, were they? Against a magical coup, it wasn't just magic that worked: the military and their arsenal of weapons were effective, too.

"I'm just getting rid of anything that can be used to summon dangerous creatures," he explained.

I nodded and then struck one of the Hearth Stones with the handle of my sai. It took several powerful blows before it chipped away to bits. After smashing three of the six Hearth Stones and two of the ten Broven crystals, I strode over to the bookshelves, my finger trailing over the various titles until I came to one that was English or Latin. I flipped through the pages, scanning them. I figured we were probably going to burn some of the books. Most spells only required objects. But sometimes, a book with certain spells was needed too. Burning books seemed wrong, but it was necessary. The more I read the spells, the easier it was to destroy them. Some of them were so nefarious I soon became okay with obliterating everything in the room.

I went back to the cabinet looking for the remaining stones and then pounded at them aggressively with the hilt of the sai until they were crushed to pieces. Calling them stones was rather generous. They were hard, but not nearly as resilient as stone. Changing techniques, I smashed a crystal against the floor. Shards of glass sprayed, and I stomped until they were nothing but sand-like pieces. It was cathartic. I shattered another one and then another until I had destroyed all ten. I whirled my finger and brushed the remains aside until they were in a little pile of glassy dust and then went after more staffs.

Gareth and I had gotten into an easy rhythm. He either

pointed to things in the cabinets, pulled them out, or told me what to look for and I destroyed the hell out of them. I came across another stone hidden behind other objects; it was a slightly darker gray, similar to the one that Kalen and I had sold to Blu. One that hadn't been logged. Another well-intending member of the supernatural community had probably turned it over. Had this stone been overlooked, a simple clerical mistake?

It infuriated me because as much as I tried to rationalize it, I couldn't do it. It had been hidden for a reason, and if this one had been, so were others. I smashed the stone to the ground. Nothing happened until I started hammering at it with the sai. The blows were more aggressive and hostile than what I'd delivered to the others.

"Destructive, aren't we?" Gareth said, looking over his shoulder. A brow raised as he watched me and then assessed the room.

"Might as well have fun," I retorted with a forced smile.

"And you indeed seem to be having fun. I guess you don't have any more concerns or apprehension about destroying things."

"I still have them, but I don't think there's a right or a wrong answer to this. If we let these exist then Harrah and the rest of them will have more power and control than I think they should." There were several beats of quiet as I considered the situation. Harrah's views, although vastly different than Conner's, were just as dangerous. The reactive and preemptive actions they took to maintain the harmonious relationship with the humans toed the line very closely to being cruel and unnecessary. It all got so blurred there was no clear moral stance to take.

As I violently chipped away at that stone I wondered if I would be considered "good" for doing this. Would the history books be kind to me as the person who demolished this? I looked over at the pile of destroyed glass. It was too freaking late to ask if we were doing the right thing, so I stopped and smashed into the stone some more. The air was now thick with magic that had been released from the broken objects, floating there unused; eventually it would dissipate. Looking into an empty cabinet, I said, "There is a very good chance you might not have a job after this is found out."

"I *will* have a job as well as maintain my position on the Magic Council. They broke the rules. These things aren't supposed to be used. Not on you. Not the way that they did. As far as I'm concerned they violated the trust of the community and for no other reason than to get rid of you when you haven't posed a threat to others."

"It was preemptive," I said softly. I lifted my eyes to meet his, which had softened. They weren't hard before, but had possessed sorrow and disappointment—not remorse.

I looked at my phone; we had been at it for nearly an hour. I moved toward the last cabinets in the room.

Gareth inclined his head slightly and inhaled the air, and when he spoke his voice was low. "Someone's here."

He didn't have to tell me. The moment the words fell from his lip the doors blasted open. Harrah walked in, power emanating off of her. It rolled over Gareth and attacked me. My shields went up. And the person behind her came through with a wave of magic that shattered it to nothing. They had enhanced magic, I'm sure the results of an object that should have been housed in the room with the other magical objects. Before I could respond I was hit dead in the chest and flew back, crashing into the wall. I quickly scuttled to my feet, returning fire just as hard. My blast of magic hit the small cadre of people she had with her, sending them out the door and into the wall behind it. Plaster crumbled, and I heard someone groan. There were three of them altogether. I assumed it was Harrah, a mage, and a witch—most likely they were the ones who'd summoned the Mors and made a preemptive strike. When magic careened through the room again my shield was up, reinforced and prepared to fight magic that mirrored mine. This time it barely wavered. I'd used very little magic demolishing the items in the hidden storeroom. My magic was just as powerful as ever.

I was prepared to end this, and I had every intention of being the only one doing it. This was the last stand, but they didn't attempt to retaliate. Instead they hovered over in the corner, their mouths moving ever so slightly. I looked at their hands and saw two gray crystals that gleamed with a harsh light, odd stones—darker than the ones we had destroyed. These had hues of burgundy that had a slight glow and an overpowering aura of magic. The mage and the witch had those objects in hand, and Harrah had a dagger, *my* dagger, a Legacy dagger. It was a Necro-spear.

Gareth glared at the weapon. He knew it was more dangerous than anything else that they were using to do the spell. If by some chance it was ever embedded in him he would lose the ability to change and his immunity to magic would be nullified. But Harrah appeared less concerned with him and more absorbed in getting the words of the spell out. The trio's lips moved fervently. Magic didn't strum through the air, it rampaged like a hurricane. Gareth and I stumbled back as the tumultuous wave tore into the room.

"Life" was all that Harrah said, and moments later she and her companions scattered away. Once again that gentle cadence, that soothing melancholy sound filled the air, ensnaring me in its magical entrapment. It dug into my mind and knocked down all the shields I put up with an overwhelming force. The alluring lilt continued. I covered my ears and screamed, temporarily drowning out the sounds, but they grew louder than my voice.

Gareth stood in front of me, a frown marring his face. His eyes were a deep well of concern. "Levy, what is it?" I didn't hear his words, I just read his lips. Refusing to be rendered paralyzed and unable to fight, I screamed louder.

The Mors entered the room in a slow saunter. The same vacuous eyes as the other one, his death song emanating from slightly open lips.

Don't let him stab you with his claws. I said it in my head but needed to let Gareth know. I wasn't sure of the effect the poison would have on him.

Before I could say anything, Gareth lunged at the Mors. He disappeared and then reappeared behind Gareth. He landed a sharp blow on Gareth's back. Turning quickly, Gareth returned the assault, hammering powerful blows into his abdomen and then jabbing him in the face. He staggered. His tall imposing body jerked as he attempted to maintain his balance. Gareth kicked him in the jaw and struck him with a semicircular kick. He lost his footing and fell to the ground. Grabbing my sai, I ran toward the creature to impale him. The Necro-spear soared through the air and caught Gareth in the stomach. He stumbled back, blood spreading over his shirt. He faltered but didn't fall. It was more than an injury—he was no longer immune to magic. His eyes widened, and I knew he heard the enchanting sound. That lulling, paralyzing sound. Gareth gave a guttural shout trying to override the sound before collapsing to the ground. The Mors focused his attention on me and the wall that I'd surrounded myself with. He slowly lumbered toward me as he worked on breaking my shield. I hoped the fight with Gareth had weakened him enough that he wouldn't succeed, but he had the others near, undoubtedly helping.

Gareth was just a few feet from me. The Mors was now right in front of me. His claws scraped against the shield as its lips formed a little *O* as if it were about to play a wind instrument. Thin lips opened wider as he cooed his melancholy sounds. I waited, letting him stroll around the shield looking for an opening. The odd gray coloring that drenched his eyes wouldn't have been scary if I didn't know what he was capable of. It walked around the shield making its haunting music, trying to render me defenseless. Just when he was to the left of me, I dropped it with a howl at the top of my lungs, drowning out all sounds. I grabbed the spear out of Gareth's stomach and embedded it into the Mors's neck. It was a clean strike; he wailed. I dropped down, rolled to my side, grabbed my sai, and shoved one into his stomach and the other into his chest. He collapsed to the ground. I pulled out the blades and chopped and cleaved until he was dismembered. When he stopped moving, I knelt down next to Gareth.

"Are you okay?"

"I'm fine," he said through gritted teeth.

Good. Because I had people I needed to see. "Stay here until it heals." I *hoped* it healed now that the Necro-spear was out of him. Tightening my grip on the sai, I ran down the hall, following the very identifiable magic. It brushed over my skin. I smiled at the devious plan to evade me—they'd split up. One wound up on the stairs to the right and the other to the left. I tracked them down by their magical fingerprints alone. Small waves of magic breezed along my arm—that familiar, devastating magic that wiped minds clean and smiled for the cameras, making magic seem innocuous and sweet. Except when you were on the other side of it, then it wasn't so nice. It was cruel and spiteful. I ran in Harrah's direction. I heard the whisper of magic in my head, but after dealing with the Mors it was nothing. I pushed back hard. Hard enough that I hoped it hurt. Enough pain to prepare her for what was coming for her. It wasn't much of a hunt. I ran, hearing the click of her heels. She was trying to make her way to the building's outer doors to get away.

At a full run, I finally caught up to her. She turned slowly, backing away, her hands raised. She revealed her palms as if she was surrendering. The placid look on her face, the gentle, wide-eyed innocence: the very features that made everyone capitulate. She was laying it on pretty thick, doing her best to look demure and incapable of any of the acts that she was being accused of. I didn't give her a chance to speak; I shoved the sai into her chest. Doe eyes widened, and her mouth slackened as she collapsed to her knees, gripping my arms. After a few moments, her hold on my arm relaxed and she fell to the floor.

I felt something bite into my side. It felt like hellfire. I turned to find the mage ready to engage again. Magic danced off his fingers, and his eyes gleamed with anger. His snarl was more intimidating than the magic. I simply smiled and pulled magic, strong magic that I'd reserved for my bouts with Conner. It shot from me like a bullet, just as lethal as it pummeled the mage. He went back hard against the wall, where I kept him pinned. I eased him away just to slam him against it even harder. I approached him slowly, trying to decide which was crueler, manipulating his mind until he was an imbecile and magic was just something he "used to do" or dealing him Harrah's fate.

I still hadn't decided. I was just inches from him, gripping my remaining sai, when I heard, "Stop right there!" I expected another hit of magic that didn't come. Instead I heard a gun cock. *Who brings a gun to a magic fight? Coward.*

"Put your weapon down!"

"I can't exactly put my magic away, now can I?"

"Drop the knife!"

I wanted so badly to correct him, but I decided against it and released my sai. It clanked when it hit the ground.

"Hands on your head!" he demanded. I complied. Someone else approached from behind, yanked my arms behind me, and placed cuffs on me. They were heavy as hell, so I knew they weren't just iron. Had they upgraded to iridium assuming if it worked on us, it would work on anyone else?

He grabbed me firmly around my arm—too firmly. My natural reaction was to retaliate, but I squashed it down and let him lead me away.

"Stop!" Gareth's voice rumbled through the room, reverberating off the walls, and everyone froze. His eyes blazed with ire as he came down the hall, his hands clenched at his sides and his brow furrowed. "Where are you taking her?"

The officers just looked at Harrah's wilted body sprawled on the floor and then looked back to him. They started to walk again.

"I said, *stop now*." Cold steel laced his voice, as if he dared them to take another step. His shirt was still bloodstained, and he kept his hand over the puncture wound, his fingers wet and colored red. Although I knew the injury had to hurt, he walked as if it didn't bother him. He rolled his shoulders back and stuck his chin out, his eyes fiery and enraged. He let his attention slip in Harrah's direction and then back.

"If she's going to be questioned, I'll do it. But there will not be any charges against her. It was self-defense and I was a witness to it."

The commanding officer's lips were pulled into a thin tight line, as thin as his eyes that were narrowed on Gareth.

"I'm sorry, Mr. Reynolds, we no longer answer to you."

"Excuse me, what do you mean?"

And then another voice rang through the air, assertive and deep with a hint of amusement. "It means, since you've been compromised, things will be handled by us."

The owner of the voice stepped into our line of sight,

along with two others. They all looked like they had been part of the military at some point in their lives. They were standing tall, squared jaws, cool eyes, and surly demeanors. Their suits were a standard black and official-looking. There were guns holstered at their waists and on their opposite hips were things that looked like the dart guns Gareth had used on Conner and me.

"And when did this become a federal situation?" Gareth asked in a low, rough voice.

The gentleman in the middle stepped forward. "We've been monitoring this clusterfuck. Mr. Reynolds, let's not be mistaken; this is the definition of *clusterfuck*. The Magic Council was tasked with maintaining civility among the supernaturals and making sure magical objects did not get out and hurt people. Above all, you were obligated to let us know when there were extreme dangers at play." His eyes jerked to my direction and seared through me. "Olivia Michaels?"

As if he didn't know who I was. Instead of answering, I fixed him with a hard stare as I tried to piece everything together. He was right, this was a clusterfuck, a huge one; and at the end of that I was truly screwed. Everything that had transpired over the past two weeks went through my mind: how many bodies I'd left in my wake, the violence, the retribution. It all boiled down to me standing in front of three men in suits with a dead body—Harrah's dead body and the mage who was about to be another victim. This didn't look good for me, and I realized that.

"It was self-defense," I said softly. And it sort of was. Harrah wasn't going to stop.

The man who had spoken gave a crooked smile. "What an interesting defense to employ. We have witnesses that put you on Carter Street killing three civilians. From my understanding it was unprovoked."

"Unprovoked? You mean the people who cornered me in the street and attempted to murder me? Exactly how were they provoked?" I snapped.

When he stepped closer, I saw the familiar little ring dancing around his pupils—the same that Gareth had. As the others moved closer to him, I caught wind of their magic as well. *Fuck.* There were so many *fucks*, and they were coming out of me rapid fire. The SG was state, they policed the supernaturals. This Federal Supernatural Reinforcement were over them. At least with the SG and a new shifter representative and Gareth, I had an advantage. At what point had they gotten involved? My heart started to race. The sneer that FSR guy sent in my direction showed that he would have no leniency for me or the situation.

"And when exactly was I going to be told that you all had intervened?" Gareth snarled.

"You haven't been officially involved in the SG for a couple of days now. Or not in the way that you should have been. The Legacy's appearance is something that should've been handled, and not in the way that you were doing it." The head guy, or I assumed he was the head of their team, spat anger that seemed to match Gareth's.

With a nod of his head the other two approached Gareth. There weren't any rights that were read to supernaturals; our system was different. Miranda rights were for humans. We had a version of the police and the Federal Bureau of Investigation but not rights that needed to be read to us because it was implied we had the right to adhere to the laws that were presented. We had the right to protect the alliance between humans and supernaturals. We had the right to do no harm.

As they released the handcuffs from their belts, a primal glint flickered in Gareth's eyes. I expected him to retaliate, to resist. Instead, he looked at me, dropped his arms to his sides, and let them put the cuffs on him.

CHAPTER 15

$\mathcal{I}$ was spending a lot of time with blood on me, except this time, the dried blood on my shirt and jeans were from a member of the Magic Council and the Mors that she had sent for me. It was hard to forget that fact with the Federal Supernatural Reinforcement agent sternly staring at me as I sat across from him in the interrogation room. I'd been there with an SG agent not less than a week ago, with Harrah in the room, and now I was being interrogated about her murder. I wasn't sure what they wanted me to say. Confess to it? Fine. I'll confess to it. But he looked at me with interest weighted by more than just a longing for a confession. No, he was looking for something else and I wasn't sure what he was angling for. There was desperation to his gaze, and as the feral animal peeked through I wanted to challenge him and refuse to allow it to intimidate me. But he was intimidating.

"I'd like to see Gareth," I said after several moments of silence.

"Not yet, we need to talk."

"Fine. You can talk all you want, however, if you want answers, I want to see Gareth."

When he smiled he bared the edges of his teeth. He was definitely canidae: wolf, jackal, maybe even a fox. His aquiline nose, narrow features, and narrowed eyes, despite their roundness, seemed more foxlike in appearance. Shifters didn't necessarily take on the characteristics of their animal, but more often than not, they did. I had a feeling I was dealing with the sneaky one. He slipped back in his chair, arms crossed, giving me his undivided attention. Attention I didn't want.

"May I have your full name?"

"I would like to see Gareth," I said pointedly. The ice in my words chilled even me but had little effect on him. He simply bared even more of his teeth. His stern gaze laid into me hard, and it probably would have worked on anyone else, but I wasn't as easily intimidated. After you've survived assassination attempts and had people whose job was to protect the supernaturals, come after you, there aren't a lot of things to fear.

"You'll find that I won't play the same games Gareth did. I don't find the obstinacy entertaining at all. Let's try this again. What. Is. Your. Name?"

"Harley ... Harley Quinn. Perhaps you've heard of me?" I immediately regretted it. Of all the comic book characters I could have chosen, perhaps a psychotic super villain wasn't the best one. He seemed more amused than I thought he would be. A wide smile blossomed on his face and the humor reached his eyes. He closed them for a long moment, the long eyelashes veiling them almost pretty, and he looked not as hard and cruel as he did just seconds ago. When he opened his eyes again they were gentler and the smile still remained. I guess he was going to use another tactic. *Now he's going to be good cop.*

"I can imagine being a Legacy is trying. Being hunted. People considering you evil without giving you the benefit of the doubt. I guess if I were in your shoes I'd choose to be bitchy, too. It will only get you so far, but at least you're having fun with it. Right?" He grinned before running his tongue over his teeth, but instead of seeming endearing, I got the impression I was about to become his meal. His narrow features sharpened and he ran his fingers over the table as though he had claws instead of fingernails. I sat up taller in my chair.

"What are you charging Gareth with?" I asked.

"Seems like you should be worried about what I'm going to charge you with rather than what's going on with Gareth. So, you're Legacy, we know that much."

"Then if you know that much there's not really much more I can tell you."

His lips twisted between a scowl and a frown. We assessed each other for far longer than was necessary to sum each other up.

"Okay, Ms. Michaels. We have no interest in making this more than just a discussion period. You walk out of here without any charges against you. But you must understand the situation you've put us in. You're sleeping with the head of the SG, a member of the Magic Council."

I made a face; was there a tape or something? How did everyone know?

He smiled. "It's not like it's a secret. You've killed Harrah, the head of the Council and the human/supernatural liaison, and were about to kill another member if you hadn't been stopped. You broke and entered the magical objects registry and destroyed a significant number of objects that we wanted preserved. You've killed three people—in broad daylight—who have been linked to an underground group known as the Brotherhood of the

Order and associated with the murder of the former head of Humans First."

Holy crap that sounds bad! "Well, anyone can sound bad if you list it like that," I offered in an even voice. "What exactly do you want from me?"

"As you can probably tell, things are getting out of control and it's a mess. And it isn't helping that now there are rumors that Legacy exist. Not to mention the escape of the Maxwells, Declan being released, and the creature that terrorized the city last week. Apparently, you had a hand in taking the last one down."

Hand? I actually did it. I get credit for murder of the so-called wrong person but only partial credit for the right one. "I'm not exactly sure where you're going with this. But since your dossier on me seems to be quite incomplete, let me help you out. My parents were killed by the Brotherhood of the Order, leaving me an orphan at sixteen. I've run into several of them on multiple occasions, and they almost killed me. I was able to manipulate them so they thought I was dead and would leave me alone or—I thought I had when no one came for me. Then I was just driving down the street, minding my own business, when another group of them jumped me. Just because I happen to be the victor, I'm sitting here in front of you being accused of their murders. I didn't murder them—I defended myself against them." *Taking creative license with the truth on that one.* I knew I could have handled it differently, but I hadn't wanted to. "And the reason you no longer have the Maxwells running around here, weird creatures terrorizing the city, or an actual Cleanse occurring again is because of me and Gareth. So don't act like you are doing me any favors by not wanting to press charges. The way I see things, the scales are very much in my favor."

He sucked in a sharp breath. "I never claimed that we don't owe you a great deal of gratitude. There's still the problem of whether or not your kind considers annihilating other supernaturals unacceptable."

"Yes, and sending someone out to assassinate us is really going to make us not want to get rid of everyone. If you have someone out there planning to do another Cleanse, know that is your own doing."

"And how is that?"

"Don't condescend to me as if you didn't know that Harrah summoned Mors to find the rest of us and kill us! So, the next time you have a group of Legacy banding together to do it again, remember that the first time might not have been warranted, but this one will be. You said you have no intention of keeping me here." I stood. "I'm ready to leave."

With a piercing gaze, he studied me for a long time. I wondered what he saw, a person inured by tragedies or a bitchy freak without cause, and for a microsecond I cared. He kept giving me long sweeping looks, and I became decidedly defiant, a scowl pulling my face tight. The agitation of having my magic restricted felt more intrusive than the large cuffs on my wrists. Protective magic brewed in me, unable to be released and used. My fingers tingled and I wanted desperately to extend them and release bolts of magic. Perhaps he sensed that desire because he leaned in, his eyes narrowed to slits as he bared his teeth like a savage animal. I'd awakened the predator and it took time for him to master it.

"Levy, you've helped as much as you've hurt, let's make that clear." He blew out a breath. "I don't dispute what Harrah did was wrong—"

"You don't get to be so flippant about her summoning a demon to assassinate me and my kind!"

"As I said, it was wrong, but she was just trying to prevent a war that is surely brewing between the supernaturals and the humans. Humans are afraid, and fear breeds paranoia and foolish groups like Humans First."

He was right—that was why they'd aligned themselves with Conner for another Cleanse to take all other supernaturals out. They wanted the same thing for different reasons.

"I want you to help us find all Legacy," he blurted.

"Then what?"

He stayed expressionless for too long. His eyes went hauntingly vacant and were hard to read. It made me feel more like prey, and I hated that feeling.

"Nothing. We form an alliance. A treaty."

"And that's it? You're not going to restrict our magic, in any way?"

He sucked in another sharp breath and considered the question. "It depends."

"On what?"

"How many. Levy, I can't pretend that we aren't concerned. But I think there is more trust when everything is out in the open. You help us find them, you become the liaison, and we will come to some kind of agreement." His voice was quiet but heavy with concern.

Although he didn't say it, the hollowness behind his gaze aptly let me know that if not, my life was about to become a living hell and he was more than willing to make it his priority to help that along.

"Gareth. I'll only do it if Gareth keeps his job and position on the Magic Council and is the person I report to."

"No."

"Okay." I stood. "Thanks anyway." I pointed to the door. "Do you need to unlock it or is it open?"

He didn't even pretend to hide his disdain. His jaws were clenched so tightly they looked locked. "Gareth will be in on this and be an intricate part of it," he finally said, but it took him a long time to concede.

I nodded. "I will agree." Headed for the door, I looked over my shoulder. "I'm sure you are a man of your word, but I look forward to our written agreement in the next few days."

That eye roll had to hurt, and he ran his tongue over his teeth as if he wished he had fangs he could use on me.

CHAPTER 16

I curled my legs under me on Gareth's sofa. My hair was still damp as I hadn't bothered to blow-dry it. It felt so good to be out of my bloodstained clothes and in clean ones, and it was even better to be in Gareth's loaned shirt. My clothes were being washed. There wasn't anything that was going to get out the amount of blood that was on them. The jeans might be salvageable but I doubted the shirt would be.

The clipped grin Gareth flashed me each time I tugged at the shirt, going to great measures to keep from exposing myself, was in vain. He didn't mind. When I once again yanked at the hem of the shirt, pulling it farther down and securing it under me to make sure it didn't ride up, he asked, "Are we back to that again?"

"Unlike you, I like to practice a little modesty," I shot back.

The delight that played at his lips and on his features was just a mask that concealed the worry. His hands raked across his head a couple of times and then scrubbed along the shadow starting to form on his cheeks.

"Do you trust them?" I asked.

"I'm having a hard time trusting anyone right now. Harrah being a skilled liar and manipulator should have been a sign. It was, but those were the qualities needed to do her job well. Skills I thought would only be used to uphold the alliance and maintain the narrative we needed. I never considered her ruthless. What they did was ruthless."

He glanced at his phone that was buzzing on the table and then rolled his eyes at the number. "Will you please call Savannah? This is the fourth time she's called. I suspect if I block her, she'll just show up at my house."

"Oh, she'll definitely show up at your house with her 'quest bag' and the knife she looks very dangerous with." Chuckling, I leaned forward to look at my phone on the coffee table. I had seven calls from her. I picked it up and dialed her number.

"At least you aren't dead," she spat out in a frosty voice.

"Nope, I'm alive and uninjured."

"Where are you?"

"Gareth's."

"Give him the phone. I'd like to speak to him," she demanded.

"You're in trouble," I mouthed to him and tossed him my phone.

His tone was silky smooth with a hint of humor as he greeted her. It stayed there, although his eyes narrowed in the confused way they did when Savannah chastised all of us in a meeting. He didn't understand Savannah's disbelief in boundaries. She didn't care about his position, money, family connections, or anything else. He'd violated her implied rule that she needed to be notified about everything. I loved Savannah, but her concern was overwhelming. I understood it—my world was scary—which was why I wanted her to have as much distance from it as possible. Life didn't work her way.

Savannah was giving Gareth an earful. "Yes, she's fine," he told her. Bemused, he gave a rundown of everything that had occurred over the past few hours. After he'd assured her again that I was fine, his wounds didn't require medical attention, and the Mors couldn't be summoned, something that I wasn't necessarily sure of, she seemed to be placated enough to let him go.

"I'm sure we'll get more calls as she thinks of more questions. Apparently, if you are within a twenty-mile radius of me, your safety becomes my responsibility. And somehow I'm obligated to keep her informed of all things. Aren't you always telling me not to damsel you? What should I do?" he teased.

Giving him a twisted sly smile, I suggested, "I'd listen to me and ignore Savannah."

"Really? Ignore her? I feel like that might be highly impossible to do."

I grinned, remembering when I was first arrested, when Savannah had camped out in the SG office trying to talk to Gareth. "Don't block her—ever. If you even for one minute think she doesn't have your address, you are wrong," I warned. I didn't think he would but I had to caution him.

"She is persistent and very enthusiastic. Maybe she should have a job at the SG."

"You want to give her a badge! Are you insane?"

He laughed at my response and sighed heavily. In a grave and overly serious voice, he said, "She's very disappointed in me. Very, very, very disappointed." As if it was too much of a burden to bear, he said theatrically, "Apparently, I'm your guard and I failed."

I rolled my eyes. "That's okay, I think she believes you're

my handler and I should run everything past you before I do it." I laughed at the absurdity of it.

His grin faltered, and his lips now drew into a thin, stern line. "You do realize that's what you agreed to. At your request, you will have to answer to me as a liaison for the other Legacy. That's why the meeting they had with me lasted so long. We were hammering out my responsibility in the role, their expectations, and some of the challenges we might face with you working under me." He was quite pleased by that.

"Not *under*. *Together*. We are working *together*," I pointed out.

"That's not what's going to happen. I must admit, I'm quite excited about you working for me." He laughed and sauntered over to me. He leaned forward and kissed me on my forehead. "I'm tired. It's been a long day and I just had a very odd dressing down by a civilian. I need sleep." He extended his hand. "It's bedtime."

I was about to take it when he added, "That's an order." He just couldn't help himself.

Yanking my hand back, I sank back into the sofa, turned the TV on, and started looking at it.

"Why don't you hold your breath until I do?"

"What am I going to do about your insubordination?"

"I suspect you'll get used to it," I said in a cloying voice, giving him a toothy grin.

"Well, I'm going to bed." He slipped off his shirt and started to back away. "I'm pretty sure you'll be in soon." And he turned around and walked away, with the swagger and arrogance that only he possessed—his special brand. I struggled to pull my gaze from him and to the TV. My stubbornness was stronger than any desire I had for him.

I didn't expect things to go back to normal so quickly. Calling it *normal* was taking creative license with the word. I didn't think things would stop being such a gigantic cluster-fuck so quickly. The FSR were still very present in my life, and weren't hard to detect, either. Like the guys that had been at Mr. Lands' office, they had that Men in Black look, suits walking around the city, generally hanging out at Coven Row and in Forest Park where the shifters usually lived. Savannah and I watched the two who'd been following us since we'd left the house. Five days since the incident with Harrah, and I'd received my contract to work with them and Gareth to find the other Legacy. Being paid for it was a bonus. Just as Gareth had stated, technically I would report to him—I worked for him. That didn't feel good at all. And the smirk that he gave each time he reminded me of it was him dancing over those buttons he loved to push to rile me up.

Despite the working relationship we now had, I had a detail on me. "Do you have any idea how long they plan to follow us?" Savannah asked, but I was more irritated by it than she was. In fact, I think it gave her some comfort.

"They aren't trying to be discreet; that's a good sign. They want my presence known. Gareth said it's until they have a handle on the Human Rights Alliance. They've been a problem."

Savannah shrugged. "At the rate those nuts are going, their stupidity is a bigger threat to themselves than to any of us. How many of them have been arrested this week? Twenty, thirty? It's just silly. But they've given the police, FSR, and SG just cause to handle them." She smiled at the idea. She was right. Humans First had become downright civil in comparison, becoming the face of maintaining the human/supernatural alliance. Whether it was the FSR position or someone using questionable magic, Mr. Lands was singing a different tune. I think it was a combination of both and seeing what had developed from him taking over. No one wanted to be responsible for the Human Rights Alliance, and at the end of the day, Mr. Lands was a politician who desperately wanted to hold on to his legacy and reputation.

Savannah looped her arm through mine; not only didn't she mind the detail, she was gaining far too much pleasure from screwing with them. The "girls' day" that she wanted was the perfect opportunity for it. After we'd gone into the wine and painting shop, she'd turned her finished artwork that looked like she'd had one too many glasses of wine during its creation to give them a look.

At the bakery, the only thing I'd made her promise to add on our day, they glared at her for several moments when she approached them with cronuts. Initially they maintained professional stoicism, and eventually took a few. *Who's turning down a cronut? It's impossible to do.*

"When are you going to start looking for the others?" Savannah asked as we entered a lingerie boutique.

"In a couple of days, after the Solstice festival."

She wrinkled her nose, and her brow furrowed. "Why? Does it affect our magic or something?"

There isn't any "our"—you don't have any magic! But I kept that to myself and felt the blush of embarrassment warm my cheeks. "No, I just like it."

I glanced over at a table of overpriced bras to avoid the satisfied beam that I knew she now had. The smile was in her voice. "I knew you liked it! Each year you made it seem like I was dragging you there. It's the best thing all year." She was right. It had started as a festival for the witches and had grown into a massive event of magic, pageantry, floats, and parades. It had been reduced to what people do on St. Patrick's Day and Cinco de Mayo: partying, drinking, staging spectacles, and having fun. Supernaturals and humans alike came for the celebration. For some it had another significance: the summer one was during the week of the Great War. The coming together of humans and supernaturals had significant meaning for some. But for most, it was another celebration.

"I know half the things you claim you hate you really like," she huffed out before giving me a face. "Just like you're pretending you hate it here." She sorted through underwear that was nothing more than strings and minimal cloth. Knowing who she was getting this for was even more disturbing.

"I *do* hate it here."

"Sure you do," she mocked. Then she held up a bra and matching underwear to get my opinion. I touched the bra, feeling the fabric and the wire underneath it. I just didn't get the idea of my breasts being hiked up with metal and contraptions or trying to walk around with a string stuck between my butt cheeks. But whenever I saw the way they made Savannah's look in her clothes, I always reconsidered—until I looked at the prices. Savannah was reasonable about a lot of things, but when it came to the pretty little things and vampires, logic went out the window. Now that she was dating a vampire she seemed to enjoy shopping at these places even more.

"What do you think of this?" she asked, holding up a different set: a pale pink bra and matching barely-there underwear.

"Isn't he a neck man? Whether or not you have on sexy lingerie or a tank and boxers as long as he can see a vein, I'm sure he'll be happy. Really rock his world and put the thong around your neck," I suggested, winking.

She gave me a naughty grin. "I can assure you Lucas cares about more than just my neck."

Well, I can't un-hear that. I made a face. Just when I

thought I was getting used to them as a couple she said something like that and I realized I hadn't.

I redirected the conversation. "Next week after the Solstice festival we'll go looking for the Legacy. Between the Trackers' dossiers and blood location, we should be able to find them all."

She smiled gently before she leaned in and hugged me. I wasn't expecting it and tensed when she did it. Responding to the look I gave her, she said, "You seem happy about it." I wasn't ever going to relax, but this was a step in the right direction.

"Okay, which one?" She held up another sexy pairing, a light apricot and black. I was about to make another neck comment when she gave me a preemptive eye roll and turned to our detail, who were seated on a bench just a few feet away. Waving until she got their full attention, she held up the two pairs of underwear and mouthed, "Which one?" I wasn't sure if they really loved or hated their job at that moment.

CHAPTER 17

The Solstice parade was the best part of the celebration. The streets cleared out as people stood on the sidelines, food or alcohol in hand for the elaborate and grand presentation. It always started with a graceful and agile group who danced in front of a float. It was hard to differentiate the shifters from humans until I got a glimpse of that telltale shifter ring. No one cared as they were drawn into the extravagant presentation. The dancers moved through the streets, their movements fluid and easy as water moving over a waterfall. They twirled and did cartwheels. The crowd cheered as they lunged into splits and moved out of them with the same ease. Acrobatics that required a lot more strength than most humans' were another distinguishing feature between the shifters and the humans. The choreography was so complementary that all the crowd saw were rhythmic back-and-forths, whirls, twirls, leaps, and sweeps of their hips as they rotated to the music.

We all stood in awe as we watched fae on a float doing tricks of magic—it was the one day they were able to use their glamours legally. We watched them shift into beautiful creatures and then change into something horrendous, changing their appearances with the same ease as shedding a shirt. People were enamored and entertained by the very magic that had once been used against them. At this moment they found a little glimpse of beauty in it and forgot the misery that it could cause.

My mind went to the discussion I'd had with Gareth and the FSR the day before. The FSR wanted him to convince us to wear iridium bands that couldn't be removed. No matter how they phrased it, it seemed like a punishment—and a preemptive one. There was no other way to look at it, but it was for the greater good. In some way, we all were being punished, and it was deceptively called restrictions; but it was punishment for having powers and magic that could be potentially dangerous to a large number of people. But no one wore bracelets or shackles unless they'd been found guilty of a crime. That was their punishment because they couldn't be trusted and were unable to demonstrate self-restraint. Everyone else was trusted at their word; why couldn't I be? I think that was what bothered me the most. How did they expect me to feel like I was blending in when I was always an exception?

Gareth was adamantly against it, and by the end of the meeting a decision hadn't been made. I gave the typical nod and platitude that I would think about it. I hadn't thought about it until I started watching the mages and their magical presentation on their float and realized the band wasn't going to stop much. I wondered if the FSR knew that and it was a false security for the public. If I had no other choice, I might be willing to go along with it if it came with freedom and sanctuary for the Legacy.

Scanning the crowd, I didn't see a city in conflict or one that just weeks ago was in the throes of one. Bodies rocked, gyrated, and bounced around to the music. The pageantry of it seemed to erase the memories of the hostile last couple of weeks. I hated that pang of guilt that I felt about killing Harrah. I hadn't done anything that warranted it. She'd had other options and she'd chosen the wrong one, but I couldn't help but feel that guilt that comes with killing someone. These festivities were exactly what Harrah had clung to: ideology and illusion. And yet things were not quite what she'd wanted because as people watched the performances they got a glimpse of magic—true magic. My eyes suddenly fixed on the pile of untidy brown hair on Avery, Gareth's nephew. A sparkle of mischief always had a place in his eyes, and the crooked smile didn't help. It was a unique mélange of innocence and miscreance. He raised his cup to me and grinned. I assessed his crowd of friends, who all had cups in hand. They were shifters, and the legal age for them to drink was eighteen. I was sure those cups didn't have juice in them. If they did, they were probably mixed with something quite strong.

Savannah saw him as well and waved. As soon as she did his grin broadened—it was apparent that like most men, he had become smitten with her, even though the last time he'd seen her, she'd been wrapped in Lucas's arms and a few minutes later throwing Molotov cocktails, trying to keep him and his uncle from attacking each other. Savannah took me by the wrist as we navigated through the crowd to get to him. As soon as we were within inches, she reached out to him and gave him a hug. When he pulled away, he looked surprised. You did have to get used to Savannah, who was overly friendly. If she met you once, you were probably getting a hug as if you were a long-lost family member she hadn't seen in a while.

"Where's your uncle?" I asked.

"To be honest, probably behind bars," he said with a hint of amusement. "He and that FSR agent aren't getting along."

I wondered if they'd reopened the discussion about the iridium band. "Why do you say that?"

He made a face. "I had to go into the office early this morning to work and saw him walking toward Uncle Gar's office. They looked as if they were ready to punch each other. I'm a little offended—I thought only I could get under his skin like that."

"Why did you have to go to the office this morning? I thought your work sentence was commuted."

Avery looked at me with soft limpid blue eyes and I had to agree with Gareth, he was spoiled to the core. He'd mastered a look that pretty much ensured that he would get away with a lot of things. Except with Gareth.

"I never know with him. Everything I do is a punishable offense. You can ask him when he gets here. All I know is I got a call last night telling me to be at the office at five in the morning. Five! Can you believe it?" He frowned. "I'm sure he'll be here soon," he said with a little chuckle that made the rest of his friends laugh as well.

A slight blush whispered across his cheeks and he shrugged. "It seems like whenever he suspects I'm somewhere having fun he has a knack for showing up and ruining it."

"Does he? Your uncle sounds like a piece of work. Maybe you should be better at finding fun that won't get you in trouble," Gareth said from behind him. I was surprised to see him, but the others weren't. Heightened senses had their advantages.

Uncle and nephew locked eyes, and I quickly ascertained they were embroiled in a battle of the wills. I didn't want to be around when everyone cleared out as they tried to thrash each other into submission.

"Are you giving Levy your sob story of why you had to work early this morning? Perhaps you gave her the same version you gave your mother last night. You know, the one where you told her you were staying at my house, which you did for a couple of hours. Coincidentally I got a call from my neighbors, surprised that I'd come to visit the loft since I had not been there in over a year."

Avery's face flushed as he looked around at his friends, all of whom looked guilty. Gareth's eyes roved over each one of their faces. "Let me guess—if I went and looked in my parking space my car wouldn't be there."

"Well, I needed a car to get here, and mine simply wasn't big enough for all my friends." He waved over the people behind him. "Thank you for letting me borrow your SUV, Uncle Gar," Avery said nonchalantly then took another sip from his cup.

This wasn't going to go well for him at all.

Gareth grinned, baring his teeth like an animal ready to pounce on his prey. "Of course. And *thank you* for forgoing your trip this weekend in order to clean it and make it ready for the next time I visit. I have to tell you it was really kind of you to agree to detail the car after borrowing it. I love that you're going to do it yourself instead of taking it to be done. And offering to clean my collection of blades was an exceptionally kind offer. Since they're in the basement they rarely get handled properly. I forget about them, so they really are going to need special attention. And since you're going to be at my house all weekend, I gave Leslie the time off so you can do the groceries and cooking."

"I know Mom did not agree to that—we've been planning this trip for over a year."

"It really sucks that you're going to miss it. All because you never learned the words *may I.*"

Avery backed away and disappeared into the crowd with his phone in hand. He reappeared a couple of feet away. All I saw was his mouth moving and the bridge of his nose streaking a ruddy color that quickly moved across his cheeks. Anger. He turned and glared at Gareth, who now was wearing the haughty smirk that had graced Avery's face just moments before.

He bounded back. "Charges. Really. You said you were going to report the car stolen and say I broke and entered. What is wrong with you? You're my uncle." Avery's defense was that Gareth was his uncle and was supposed to allow him to get away with things. It was as if he'd just met the man.

I really wanted to introduce them. *Avery, this is Gareth. Gareth, Avery.*

"The car was stolen, and you might not have broken and entered but you didn't have permission. You stole my keys," Gareth pointed out. "I was at work, never gave you permission to use the loft, and you took one of my cars for the second time without asking. That's theft. It's not like I wouldn't have let you have it if you'd asked."

Avery was seething. Flicks of anger bounced over his eyes and the more perturbed he became, the more amusement Gareth found in it. "Let's use this as a teachable moment. Ask."

"You're the cool uncle, I knew you'd be fine with it," Avery said, plastering another sheepish look on his face, and his friends started to nod emphatically in agreement.

Really. Clearly this is your first time meeting your uncle. Do you have amnesia?

"Come on, Uncle Gar, if I would've asked, you would have had someone checking in on me and I didn't want to put you through all that trouble. I was really helping you out. You've been through so much with the FSR, the whole job thing, the city imploding, HF, I didn't want to burden you with something else."

Now I was the one amused at how easily he spewed his

lie, the docile and genuine look. I started laughing and tried to cover it up with a cough. If nothing else, Avery was persistent and full of it.

"Wow, that sounded authentic. Kudos. Now if only I was as bad at detecting lies as you are at telling them," Gareth said sarcastically.

Again they were at a standoff, eyes narrowed as they studied each other. Even Savannah was distracted by their show of obstinacy and defiance. Avery's glares at his uncle had little to no effect on him. His smile widened the harder his nephew glowered.

"You're ruining my summer," he grumbled under his breath.

"That's okay, you're ruining my tolerance for teenagers," he retorted. Then he flashed him a half-grin. Avery's defiance quickly dwindled to acquiescence and then defeat. It was a short battle, and I was never confident he would win. After spending any time with his uncle, he should have known better. I had a feeling this was just one of the many they would have.

Savannah split her attention between watching Gareth and his nephew and the presentation in front of us. The sides of the streets were getting even more crowded. It was easy to become immersed in the festivities, and the crowd was.

Gareth had inched closer to me, the heat of his body brushing against my back and his hands resting on my hips. It was weird, and my overactive and cautious mind went to work. It wasn't as if people didn't know about us, but I didn't want to flaunt it. It seemed like everything had been swept under the rug. Our breaking into the Magic Council's storeroom had never been reported, and Harrah's death became a story of a random act of violence. Cities had crime, and supernaturals as well as humans died. I wondered how it was cleaned up so neatly—who else did they have in reserve to take over Harrah's job? Politics. I hated everything about the illusions presented in the effort to maintain an amicable relationship with the humans. At some point all the lies and manipulation would devolve us into nothing more than fun house mirrors where nothing was what it actually was.

I tried to push those thoughts out of my head but couldn't help but wonder if people speculated about the influx of men in suits roaming around the city. Perhaps they went unnoticed. If they didn't flash their guns you wouldn't know they had them. Their badges were kept concealed. Maybe they were seen as nothing more than men in business attire.

Eventually I allowed myself to be distracted by the vampires who'd arrived at the parade and whose appearance made the men in suits look less audacious. The older vampires seemed to have an aversion to casual wear, women and men alike. I didn't see it as much with the younger ones, who transitioned well into the casualness of society, but the older vamps seemed too resistant to give into it. The men showed a preference for expensive suits, and the women favored delicate fabrics that molded to the curves of their bodies. Their clothes were modern, although some seemed to hold on to anachronisms like a pocket watch, pearls, or an antique broach. Some liked large outdated hats, like those I remembered seeing in old Western movies, but with today's fashion it was easy to think they were being ironic or ultra-trendy. One thing that remained consistent with the majority of vampires was that they dressed a little too extravagantly.

When one of the vampires held my gaze too long before allowing her eyes to rove over Gareth and his placement of his hands on me, I became aware that I wasn't just being caressed by any man but by the head of the Supernatural Guild. I wasn't sure if it meant anything to the vampires or not. Savannah was very enthusiastic about the public display of affection since she was the founder of Team Gareth and me not being single.

The floats with supernaturals performing continued down the street. This time it was another mage. A beautiful kaleidoscope of colors danced over his fingers as things disappeared from the float, reappeared and skated across it, and then had their own little performance. Suddenly the mage dropped to the ground. A mage behind him succumbed to the same fate. I watched bodies drop in front of us, one after the other. The float came to a complete stop. Navigating through the crowd, I ran to the front. Dancers were now sprawled out in front of the float. I didn't see any blood or bullets, and everyone was still breathing, a light rise and fall of their chests. Each one of the fallen had a small entry wound but not an exit. Not one of them showed signs of trauma or distress. Instead, they were in a state of deep sleep. As Gareth and I examined them between glances around to see where the shots had come from, they began to sit upright, rubbing either neck, shoulder, or arm. Some stood and tried to go back to business as usual. The mage flicked his fingers, and the spark of magic that should have come to life didn't. He furrowed his brow again and gave another flick—nothing. His face strained with effort, the muscles of his neck bulging out as he made another unsuccessful attempt. He collapsed again and didn't move. I couldn't tell if he was breathing.

People scattered, and an SG officer moved through the remaining crowd with an FSR agent beside him. The officer pressed fingers against the mage's wrist. The grimace remained on his face before he moved to the neck and nodded once he found a pulse.

Other members of the FSR edged out of the crowd to get a better look. Some of them had their hands at their sides touching the guns holstered there while scanning the crowd and the buildings above it. I knew one was a vampire because he couldn't resist, like most of them, drawing back his lips—bearing his other weapons. For anyone who wasn't a shapeshifter or vampire, the distance of the buildings, nearly forty feet away, would've made it difficult to get a good view. The vampire squinted, and I realized that he couldn't see anything, either. I trailed his eyes as they skipped along the roof of the building. There had to be more than one magical sniper. I counted at least twenty victims.

I continued to scan the buildings as more people were targeted in the crowd. The assailants were indiscriminately shooting. I wasn't sure how it was affecting the humans, but I could see the effect it had on the supernaturals.

Shots whizzed through the air and more bodies fell. Chaos ensued as people scattered, running through the streets, screaming as they tried to take cover. Gareth instructed Avery and his friends to go. Just as he started to walk away, Gareth heard the sounds and instructed them to get down, but it was too late. A shot hit Avery and another one hit his friend just a couple of feet away. They both fell to the ground. After a few moments, just as the mage had recovered, so did they. Gareth and I quickly moved in Avery's direction, and Savannah went for the friend. We scanned their bodies trying to find the entry wounds. Gareth's sight being much better than mine, I stepped aside and let him assess Avery.

"What exactly are they shooting?" Gareth asked, his fingers moving along his nephew's arms and legs, still unable to find the entry point. Was it that small? What could be shot from a distance and not leave a significant mark?

"Can you stand?" he asked his nephew. Avery nodded, but when he made an attempt he lost his balance. Gareth studied him and lowered him back to the ground. "I want you all to try to change now."

Having seen Gareth change a couple of times, as well as Avery, I knew it was a process they did with the ease of shedding clothing. Avery and his friends were having problems changing. Strained grimaces stretched over their faces, panic in their eyes, and their mouths parted slightly, aghast. They couldn't change.

Gareth fished a set of keys out of his pocket and handed them to Savannah. "I don't want to take any chances Will you take them to the Isles?"

"And what are you going to do?" she asked.

I knew he was going to try to find out who'd made the shots. When he stood, I rose to my feet as well. "You go with Savannah," he instructed.

I made a face. "No. I need to find out who's doing this."

I needed to know who it was—there was a new player in town. Most of the Trackers had been taken into custody, along with many of the militant HF and Human Rights Alliance members.

"Do you think it's the Human Rights Alliance?" I asked, increasing my pace to fall in step with him.

"Possibly. Over the past few weeks, Lands has been vocal about his dedication to maintaining an alliance with supernaturals, and his goal to work closely with us. It didn't sit well with their more enthusiastic members."

I'm not sure why he had a problem calling them batshit crazy militants. But fine, let's go with "enthusiastic."

"They've been involved in a lot of violence and destruction of property. Most of them have been arrested by the police, and the others we've been keeping a close eye on." He was at a slow jog.

"You think there's a new player?"

"I don't know what to think." With each passing moment, his anger heightened, and I understood it perfectly.

There were still shots being fired from several directions.

FSR agents and SG officers started to navigate toward them, their eyes narrowed to scopes as they peered at the top of each roof and at open windows. One of the FSR agents called for Gareth's attention, giving him a hand signal to let him know which buildings they planned to cover. Gareth was directed to go to a building just a couple of feet from where we were. Although it was doubtful that the shot that hit his nephew had come from that direction, at least we could find out who was involved. I knew Gareth wanted the person who'd shot Avery. Sirens blared off in the distance, I assumed the Isles' ambulances and perhaps human ambulances as well. Humans' injuries were from the impact of the objects and didn't seem to have any other physiological effect.

Faces whizzed by as we ran through the oncoming crowd scrambling to get out of the area. I wondered what was in the shots, angrily remembering Conner poisoning me. If it was just iron or even iridium it would prevent supernaturals from doing magic without killing them, but if it was something that drew out their magic then they would surely die. I took a ragged breath, and Gareth slowed to turn and look at me.

"Are you okay?" he asked. His preternatural speed made it hard to keep up with him, but I was able to as long as I pushed myself. We bounded up the stairs, winding around each flight and going through each of the higher floor levels where the shots could have come from. Nothing. The noise from the street was frenetic and distracting, and I wanted to look out the window to see what else was going on. I really wanted the perpetrators not to be from Humans First. They'd never done anything like this before. Two years ago they'd led a protest, which was nothing but a few guys spewing their rhetoric being drowned out by the sounds of the festivities and people booing them, offering them a drink or witch weed, or telling them "to chill the fuck out." They'd gotten the hint that most people didn't care and hadn't tried it last year.

The second building we went to was taller, giving the shooter a better vantage point. We pounded up the stairs to the second-to-last floor, searching offices to find where someone might be stationed, when we saw the open window. Gareth inhaled, made a face, and directed me to go to the next room. He went in the opposite direction to another. I opened the door and found two men dressed in dark blue camouflage packing away their guns. I waved my hand and one crashed into the wall, where I kept him pinned. The other reached for his gun, but before he could I kicked it out of reach while trying to focus as I held his partner to the wall. He attacked me, clipping my leg and sending me crashing to the floor. My shoulder hit against the hard wood floor. Pain seared through me. I didn't allow it to break my concentration as I continued to hold his friend. That man's face was bright red as he strained to rip himself off the wall. His amber eyes fixed on me: narrowed, angry, and vengeful. They were definitely new players, but I wasn't sure if they were part of Human Rights Alliance. At least they weren't HF. They were missing the whole brotherhood of spies attire or even the more recent suited look, which was a new spin on the old cliché. These men were sporting fatigues and ready to go to war with the supernaturals. I rolled to my knees and punched the man who'd swiped my leg in the groin. There weren't any rules of engagement. He grabbed his family jewels, doubling over, and I struck again in his inner thigh.

He wasn't going down easily. He was quick and kicked me with his steel-toe boots in my ribs. When I went to punch him again, there wasn't any doubt he'd done a number on my ribs. The pain was distracting, but I still managed to keep his friend pinned to the wall. Grimacing, he clawed at me and took hold of my hair, pulling me to him and hammering blows into the side of my face. I held the one with magic because I knew I wasn't going to be able to fight both of them. The active combatant pushed me to the ground, recovering enough from the groin assault to try to stomp me while I was down. I punched up, landing a heavy blow to his stance leg. He crumbled to the ground. I jabbed my elbow into his stomach, he let out a gasp. Another one went into his chest. He tried to get to his feet, and the next strike went into his throat, making him gasp. Then I crushed the heel of my hand into his nose. Blood splattered from the impact.

I was starting to think I was dealing with someone who wasn't human when he made a feeble attempt to swing out at me, unable to make contact through his blurred vision. Wiping the blood from his nose with the back of his hand, he smeared it and left bloody lines down his arm. He glanced over at his friend through watery, red eyes, probably still unable to focus.

"You are all alike. You cheat. You would not have us if it weren't for your magic. There wouldn't be an alliance if it wasn't for your magic. We know what you're doing to us: manipulating our minds, making us forget how horrible you are, but we won't forget. We were here first and we will be here last." I didn't feel like giving him a history lesson about how supernaturals were found to exist far before humans came along. I was sure his revisionist history had his ancestors here, and supernaturals the result of them, and not the reverse, which was true. I prepared myself for the next few moments of his rhetoric of how we were wrong and he was going to rid the world of our kind. The same boring monologue they always gave. But he didn't. It was almost as if he had given up.

I maintained my defensive stance, waiting for him to attack again. He stood, scowling at me and his friend who was fixed against the wall. Both of them were seething and glaring at me. If looks could kill I would've died a thousand times over. When Gareth walked into the room, the man whose nose was still running blood fixed on him with the same hostile look he'd given me. "Animal. Fucking animals."

Gareth advanced slowly with lithe, padding movements. The shifter ring flitted across his eyes and his lips were drawn back baring his teeth.

"What the fuck did you shoot them with?" Gareth asked through gritted teeth, rage unrestrained, volatile and ready to destroy everything in his path. Both men pressed their lips tightly together, sealing them in silence as if they'd made a pact never to reveal anything. They just waited patiently. I was especially gifted when it came to making Gareth angry—but never this angry.

"I will only ask you this one time. What the hell did you shoot them with? Will they die?"

The man made a dark chuckle. "I hope so."

Before the last word fell from his lips Gareth was on him. His hands closed around the man's throat before shoving him into the wall. "You better hope they don't." The man made gasping sounds as he struggled to breathe, the muscles of Gareth's arms protruding as he squeezed tighter and tighter.

"Gareth." I said his name softly not wanting to further agitate him. I imagined the only thing he was thinking about was his nephew and whether or not he was going to live. "Gareth." This time I whispered, gentle and soothing. I had limited experience with shapeshifters but my assumption was to treat them as you would any animal who was on the verge of attack. Don't make any sudden movements, speak in a soft soothing voice, and stay still.

I went to the guns that they had started to pack away and took out the cartridges to examine what they'd been shooting. They weren't bullets They were similar to what Gareth had used on Conner and on me. I figured, based on what had happened, that upon impact the casing dissolved and dispensed the serum in the target's body. I gave one more look at these brutes. They were not the masterminds behind this. They wouldn't have the resources and money it would have taken to make the ammo and modified rifles. I doubted any small organization would have the resources for it.

"Where did you get these from?" I asked, holding up a cartridge. They simply pressed their lips tighter together refusing to let any words pass through them. I shrugged and walked toward the gentleman I had fixed to the wall. I clenched my teeth and worked hard not to show the pain from my ribs. With each step it was getting harder and harder as the throbbing persisted, but I didn't have the energy to direct to healing because I needed to gather information from him. My lips curled into a smile but it was mirthless, and I must have been a scary sight because his eyes widened just a bit before returning to their narrowed position.

"I'm not going to tell you a goddamn thing," he hissed out.

"You don't have to," I said in a low voice, hardened by my anger. Anger that predated anything he was doing but was reignited by it. I was tired of xenophobes trying to get rid of people who couldn't help the way they were born. And people trying to nullify others' magic. The past couple of weeks had really started to wear on me and I knew my rage was misdirected, but I didn't care.

I asked again, my voice blistering, "*Who* gave this to you?"

Again, he fixed me with a defiant glare, his lips furled into a snarl. "I'm not going to tell you anything." His voice was just as gruff as his appearance. I smiled, cloying and gentle. His eyes fixed on the swirls of color that danced around my fingertips. He was human and probably couldn't feel the influx of power I put in the magic or how it draped through the room. But he could see the menace in my eyes, and that was all that mattered.

"Fae magic allows them to do a lot of things, cognitive manipulation, charming people, and even the manipulation and erasing of memories. I'll leave you as though you were a child, without the essential skills to survive in this world, and it won't be able to be reversed." A fae didn't need to draw blood, and perhaps I didn't, either, but I'd never tested it. I knew blood made the spell powerful and definitely ensured that it would work. Today, I didn't have time to practice. I pulled the small blade from my ankle holster; it wasn't much for fighting, barely enough to make a fatal cut, but it served its purpose. It sliced across his arm, blood welled, and I whispered my incantation while watching the magic that swirled around him. I pushed just a little bit into his mind, letting him feel me slowly wrapping my magic around it, caressing those memories, and giving him a slight taste of what I could do. He screamed shrilly. Not out of pain—I didn't think it had hurt—out of anger.

He wailed and screamed and cursed me, calling me every vile name he could think of under the yoke of fear.

"Stop that. I haven't even really started. Save that for the real thing."

"You bitch."

"Seriously, that can't be the best you could come up with. You have to know I've been called worse."

"Don't tell her anything," said the man from across the room whom Gareth had a hold of. I assumed that's what he said. I couldn't really make out his garbled and barely audible words.

"Apparently you haven't been paying attention. I'm going to go and play in his mind. Hopefully, I'll find what I want. If I don't, he's going to be a mess afterward and no good to whoever sent you. It's going to be quite unfortunate how he's left. And when I break him, you'll be next."

I shot my guy a look. His eyes widened, and I hoped I'd struck enough fear in him that he would spill it all. He briefly allowed himself to show his fear before he quickly accepted whatever I was going to do to him. Dying for his self-righteous cause.

Fine, be a martyr. The vibrant colors of blue, teal, pink, and orange engulfed him for a few moments before pulling together and concentrating on just the upper half. I moved languidly through his mind, getting a glimpse of what was there. Defiance had made this harder—it was like approaching a steel wall. I drew more magic, whisking him off into a somnolent state. His body eased and his head relaxed back against the wall as he gave in to his fate. At one point in going through his mind, I was trying to take care to preserve everything I found, but soon I didn't care. I rummaged through, finding absolutely nothing of use. Just faces that I couldn't make out. It was as if the man had known a mind search was a possibility if he was caught and had gone through great pains to make sure he didn't reveal anything. *Dammit.*

"Ms. Michaels!" barked an FSR agent. "What the hell are you doing?"

"Trying to save the victims. And find out who did this." I blocked him out and continued navigating through the folds of my guy's mind, moving inch by inch trying to pluck those memories and make sense of them. Once again I came up empty. The man slumped down—mental fatigue. I wasn't sure if he'd be the same person when he woke. Perhaps he'd be less hateful, but he'd probably be more, remembering this violation and adding it to the long list of things he held against the supernaturals.

"That is not how we handle things," the FSR agent said.

That's exactly how you handle things. I wasn't naïve enough to believe him, but for some reason he was putting on a show for the humans who had just shot and probably killed over twenty supernaturals. Their lives, their mental states, and this pseudo-alliance that we shared was what he was trying to protect. I knew it wasn't about these guys or their safety, but if they were apprehended and treated badly, the world would be watching and judging. When my guy lifted his head again, I directed my attention to him, ready to give it another try.

One of the FSR agents drew his weapon and aimed at me. "Let them go."

"We're on the same side," Gareth growled at him.

"Then she'll release him as I asked," he countered, his voice just as grating and rough as Gareth's. "And you, too. Release that man."

Almost at the same time, we released them and let them collapse to the floor where they folded into themselves before sliding down to their sides. More FSR agents spilled in, and not far behind them were three human policemen. They looked at the men, checking them for injury before handcuffing them and escorting them out.

The lead FSR agent grabbed the cartridges as the police tried to get a hold of them, shaking his head. "We need samples of this to see if we can find an antidote. The people shot with this aren't doing well. It seems like it's slowly drawing the magic out of them, and if it does they will die. "

I looked over at Gareth. His eyes landed on the spot where the men once were, his anger prominently displayed on his face. He walked over to the agent, took a cartridge and took one of the bullet-needles out, and headed out the door without another word. I knew he would probably get to the Isles before the FSR.

Running to catch up with Gareth, I fell in step. "They

have the best doctors there as well as powerful mages. They will be able to find something."

"I really hope you're right," he said quietly.

Of course, we were going to get to the Isles before the others because Gareth had broken every speeding law there was as he drove through the city trying to get there. A drive that should've taken us twenty minutes was reduced to just over twelve.

The Isles was hectic. Probably more so than it had ever been. They dealt with supernaturals, which meant they didn't have a flux of injuries very often. Shapeshifters rarely were injured badly enough to require medical intervention. Mages and witches could use healing spells, and even fae had their version. Vampires were nearly indestructible, with the exception of a stake through the heart. Generally, the Isles patients were humans injured by supernaturals. Wounds were healed fast, and depending on what happened, a nice fae might be there during checkout to help the person with a more palatable recounting of the event that had led to the visit.

The panicked look on the nurses' faces was an indicator that this was something they weren't prepared for. People moved around with supernaturals on stretchers, taking them to the various rooms, nurses scribbled on their pads as physicians gave med orders, people were nearly running back and forth through the hallway. Codes screeched over the intercom. This reminded me of a regular hospital—a human hospital. Whoever was behind this seemed to want to reduce us to nothing more than just fragile humans. Eventually, one of the doctors came to Gareth and pulled him aside and started talking to him. I inched closer trying to listen, but they spoke so low I suspected they were trying to be discreet, even though the privacy laws that the human world had weren't applicable in that of the supernatural. I watched as Gareth tried to take control of his emotions. He wasn't doing a very good job of it. His tense but fluid movements made it obvious that the predator was in the driver's seat. He handed the physician the bullet-needle and as soon as he did, the physician made a phone call. Moments later someone was taking it away.

I was just about to approach him when a tall woman with light brown hair ran through the front doors. "Gar, what happened?"

Where Gareth's features were striking and defined, hers were delicately curved and rounder. But the piercing crystalline blue eyes with the darker cobalt-colored ring that bounced around them were the giveaway—the familial distinction. I knew from a conversation he'd had with her while I was in the room that she was about ten years older than him, but I couldn't see the age difference. One of the benefits of being a shifter—they didn't seem to age as others did.

This was Gareth's sister, Charlotte, and she was just as distracted as I was by the people moving about, the chaos, and the constant blast of codes over the intercom. She stood frozen, unable to respond as tears rolled down her face. Gareth's thumb swept across her cheek wiping them away. They kept coming, and eventually he just stopped trying. I didn't know what to do, so I watched him as he tried to comfort her. Eventually, they took a seat next to each other, his hands on her thigh, patting soothingly. He waved me over, and I hesitated, feeling like I was an intruder on their moment. It had to be invasive to have me there as she tried to deal with the tragedy. Well, it wasn't a tragedy yet. They just needed to stop whatever was happening to the shot supernaturals.

We had been there two hours, and I was afraid to ask questions. I'd heard too many codes, watched too many nurses run to the different rooms, and seen too many doctors walking past us with their faces twisted into a mélange of confusion, anger, and frustration. Gareth was so preoccupied with comforting his sister he didn't seem to be concerned that the FSR wasn't anywhere to be found. Another hour passed with nothing different, and eventually Victor, the first agent who'd interrogated me after the incident with the Magic Council, slowly approached me.

"Ms. Michaels," he said in a flat, pensive voice. He frowned. "Can we speak with you for a moment?"

I nodded and came to my feet, and Gareth did moments later and started to follow them as well. Victor stopped, addressing him. "We just need to speak with Ms. Michaels."

"If it has anything to do with the situation, I want to be involved."

"We only need to speak with Ms.—"

"If it involves anything that happened today, then I need to be in on this. Not only does it involve my nephew, it also concerns the people that I want to protect. So I will be on this," he said firmly.

I figured if this wasn't so urgent there would be a battle for dominance and everyone would be tossing around their credentials and badges, but no one had the time for it. We followed him down the hall, and as we walked past one of the desks, a physician joined us. We were escorted into a private office and then the physician closed the door and directed us to take seats. I sat down first; Gareth took a chair next to me, and Victor and the agent with him took up a position opposite us against the wall. Everyone directed their attention to the physician, who I assumed was a mage. "Whatever was injected into them is in their system and eating away at their magic almost like it's a cancer. Once all magic is gone, they will die. I have no idea what this is, and it keeps mutating so we can't find anything to cure it."

"How fast is it changing?" I asked.

"Rapidly, at least four times since I've tried to find something."

"What if you try magically?" Gareth's voice was strained. This was an exceptional situation. Shapeshifters didn't respond the same way to magic as others did, and I'd never considered that restricting their ability to change would do the same as restricting magic—or rather removing magic— that was so entwined in each of us it was the very essence of our being. Removing a person's magic killed them. I kept trying to listen to the physician speak, but my mind kept drifting off to who would have the resources to do something like this.

"This is where you come into play. Your magic is different, and we wonder if you can actually help." He hesitated, and I didn't blame him. Blood was quite powerful and asking someone to give it so freely was a very intrusive thing to do. They had to be desperate. My being out was definitely a thing—people at the Isles knew what I was, as did the FSR, the Supernatural Guild, Gordon Lands, some members of Humans First, and the new extremist group of the month that stemmed from the latter. And those extremists who didn't know certainly would after their member told them that I almost erased his mind and plucked out his memories. I was pretty sure there weren't too many people who could do that. My old life was *so* over.

The doctor hadn't officially asked for my blood, and when he did, all eyes went to me. Relief fell over all their faces when I agreed, but it took longer than I wished. It should have been immediate, but I'd thought of the Mors and that my blood was what allowed it to track me down. But I had to do this.

Gareth rested against the wall, his arms crossed. He gave me a sympathetic smile. I had to put my trust in people who for years had believed my kind was extinct. Gareth held my gaze as they inserted the needle, and I wondered if he knew what I was thinking. Did he sense my anxiety? I ushered a wry smile onto my face. Focusing on Gareth was better than watching the doctor, who'd decided to draw my blood instead of having a nurse do it. Hiding his look of intrigue and disgust seemed too much of an effort for him to bother trying.

Ignoring the three other people in lab coats, gawking as though they'd found a unicorn doing the flamenco in the park, wasn't helping either. So, I focused on Gareth and the crapstorm of things that were happening. We had another formidable radical group that was organized, strategic, and had resources. While the other groups were blathering about their tenets, annoying people with their brand of crazy and proving to be more bark than bite, the new one moved in silence. Who would have thought they would have struck so efficiently? How long had they been working on their virus?

Once the doctor had drawn my blood, he looked at it in the vial hopefully. He gave it to another man in a blue coat who seemed to have melted into the background so much that I hadn't noticed him until he moved into my line of sight.

Gareth and I stepped out into the waiting area, and when he pressed his hand to the small of my back, I stopped walking. Giving me an appraising look and a half-smile, he nodded before mouthing a thank-you. I guess he understood my concern, but I didn't really see it as a sacrifice as it might save so many people—it was an obligation. And yet we knew nothing about those doctors I'd just handed a vial of my blood to. I blocked out the worry; it wasn't going to help or change anything. I wasn't going to deny people a potential antidote on a possibility of a threat.

It was good to see Savannah's smiling face when we entered the sitting area. I wasn't surprised to see Lucas next to her.

"Where were you?" she asked, coming to her feet and giving me a hug. Before I could answer, she directed her attention to Gareth. "You should probably go check in on your sister, she doesn't seem to be doing too well." In response to his inquiring look, she said, "I went in to check on Avery and she was in there."

Gareth nodded his head and left. As soon as he did I explained everything to her, including offering my blood as a possible option for curing everyone. She sucked in a ragged breath and held it for a long time before exhaling. "So everyone knows now?" she said in a strained voice.

"I don't think there's a way to hide it. Too many things have happened." I tried to keep my voice level and the expression on my face neutral, but I'd known Savannah too long for that to actually work.

"Well, whoever did this hasn't done themselves any favors. They're now not only targeted by us but by humans as well." It bothered me how fast she'd identified with her nascent abilities and assimilated herself into the supernatural world, no longer identifying herself as human. I wanted her to be human, but no matter how little magical ability she possessed, she wasn't *just* human.

Two hours later Victor and the doctor returned to me. The pensive look on the latter's face was more than enough of an answer.

"I didn't work," I said.

He just shook his head. The hopelessness of the doctor drove it home. The injured were going to die. *Dammit.*

"I really thought it was. It started to. For several minutes it seemed to be working, changing with the mutations and stabilizing them. We thought it would reverse them. It started to show signs of it, but then everything stopped. It did keep the virus stable, so the patients won't get any worse. As long as they have some magic, they won't die."

"But they won't be the same?"

The doctor shook his head.

"It did work. You said it started to reverse the process and stopped. The antiviral just needs to be stronger, right?" Savannah theorized.

"Technically, yes."

"It just needs to be stronger, right?" she repeated, her eyes brightening, the way they had when she'd suggested I use her during magic. She wasn't magical, but she could give a magical boost.

"If you had access to an *ignesco* that would help."

They gave her blank looks. So few people knew what that was because it was rare. And when she explained it, the doctor looked as though she was a child and was telling him one of her tales about the time she met a dragon and rode it to Neverland or something equally fantastical.

"Well, sure, if we had a magical 'booster,' I'm sure that could work." His tone was heavy with condescension.

Savannah's eyes narrowed on him, and I watched her throat bob as she swallowed what she wanted to say, which probably wasn't pleasant. "I'm going to ignore that tone and offer my assistance. I am one."

The doctor looked at Victor and shrugged. "I can't imagine she would make something like that up. Thank you," the doctor said. "Please ... please follow me."

We were escorted to the same room where they'd drawn the blood, and we waited. And waited. And waited for someone to come. We'd been in the room for nearly an hour.

"How much you want to bet they are Googling the crap out of *ignesco* and calling every supernatural expert they know?"

"Definitely," she said, but for some reason it didn't bother her. Her optimism was contagious, and I really hoped she was the answer.

Humility wasn't a good look on Dr. Condescension at all, and he wore it poorly over his features. "Savannah, if your offer still stands we would very much like to use you and Levy. Mr. Reynolds confirmed that your skills have been invaluable in the past."

I would love to say that Savannah didn't have the smuggest of all smug looks on her face, but that would be a lie. If she had an "I told you so" or "in your face" dance, she definitely would have been doing it. There was a special dignity to her as she slipped into the chair they used to draw blood and extended her arm, exposing her vein to them.

Everything came to a halt and we waited. Silence could be a good thing or it could mean that there was nothing else to do. Gareth was still in the room with his sister, so it was just Lucas, Savannah, and me waiting in the room they had allowed us to stay in. The Isles was quickly filling with family members and friends. My stomach knotted when I realized that we didn't know what would be boosted, the Legacy blood or the virus.

I found comfort in that fact that I didn't hear mourning. That was something, and I clung to it for all it was worth. When Dr. Condescension stepped in, beaming, his eyes went straight to Savannah. "Thank you!" Then his eyes slipped in my direction. "Thank you both."

Savannah and I were out. This wasn't going to go unnoticed.

We made our way to the room where Avery was and found him sleeping in his bed next to his mother with his arm wrapped around her. Sweat had matted his hair to his face, and I could see how he got away with so much. He looked innocent and nothing like the car-stealing miscreant who gained a special pleasure from irritating his uncle.

"He wore himself out. He's changed three times since the treatment. I guess he needed to make sure."

Savannah and I both sighed, heavily. We didn't have any reason not to believe the doctor, but for some strange reason, we needed to see it.

CHAPTER 18

"*I*t's not a vacation, it's work," I groused, tossing out the dresses and swimsuit that she had placed in my suitcase.

"You won't be working the whole time. Legacy searching by day, fun and naughty times by night."

I reminded myself how much I loved Savannah, although she was more annoying than adorable at that moment.

"And these." She pulled out two of my bras that didn't have all the wire, padding, and lace that hers had but did what they were supposed to, which was hold up my tatas well.

"It's work, Savannah."

She plopped on the bed as I continued to pack, peeking up at me every so often. She'd settled quite nicely into her role as the quiet hero and I think was perfectly fine with the Isles and its staff taking full credit for curing everyone four days ago. We both seemed content with just the smug look of indignation she'd given the doctor before we left. Fading into obscurity seemed like a good plan, although we weren't ever going to be unknown. For now we weren't the face of the Legacy and some weird magic that no one had heard of.

"I wish I could take the time off to go with you two."

I simply smiled and gave her a look. But it saved me from telling her she couldn't go. I wasn't too keen on Gareth going, but he'd be easy to reason with, as opposed to my enthusiastic roommate who was always ready to grab her "quest" bag and go on an adventure.

"Me, too," I offered with very little enthusiasm. "I'll miss the quest bag," I teased, closing my suitcase before she could try to add anything else. Gareth rang the doorbell just as I was heading out of my bedroom.

Savannah answered the door, and he greeted her with two bottles of the same wine he'd brought to dinner earlier. "A gift from my sister. Just expect a lot of them for a while."

Taking the bottles, Savannah said, "Tell her she doesn't have to do this. I'm glad we were able to help and things worked out."

He flashed her a half-grin. "Good luck trying to get her to stop. Avery's grateful, too. When he's not milking convalescence for all it's worth, he's been in animal form."

"Have you found out anything else about who is responsible?"

He shook his head. "No, the men responsible for the shootings didn't offer anything. Even when we used fae magic to coerce truth out of them, we only got the location of a building where they were given the virus and the weapons. It was just a warehouse. We've questioned the owner of it, and he doesn't know anything. Whoever is behind that is very strategic. The shooters are martyrs for a cause who don't have enough information to lead us to anyone else. They aren't linked to the Human Rights Alliance," he said, frowning.

Should we wait on looking for the Legacy?" I didn't want

to put it off, but I wanted to find the people responsible for the mass attack more than I wanted to find my kin.

He shook his head. "No, we are only going for three days. Let's do this. I'm confident they can handle it."

"Have fun," Savannah offered, waving at us from the door.

Gareth smirked, giving me a salacious look before glancing back over his shoulder. "We will."

"It's work," I reminded him, giving him a nudge with my elbow.

"Of course, it's work where I am the lead and you are my subordinate. I guarantee, I'm going to have a lot of fun." His teeth gripped his lip, fighting the wolfish grin that was threatening to emerge.

"We'll see," I challenged, getting into the car, my eyes narrowed on him.

But the haughty look of mischief remained, tugging at my defiant nature. "I can ask for another handler," I offered.

Chuckling, he pulled the car away from the curb. "Yet, you won't."

This guy.

Gareth split his attention between me and looking down the road. Once we were several blocks from the house, he leaned forward and his eyes narrowed, studying the images in the rearview mirror. He stopped the car abruptly and turned around, speeding back to the apartment. It wasn't until we were closer to the apartment building that I saw a van pulling away and the door to my apartment wide open. He increased his speed, closing the distance between our car and the van. A hand slipped out the window of the van. When it waved, swirls of color raged through the air, and our car swerved out of control. Gareth pumped the brakes but couldn't stop, going over the curb and hitting a tree. We both got out of the car and ran through the grass, hoping to cut the van off in its oncoming direction. Gareth gave chase and midstride he shifted into that massive cat and pounded down the street. I moved between the neighboring apartment buildings and houses and hopped over gates until I got to the street. I saw Gareth gaining on them, too far away for me to run. The distance between Gareth and the van was now just a few feet when it braked and turned at a speed that I hoped would tip it over; it didn't. Instead, it swiped into Gareth, knocking him several feet away. The van did a full circle and sped away.

Gareth was in human form by the time I reached him, a frown deeply embedded on his confused face. He shook his head.

I closed my eyes for a moment, and all I saw was the broken door. Gareth still seemed disconcerted.

"Did you get a look at them?"

He nodded, slowly. "It was Conner."

MESSAGE TO THE READER

Thank you for choosing *Renegade Magic* from the many titles available to you. My goal is to create an engaging world, compelling characters, and an interesting experience for you. I hope I've accomplished that. Reviews are very important to authors and help other readers discover our books. Please take a moment to leave a review. I'd love to know your thoughts about the book.

For notifications about new releases, *exclusive* contests and giveaways, and cover reveals, please sign up for my mailing list at mckenziehunter.com.

Happy Reading!

www.McKenzieHunter.com
MckenzieHunter@MckenzieHunter.com

35101293R00146

Printed in Poland
by Amazon Fulfillment
Poland Sp. z o.o., Wrocław